D1132430

CALLIE

The Bayou Hauntings
Book One

Bill Thompson

Published by
Ascendente Books
Dallas, Texas

Books by Bill Thompson

The Bayou Hauntings
CALLIE

Brian Sadler Archaeological Mystery Series
THE BETHLEHEM SCROLL
ANCIENT: A SEARCH FOR THE LOST CITY OF THE MAYAS
THE STRANGEST THING
THE BONES IN THE PIT
ORDER OF SUCCESSION
THE BLACK CROSS
TEMPLE

Apocalyptic Fiction
THE OUTCASTS

The Crypt Trilogy
THE RELIC OF THE KING
THE CRYPT OF THE ANCIENTS
GHOST TRAIN

Middle Grade Fiction
THE LEGEND OF GUNNERS COVE

*This book is dedicated to Gretchen
and the gals in the Lafayette book club.
The inspiration for this novel arose entirely
from my experiences when I came down to visit you all.
Many thanks.*

*I am grateful to attorney Douglas Smith, who provided
valuable insights into how the legal system works.*

I probably spent a hundred nights in this house during the endless summers of my childhood. I loved coming to this place more than anything I can remember. Today, standing on the familiar front porch, why do I have goosebumps? Why am I afraid to walk through that door? What's inside that scares me?

Many afternoons my grandmother and I would spend time together in the kitchen. Mamère Juliet would pass me the bowl and spoon to lick when the cake was ready for the ancient cast-iron stove. I remember the smells, the song she hummed while she worked, and how much fun it was to be with her. But now, after all these years, there's something in the kitchen so menacing that I'm afraid to go in there. What's wrong with me? What's making my skin prickle?

I loved playing dolls way up in the third-floor ballroom. I pretended the cavernous room with its dormer windows overlooking the bayou was my house, and I rearranged the dusty furniture over and over. Today as I stand at the bottom of the dark, narrow stairway that leads to the top floor, why are my hands trembling so much I can hardly hold the rail? There's nothing frightening up there – nothing that should make me feel this way ... is there?

CHAPTER ONE

Callie was jarred from a very pleasant dream into the meaningless reality of her life by the incessant ringing of her phone. What time was it? As she reached for the phone, she glanced at the clock on her nightstand. It was 11:15 a.m.

Crap. I overslept again.

This was it. Her boss had almost fired her the last time she was late, and that had only been two weeks ago. The old bastard wouldn't give her another chance. The phone rang again. Although she didn't recognize the number, the area code was instantly familiar. St. Landry Parish, Louisiana, where her family was from.

"Hello," she mumbled, thinking how she'd screwed up her life once again.

"Calisto Pilantro? Is that you, honey?"

Nobody called her Calisto.

"Who the hell's this?"

"Well, I know now I've reached the right party," a silky-smooth voice said in a Southern accent much like her own. "Your momma never did teach you any manners, now did she? This is your dear old uncle Willard, darlin'. I'm wonderin' if you're on the way down here to see me."

There was nobody she detested more than Willard Arceneaux. He was her great-uncle – her grandmother's brother – and everything about the sleazy lawyer made her cringe. When she was a child staying at her Mamère's plantation house near Point Charmaine, he'd come around now and then and speak to her in that syrupy, creepy voice. Something about him scared her even as a little girl, and hearing his voice now brought it all back in a rush of feelings.

"I have no idea what you're talking about, Uncle Willard."

"Ah, that's what I was afraid of. You didn't get the registered letter I sent, I suppose. Move around a lot these days, do you?"

None of your business.

"Where'd you send it?"

"Richmond, honey. Are you still in Virginia?"

"Yes, but not in Richmond." She had no intention of telling him where she lived. "Why should I be coming to see you?"

"For the readin' of your grandmother's will."

Callie's grandmother Juliet Arceneaux had borne an illegitimate child she named Simon Pilantro. All Callie knew was that Simon's father – whose last name was Pilantro – had disappeared without marrying her grandmother. Apparently, the predisposition toward shirking responsibility was passed down to the next generation, because the minute her father, Simon, had found out that Callie's mom was pregnant, he'd skipped town too. Her mother had always struggled, but with Mamère's occasional help, they got by, if only barely. Juliet didn't care much for Callie's mother, but she doted on her only grandchild. Callie got a check on her birthday and at Christmas – money which had helped more than Mamère ever knew. And high school would have been the end of Callie's educational career if her grandmother hadn't paid for college.

After graduation, Callie had decided to grow up. She wanted to make it on her own, so she'd made a conscious decision to stop communicating with her grandmother, lest the subject of money come up again. Callie had cried when she learned Mamère had died, and she was ashamed that she hadn't spoken to her in years. After what Mamère had done for her, it was inexcusable – far worse than simply confessing that she was a failure at life like her mother had been. Callie couldn't consider coming back for the funeral. She didn't have the money. How pathetic was that, she'd told herself over and over.

4

"Are you saying she left me something in her will? I can't afford ..."

Willard interrupted. "You can't afford *not* to come, Calisto. Accordin' to my sister's will, the heirs have to be present to inherit anything. My kids are planning on being here and I'd suggest you come too."

Of all people, she hated to admit her situation to her uncle, but there was no way around it. "I don't have any money. I don't make enough to live on, much less take a trip halfway across the country. Can't you just tell me what she left me?"

"I was afraid you might be broke again," Willard said condescendingly. "You never were good at much, just like your momma and that bastard father of yours. You have to be here. It's part of Juliet's instructions. So I'm gonna wire you two hundred dollars. That's more than enough for a bus ticket. You have three days to get to Opelousas – the meeting is Friday at ten in my office. I couldn't care less if you show up or not, but I'm trying very hard to be fair. If you don't come, you'll get nothin', so I'm sure I'll see you on Friday."

Uncle Willard had never been fair in his life. There was more to all this, but to find out what, she had to go to Louisiana. She told him she'd come. Hating herself for the situation she was in, she asked, "Is there a place I can stay while I'm there?"

He was curt this time. "I'm sendin' you two hundred dollars, girl. I'm being generous, but you want more, don't you? You're a grown-up now. You don't have Juliet to take care of you. So figure it out for yourself. Try the Salvation Army. Maybe they have an empty cot." He hung up, leaving her sitting in the middle of the bed in her crummy apartment in Petersburg, Virginia, probably fired from her dead-end job as a reporter for the local newspaper, and with a bank account that would have two hundred and twenty-one dollars in it ... after Uncle Willard's deposit arrived.

She looked up the bus schedule. The trip would be a grueling thirty-two hours, but if she bought an economy ticket, she'd have nearly seventy dollars left, plenty for food and a few beers along the way. She couldn't afford a motel room in Opelousas, but she'd come up with something. She had plenty of time to think about it, for sure. That afternoon she got a call from Western Union. Her two hundred dollars was waiting for her at the Piggly Wiggly downtown.

The next morning at 7:05 a.m., Callie checked her suitcase and climbed the stairs onto the bus. There were thirty-seven other passengers, representing a broad swath of humanity. Hoping to avoid a seatmate, she slipped into the window seat, put her backpack on the one next to her and pretended to be asleep. The clerk had told her the bus would be half empty on the first leg, and she felt fortunate to be alone, at least for now.

The huge transport pulled out on time and she put on her headphones and ate a protein bar. She dozed now and then as they passed through one little town after another. When the bus arrived in Raleigh almost three hours later, Callie reflected that the trip had been less grueling than she'd expected.

She had to change busses here, and when she boarded, she saw that most of the seats were taken. There wasn't a window available, so she slid in next to one of the few relatively thin people on the bus. This was a long stretch – ten hours from Raleigh to Atlanta – and she hoped a lot of people would get off along the way.

Every hour or so there was a fifteen-minute stop so almost everyone except her could get off and smoke. She stretched her legs and talked to another nonsmoker, a girl named Jessie, who was younger than Callie and had a baby in tow. They were coming from New York City to Greenville, South Carolina, to live with her mother. Her boyfriend had walked out after the baby was born, and she didn't have money or a job, so she had panhandled until she had the money for bus fare, milk and diapers. She hadn't told her mother she was coming, the girl confided, and she was afraid she wouldn't take them in.

"She thinks I'm going to hell for having a child without being married," Jessie explained.

Since her own father had abandoned her, Callie felt compassion for the girl's situation. She was embarrassed she'd been feeling sorry for herself, but compared to this poor, scared girl she had a lot to be grateful for.

At three p.m., the bus arrived in Charlotte and the driver announced they'd stop for an hour. Callie asked if Jessie wanted to go to a Wendy's across the street and get lunch. Jessie shook her head.

"I ain't got any money. Belle here can drink her milk – I brought plenty of that. I'm not hungry anyway."

"Come on," Callie insisted. "I'll buy lunch."

This time Jessie accepted. She ordered a burger, fries and a milkshake and ate ravenously. When she finished, Callie asked if she wanted more, but she shook her head.

"I've taken advantage of your hospitality enough already," the girl said sincerely. "I don't need to be takin' your money."

Back on the bus, Callie saw that there were more open seats on this leg, so she moved across the aisle from Jessie and Belle. She said she was heading into the unknown too. She was going to Louisiana for the reading of her grandmother's will. She was one of three heirs and she had no idea what to expect.

"Maybe you'll be rich." Jessie smiled. "Maybe she left you a million dollars!"

"That would be nice, wouldn't it? Back in the old days I guess our family was rich, but nowadays not so much, except for one uncle who's a scumbag lawyer. We didn't lack for anything, but my grandmother lived in an old run-down house on the river that has been in our family since before the Civil War. I'm hoping I get something I can use, but I wouldn't be surprised if it's a set of silverware or old dishes."

Three hours later they arrived in Greenville, and Jessie gathered her carry-ons. It was only a ten-minute stop, but Callie got off and held Belle while the girl claimed her bags. Jessie hugged her and thanked her for lunch. Callie said she hoped things went well and pushed some money into her hand.

"No, no," she protested, but Callie insisted. As hard as it was, she knew Jessie and Belle needed it more than she did.

"I'm fine," she lied, having just handed this stranger eighty percent of her remaining funds. "Buy Belle something nice and think of me when she wears it." She boarded and waved out the window as the bus belched diesel and pulled into traffic. She settled in, sprawled across the empty seat beside her, leaned against the window with her backpack as a pillow, turned on music and slept until they arrived in Atlanta.

The next leg – Atlanta to New Orleans – would take more than seven hours, from around midnight until seven tomorrow morning. This part – the overnight stretch – was one she'd hoped would be half empty too, but it wasn't to be. The bus was full, and the aromas of body odor, cigarette breath, marijuana, take-out food and humanity in general wafted through the bus like a nasty breeze from a cesspool. The man next to her was obese and his muscle shirt and shorts looked like they hadn't seen a washer in a while. He settled back, took the armrest, extended his belly into her space, belched and began to snore. She attempted to establish her territory, but eventually she gave up and tried to sleep. She was grateful when he and half the others got off the bus in Mobile at 4:25 a.m. and finally she had room to stretch out.

She grabbed a donut and coffee in New Orleans, stretched her legs in Baton Rouge, and at 2:40 p.m. the driver announced their arrival in Opelousas. She stood on the sidewalk, counted her money – nine dollars and forty-two cents – and she wondered what to do. The meeting at Uncle Willard's office was at ten tomorrow morning, and after how he'd treated her on the phone, she damned sure wasn't asking him for anything.

There was one possibility – someone she hadn't spoken with in more than five years. She had no idea if he was around, but she recalled his moving here after high school. On the bus, she had searched the web for Mark Streater in Opelousas and got a hit. The guy who might be her old high school friend owned Streater Realty, and his office was just three blocks away.

Having nothing to lose, Callie put her backpack on top of her rolling suitcase and walked to his office. A little bell tinkled when she opened the door, and an older lady looked up with a smile.

After thirty hours on a bus, I must look like I just crawled out of the bayou.

The woman introduced herself as Mrs. Collins, and Callie said she was an old friend of Mark Streater's, if he was the right one. She asked if Mark was from New Orleans and had moved to Opelousas after high school. The lady confirmed she had the right person, but he was out on a job right now.

"He fixes up old houses and flips them," she said. "Sometimes the real estate business can be a little slow, so the flips keep Mark busy! How about I call him and let him know you're here ... uh, what's your name, honey?"

"Callie Pilantro. Please tell him I went to high school with him. We were in science class when he almost blew up the chemistry lab."

She laughed and placed a call. Ten minutes later she was air-kissing her old friend and thinking to herself that he didn't look half bad. He was taller than she remembered and had a deep tan from working outdoors. He was wearing a Saints T-shirt, shorts and a pair of old black Pumas.

"Wow, Callie. What brings you back to God's country?"

She explained what was going on. "I look like a train wreck," she admitted, explaining that she had hardly slept in two days. She wasted no time playing all her cards. There was no point in sugarcoating anything with this man she hadn't seen in years anyway.

"I've been going through a tough spell, to be honest. My uncle Willard told me I had to be here in person for the reading of my grandmother Juliet's will or I'd be cut out of my share of the inheritance. I have no idea what she left me – he won't tell me anything – but here I am with ten bucks to my name."

9

BILL THOMPSON

She does look a mess, he thought to himself, *but she's as beautiful as ever.* There had never been anything romantic between them – they'd run in the same crowd, taken some of the same classes and worked together on PTA garage sales and fund-raisers. They were both from New Orleans, and although her last name was Pilantro, everyone knew she was related to the Arceneaux family in St. Landry Parish. Her uncle Willard had made a name for himself chasing ambulances, and no one could miss his prominent billboard presence along the Louisiana highways.

Mark had decided to go into business instead of attending college, and he got his real estate broker's license. He loved the outdoors far more than the classroom and he moved to the heart of Cajun country, where his own family had a connection, like Callie's did. His parents had died in a car wreck, and a small inheritance allowed him to begin buying dilapidated houses, fixing them up and selling them to new owners. He had crews, but he also did a lot of the work himself, and house-flipping was a bigger part of his income than his sporadic real estate sales.

"How long will you be in town?" he asked, and she said she wasn't sure.

"I have to go to the reading of Mamère's will tomorrow. Once I know about that, I can decide what's next." She admitted that although she'd been working for the newspaper in Petersburg, she was certain there was no job now since she hadn't even bothered to tell her boss she was leaving.

He offered his spare bedroom for as long as she needed it, and she asked if there was a wife or significant other in the picture. He shook his head with a rueful smile and she accepted his offer, promising to stay for just one night. There was no reason to be here longer than necessary. She had a return bus ticket and her rent wasn't going to stop just because she wasn't at home. There was nothing for Callie Pilantro here, especially now that Mamère was gone.

Mark drove her to his house, an eighteen-hundred-square-foot bungalow on a tree-lined street that looked as if Beaver Cleaver had just run out the front door to catch the school bus. It was cleaner and neater than she'd expected a bachelor pad to be; even the guest bedroom was dusted and bright, with its windows slightly cracked to allow the breeze inside. It was as though he knew he was going to have company, she remarked, and he laughed, explaining that he kept the windows open in warm weather. The cross-breeze kept the entire house cooler and saved on air-conditioning.

After an hour soaking in the bathtub, she finally felt human again and he took her to Applebee's for dinner. Over a couple of beers, they talked about why she was here.

"How long ago did your grandmother die?"

"A few months ago. I was close to her, but I couldn't make it to the funeral. Same financial issues then as now, I'm sorry to say. I feel awful that I didn't come to her service, but when I learned I was in her will, I jumped right on the bus and came down here. How hypocritical is that?"

"You can't blame yourself. She obviously thought a lot of you because she left you something in her will. She'd have understood."

They talked about his business. He explained how hard it was for a newcomer to compete with the well-established real estate companies. He got a listing here and there, but there wasn't enough income to live on. He had listed a small older home and decided to buy it himself. He put a few thousand bucks in it and flipped it. It worked, and he'd done it a dozen times since. Right now, he was working on four run-down houses that needed a lot of TLC.

She asked, "Have you heard of Beau Rivage Plantation, my family's place out on the river?"

She noticed an odd look on his face for a moment and she wondered what it meant.

"Sure. It's an old antebellum mansion out on River Road, one of the few in this parish, if I remember correctly. It's been abandoned for decades – right?"

"I don't think so. As far as I know, it was Mamère Juliet's home until she died. I haven't seen it in twelve years and I'm planning to go tomorrow afternoon. I have to be at Uncle Willard's office at ten. Do you want to go with me when I'm finished?"

He told her he'd like to go, since old houses were his passion these days. They talked about old times, friends from high school and crazy things they'd done. At last everything caught up with Callie, and by the time the check arrived, she could hardly keep her eyes open.

"I'll pay you back for the meals," she slurred sleepily, and he told her not to worry about it. He took her to his house and escorted her to her bedroom. The moment he was gone, she tossed her clothes on the floor and slid between the sheets. She stretched languorously, fell asleep immediately, and only awoke when she heard a rooster somewhere announcing the dawn.

CHAPTER TWO

Willard Arceneaux was the slimiest, slickest, nastiest and – to the insurance companies – the most fearsome personal injury lawyer in Cajun country. Along the interstate highways from Shreveport to New Orleans and from Houston to Biloxi, one billboard after another featured his flashy smile, his fancy pin-striped suit and the fat cigar in his mouth.

Car wreck? Hurt on the job? Laid off and injured? The Cajun Crusher can help!

I put $180,526.44 IN MY CLIENT'S POCKET, Uncle Willard bellowed intrusively on daytime TV ads, flashing gold cuff links and a fancy Rolex. He was rich and he made sure everyone knew it. But if it hadn't been for that poor old lady from Kaplan, he'd still have been a small-town ambulance chaser.

One afternoon an elderly woman's car was rear-ended on Interstate 49 a few miles north of Opelousas. Willard was at the hospital before she was out of the ER, thanks to the police radio scanner his paralegal monitored all day long. When she heard the first responders say to which hospital Eunice Barber was being taken, Willard jumped into his BMW and headed off, as he'd done dozens of times previously.

She had a broken leg, several broken ribs and a lot of bruises, but she was awake when Willard popped into her room with the flowers he'd bought downstairs in the gift shop. She'd never heard of him; back then Willard wasn't rich and famous. Eunice didn't have any family left, and she was grateful that someone had come to visit her. He seemed like such a nice young man, she thought.

Willard listened patiently, shaking his head in commiseration as she recounted her horrifying experience. He grimaced as she lamented her beloved 1998 Oldsmobile that was a total loss. When she finished, he gently patted her hand and told her everything was going to be all right. She was a victim and he would be proud if she'd let him be her attorney. He promised to take care of her hospital bill, get her a nicer car and put forty thousand dollars in her pocket.

"If the judge doesn't award you that much, I'll give it to you myself,' he had said soothingly. "You didn't deserve what happened to you and I'm glad I can help." His words were comforting, and she could tell that he really cared. She was living on a tiny Social Security check and had never seen forty thousand dollars at once in her entire life. Eunice thanked God this kind man had appeared in her room to help her get through all this.

She said she'd be honored to have him as her lawyer and he walked out ten minutes later with a signed representation letter. He stopped by the hospital's accounting office, left his credit card number to cover any expenses Medicare didn't pay, and returned to work.

Willard hadn't gone out on a limb when he guaranteed her forty thousand plus a car. Since the accident had happened in St. Landry Parish, Willard knew he could get a hundred grand minimum. The up-and-coming personal injury lawyer knew the judges here. He'd handled maybe fifty cases and his win rate was a hundred percent. Only one lawsuit in a hundred ever went to trial anyway; insurance companies knew better than to come down to southern Louisiana, sit in front of a Cajun lawyer, judge and jury, and maybe get socked with a million-dollar verdict.

Eunice Barber's case had a twist that became Willard's path to fame and fortune. He got a copy of the accident report and made initial contact with the company who insured the other driver – the man who had rear-ended her car. Then his paralegal found something very interesting on the internet. There was a recall notice for the vehicle that had hit Eunice's; there was a chance that the brakes could suddenly fail. It took a few weeks to get through the red tape, but eventually he learned that the brakes on that vehicle hadn't been fixed because the driver had bought the car from someone else. He had no idea there was a recall notice. That vehicle was absolutely going to cause an accident sometime, and fortunately for Willard, it had happened to Eunice Barber.

By now, Eunice was on the mend and driving around town in the 2005 Honda Willard had given her, but Willard made her out to be a helpless old lady, permanently crippled and in constant mental anguish because of the accident. She was afraid to leave her house, terrified of every car around her, and a shell of her former vibrant self. According to Willard, at least.

He wrangled and battled with the other driver's insurance company. He accused them of bad faith and refused to consider their offers to settle. When the claims manager said his company was prepared to go to trial, Willard laughed in his face. Each of them knew that would never happen. The insurance company was in a serious predicament and it was just a matter of time until the claims manager came up with an offer that Willard would accept.

One afternoon eight months after her accident, he stopped by Eunice's house, telling her he had good news. The other driver's carrier had settled.

"Do I get my forty thousand dollars now?" she asked eagerly, hoping against hope that he remembered that offer. Back then he had told her he couldn't put it in writing, but she trusted him. After all, he was her friend and he cared about her.

"Eunice, honey, I have your money right here." He handed her a cashier's check. It had her name on it, but it was in the amount of fifty thousand dollars, not the forty she'd been promised.

"Is there ... is there a mistake?" she asked, but then she understood. "I guess that other ten thousand is for your legal fee. Am I right?"

"No, no, darlin'. The insurance company paid me already. I wanted to be sure you had plenty, so I demanded they give you even more. You were the victim here, and you deserve this money." He smiled and squeezed her hand as she wept. She was rich beyond her wildest dreams, and this nice man had made it all happen.

"Is there anything else I have to do?" she asked. "I should go to the bank right now so I don't misplace this check."

He pulled out another piece of paper – the check from the insurance company made payable to Eunice – and handed her a pen. He never showed her the front of the check and she endorsed the back just like her wonderful lawyer told her to do. Willard put it in his pocket, kissed her lightly on her wrinkled cheek and told her how glad he was that things had worked out well.

She was the happiest woman on earth. And Willard was ecstatic too.

He drove straight to the bank and made a deposit. He put Eunice Barber's $4.5 million settlement check into his personal account.

Word got around and some people claimed Willard had cheated the old lady. A couple of attorneys started talking about bringing him up for disbarment, but it didn't happen. Eunice Barber was his biggest fan, and she refused to let anyone speak badly about him, even after she was told how much money she'd given up by endorsing that check.

"He promised me forty thousand dollars and got me fifty," she claimed proudly to anyone who questioned Willard's ethics. "I don't understand business, but I know he worked hard for me. I'm happy and I would hire him again."

With only a few battle scars on his reputation, Willard Arceneaux launched his career and became the preeminent personal injury attorney in the state. Now, forty years later, Willard was seventy-nine, fat and happy. He had made millions since that first lucky break, and life was good indeed.

CHAPTER THREE

At ten in the morning, the humidity in Opelousas was oppressive, but inside Willard Arceneaux's conference room, Callie's skin prickled from a coldness that wasn't caused by the air-conditioning. Willard hugged her in a contrived show of affection and motioned for her to sit. He took a chair on the other side between his two girls, Madeline, aged forty-four, and Carmine, forty-seven. Neither made even a halfhearted effort to be cordial, not that Callie had expected it. She was more than a decade younger than Willard's children, and they had always treated her with contempt because of her financial situation. While they had been raised in true Southern luxury, her mother's handsome-but-worthless boyfriend had gotten her pregnant and skipped town. She never had much, and the Arceneaux girls always made sure everyone was aware of what little she had compared to themselves.

Ever since she was a child, she had never known Madeline and Carmine to be anything other than the same pompous, spoiled bitches who sat across from her today. It only took a moment to see that nothing had changed. They might be older, but they were still the same.

"Heard you rode the bus," Madeline said with a smirk. "That must have been exciting! I've never been on a bus in my life!" She and Carmine laughed as if they'd just heard the best joke ever told.

"I helped a girl with a new baby ..." she replied defensively, regretting the words the moment she said them. She had always felt compelled to respond to their taunts, but that had never ended well for her.

"Maybe somebody should have helped your momma when she had *you*," Carmine shot back. "Aunt Juliet's bastard son was no dummy. He got out of town as soon as he knocked your momma up."

Callie blushed, angry that she couldn't think of a response, and Willard said, "Let it go, girls. Callie's come a long way and I had to send her money so she could join us. Maybe my sister's going to give her something that'll help her out."

Even old Uncle Willard had joined the Callie-bashing party. There were snorts of derision from the girls, and she wished she were anywhere else but here.

"Can we just get to the reading of the will?"

"Yes, let's," Madeline replied. "Callie needs her inheritance right away so she can afford a bus ticket back to whatever hole she crawled out of!"

Willard opened a folder and took out several legal-sized pages. "Before I begin," he said, "I want to let you all know that I wouldn't have done things the way Juliet did. My sister never had a head for business or money, but she was also too damned stubborn to ask for help. She left this envelope with the bank a few months before her death. After she passed away, the trust officer opened it, read the will and sent it over to me since she appointed me as her executor. Her instructions were that all three of you had to be present for the reading of the will. If any one of you wasn't here, none of you would inherit anything. Whatever she had would go to charities."

Now I understand why it was so important that I be here. If I hadn't come, Madeline and Carmine wouldn't have gotten their hands on Mamère's bequest.

Unaccustomed at having to wait and disgusted at having to occupy the same room with their destitute cousin Callie, Willard's daughters squirmed in their chairs like worms on a hook.

It took less than ten minutes to read the will. Juliet's wishes were clear. She had divided whatever she was giving away into thirds. Willard's children – Juliet's nieces – would each pick a sealed envelope, and a third would go to Callie. Juliet's only other heir, Willard, wouldn't inherit anything since he had plenty already.

Willard removed the envelopes from the folder and said to Madeline and Carmine, "Girls, these envelopes are marked One and Two. You'll each choose one. Callie, yours is different. Your name's already on it. Why Juliet did that, I have no idea." He handed the envelope to her and she saw her name in Mamère's instantly recognizable handwriting.

Callie wondered if her uncle had steamed open the envelopes to see what was inside, and she smiled when he explained that there was a duplicate set of envelopes that the bank trust officer would use to verify the disposition of assets. Obviously, Juliet had known her lawyer brother well. Although she had made him executor, she hadn't trusted Willard and she made sure someone independent would keep him honest.

Madeline grabbed an envelope and said, "This one's mine!"

"Bet mine's better," Carmine sneered. "Sure you don't want to trade?"

"I want to trade!" Madeline grabbed Carmine's envelope and tossed her the other one.

Callie sat silently on the other side of the table, watching two grown women arguing over whatever was in an envelope. Hers lay on the table, unopened.

Carmine ripped open her envelope and found a small key with a number on it. "What's that?" she said petulantly, tossing it on the desk. "She left me a key? Thanks a lot, Aunt Juliet. I thought it would be a check."

Willard picked up the key, examined it and said, "It goes to a safety-deposit box, honey. Depending on what's there, it might be even better than a check!"

To build the suspense, Madeline took her time, but Callie couldn't have been less interested. A small slip of paper fluttered from Madeline's envelope and she picked it up. "It's a claim check from a car repair shop in Baton Rouge. It's a year old. What did she leave me? Her damned old Pontiac that's in a fix-it shop? Thanks a lot, Auntie Juliet. I want yours, Carmine! You took it from me!" She tried to grab the little key, but her sister snatched it away.

19

She sneered, "You wanted to trade. I get the safety-deposit box. You get the Pontiac!"

Callie could see Willard's patience was running low. "Madeline, this may be something else entirely. If the car needed repairs, why would an old lady drive all the way to Baton Rouge? My advice is to call them and find out."

He looked across the table at Callie. "Aren't you going to open yours?"

"Is this it?" she asked, holding up the envelope. "Whatever's in here for me, that's all there is – correct?"

"That's right. The will makes no other provisions."

"Then I'll open it later." She stuck the envelope in her backpack, stood and walked to the door.

"No fair!" Madeline whined. "You got to see ours. You have to show us what old Auntie left you."

"I don't have to do anything," Callie replied calmly. "I have no idea what she left you, and you don't know either. So we're even."

She walked to Mark's office. He was out, so Mrs. Collins showed her into a tiny conference room and gave her a cup of coffee. Callie took out the envelope and stared at it for several minutes. Whatever was inside had to be good, she thought. Things couldn't get much worse. Cautiously optimistic that she might be on the verge of a positive turn in her life, she ripped it open.

There were two things inside it. She saw a printed road map of the Atchafalaya Swamp area. The map covered the area between Interstate 49 going down through Opelousas and Lafayette on the west, and St. Francisville and Baton Rouge on the east. Down the middle was a highlighted route that ended near the town on the Atchafalaya River called Point Charmaine.

She didn't need a map to know where this route would lead her. She'd spent many summers as a child at Beau Rivage, the majestic Arceneaux family home built in 1835 by Henri Arceneaux and most recently occupied by her grandmother Juliet. The tiny village of Point Charmaine was a mile or so from the house. The last time she had come out here – twelve summers ago – Point Charmaine had dwindled to one store with a gas pump, a few snacks and a Coke machine. The map Mamère had enclosed would take her to the old plantation home, which as far as Callie knew had sat empty since Juliet had died eight months ago.

She turned the paper over and found a hand-drawn floor plan. There were several rooms; one was quite large and one of the smaller ones had a red dot inside it. Settling down after the realization that her inheritance was reduced to some kind of clue just like Willard's girls' had been, she composed herself, admitting that three days ago she'd expected nothing from Mamère, so she should be grateful for whatever this was. She'd have to follow the map to find out what was there.

The other thing in the envelope was the business card of the trust officer at the First National Bank of Opelousas – most likely the same man to whom Mamère Juliet had entrusted her will. She called the number, got voicemail and left a message giving her name and number and explaining that Juliet Arceneaux had left the card for her, but she didn't know why.

She heard the front door open and the sound of Mark's voice. He came into the conference room and took the chair next to hers. Since he had dropped her at Willard's office only a couple of hours ago, he was surprised she was back so quickly.

"Tell me what happened! Are you flying first class back home instead of taking the bus?"

"Not exactly." She laughed. "I'm no wealthier than when I left you earlier. Here's my inheritance." She handed the two-sided map to him.

He glanced at it, and then handed it back to her. "What's this?"

"One side's a map that'll take me to her house. From memory, I'd say the other side is the third floor of Beau Rivage. I think that's the ballroom, and I have no idea what the red dot means."

"You inherited the house?"

"I don't know that. I don't know anything at this point. There was also this business card; I left a message."

Mark looked at the card. "I know this guy. I've played golf with him at the public course. Maybe your grandmother gave him something that'll shed light on all this."

"Meanwhile –" she smiled "– want to take a ride out on River Road?"

Fifteen minutes later he was driving very slowly along the highway, looking for a turnoff Callie remembered from the past. Back then it had led to Beau Rivage, but they couldn't locate it today. Instead, they looked for another intersection – the road to Point Charmaine.

"I wonder if the town's even there," Callie said. "There used to be a gas station, but that was it. If there's anything left, surely there's a road to get to it."

They backtracked until they found it. What once had been an asphalt-paved road was mostly dirt now, and a sign that read, "Point Charmaine – 1 mile" was lying in the tall grass beside the highway.

Before the Civil War, Point Charmaine had boasted over two thousand residents and had been a busy stop along the Atchafalaya River. Callie remembered Mamère telling her own grandmother's stories about hearing the steamboat whistles in the distance. Kids living along the river would run to the shore and watch the grand riverboats as they sailed by. They would dock at Point Charmaine, unload passengers and freight, take on more and head off toward New Orleans.

I heard those same stories once myself, Mark recalled, but he said nothing.

The once-paved Main Street was in as bad shape as the road from the highway, and there were only a few shells of buildings still standing. The bank had been a stately two-story building with a clock tower. Now it was a pile of lumber and brick lying inside four crumbling walls. There had been other stores on both sides of the three-block downtown, but only two were more than rock foundations.

The same store was still on the corner, and it was the only business open these days. The name had changed sometime in the twelve years since Callie had been here. Now it was Phil's Quick Stop, a corner gas station and c-store. It had two fuel pumps on the street side for cars, and a couple more on a dock alongside the river to serve boaters who might need a fill-up. There were no customers today and they wondered whether Phil had much business at all these days. They went inside to see what they might find out about Beau Rivage.

"Mornin'," said a man with a smile and a white beard that made him look like Santa Claus. "Don't get many people from the highway. You all lost?"

"No." Callie laughed. "We're on our way to Beau Rivage."

The man's smile and friendly demeanor disappeared in an instant. "What in hell for? Nothin' over there since old Juliet died. Strange things happen over there, people say. Lights and stuff. They don't take kindly to trespassers either, so I'd be careful nosin' around where you got no business."

"I'm Juliet Arceneaux's granddaughter, Callie Pilantro." She stuck out her hand and he shook it hesitantly, as if it were going to shock him. "This is my friend Mark. You said they don't take kindly to trespassers. Who are 'they'? Is someone living in the house?"

He shook his head. "No," he said curtly. "I just made that up in case you were going over there to tramp around. People stop in here sometimes, asking me how to get there. They've heard the same stories everyone else has."

"What stories would those be?"

He turned his back to her and fiddled with some things on a table. Without turning her way, he said, "All the old houses got tales. The more run-down and decayed they are, the scarier the stories. People boating on the river say they've seen things inside Beau Rivage at night. Lights and stuff. Maybe people walking around. Hogwash, I guess."

But his face didn't look like he thought it was hogwash.

"Have you seen anything unusual yourself?"

He changed the subject. "Used to see Miss Juliet now and then. When my store had more things to offer, she'd stop by sometimes for gas and provisions. I figure she must have quit driving at some point. I didn't see her for maybe a year before she died."

"Nobody's in the house?"

"Nobody *lives* there. That's what you asked me and that's what I told you." His answers were getting increasingly curt, as if she was pushing too hard, and it surprised Callie. She really hadn't asked him anything specific at all.

"Do people come and go during the day? Is that what you're saying?"

"Nobody comes and goes during the day, far as I know."

She remembered how exasperating trying to have a conversation with a Cajun could be. Mostly they gave you exactly what you asked for, but nothing more.

"Do you know anything personally about Beau Rivage? Have you ever seen anything unusual?"

He looked up and stared her in the face. His eyes bored into hers, and she recoiled in shock at how riled up he appeared to be.

"I've answered enough questions. I have work to do."

"Thank you for talking with us, Phil. Maybe I'll see you again," she said, trying to sound more cordial than she felt.

"I ain't Phil and I doubt I'll see much more of you," he shot back. "No reason for anybody to hang around at Beau Rivage. Ain't nothin' but problems out there ..."

"What do you mean by that?"

He shook his head and said, "You said you're an Arceneaux. Go find out for yourself."

CHAPTER FOUR

That was strange, wasn't it?"

"No kidding," Mark responded. "Some of these river folk aren't the friendliest, but I'd think with his having a store a mile from the house and seeing Juliet from time to time, he'd have had more nice things to say about her and the house. Maybe it's just him – sometimes these old bastards get cantankerous."

"It just seemed strange to me. He was getting hostile at the end."

As they left the Main Street of Point Charmaine, the road toward the mansion deteriorated into a rutted one-lane trail. It was clear no one had driven on it for a long time. Limbs brushed Mark's Jeep on both sides and he maneuvered around rain-filled potholes. Abruptly the lane opened into a broad field of tall grass with a fence running alongside the road. What had once been imposing six-foot-high brick columns every twenty feet, with black wrought-iron fencing in between, was now deteriorating quickly. Some of the columns had collapsed and the railings were a rusty brown.

Callie bit her lip to keep from crying as they passed under a gate with the family name on it and drove down a narrow lane that was lined with tall magnolias. The trees had once been neatly trimmed, but now there were masses of jumbled limbs stretching in every direction. When she had come here as a girl, the house had been visible from the gate, and its white facade had gleamed in the sunlight. Today there was so much unbridled growth and vegetation that the house was hidden.

"Mamère's only been gone eight months," she mused. "I can't believe this place could have deteriorated so quickly. It's almost like she had stopped keeping it up before she died."

Mark concentrated on the sharp right and left turns through brambles and bushes until they came to the broad expanse of yard and finally saw the house and the Atchafalaya River just beyond it.

"Oh, God," she whispered. "Oh, my God." She could hold back tears no longer. She put her hands to her face and wept uncontrollably for a minute or so.

"I'm ... I'm sorry," she said with a sigh as she composed herself. "I didn't think it would have that much effect on me. I should have expected this ..." She paused.

"That it was in pretty bad shape?"

"Yeah. I guess that's somewhat of an understatement," she said, trying to make a joke out of something that was tearing at her heartstrings and her memories.

Even today there was no mistaking what a showplace Beau Rivage must have been when Henri Arceneaux built it in 1835. The facade they faced – the side of the house you saw when you came down the road – was in fact the back of the structure. There had been no road then. The river was the means of transportation in those days, and there would have been steamboats, barges and pleasure craft. The front of the house faced the river, and until right now Callie had been looking forward to seeing it again. The majesty of it always took her breath away, but today her breath was coming in short gasps for an entirely different reason.

The old mansion was in far greater disrepair than could have happened in the eight months since Juliet's death. The paint was peeling everywhere, limbs from huge dead trees lay across the roof, windowpanes were missing in places, and the entrance – the back door that the servants would have used – was hanging off its hinges, drifting back and forth in the breeze.

"It's just so sad," she said over and over. "She must have let it go. I wonder if she was sick ..."

"Your uncle might be able to tell you about that," Mark said. "Ready to go around to the front?"

"Why not? It can't be any more depressing than this view is."

They got out, and as they walked in the knee-high-tall grass, he pointed out more problems on the side of the house. Several panes of glass on the first floor were broken, which had likely been caused by rock-throwing kids. "There's no telling what the inside looks like," he commented as they passed a side door that was ajar.

Even in sad condition, the front of Beau Rivage still displayed its majesty. Eight massive white columns ran from the ground to a broad second-floor porch that stretched the length of the house. Similar columns on that level supported a roof. Above that, Callie pointed out the third-floor balcony that was accessed through a door in the ballroom.

The mansion had been built in the same Greek revival style as many other pre-Civil War homes in the South. The huge verandas provided both shade indoors and a cool sitting area outside where the owners and their guests could watch the river traffic heading down to Point Charmaine.

After seeing the rear of the house, Callie steeled herself for how bad the front side might look, but she was happily surprised to see that the columns and porches looked good and fewer windows were broken. To a boater on the river who glanced at Beau Rivage, the only signs of neglect he'd see were a house in need of a paint job and a yard that once had been carefully groomed by a staff of gardeners but now was full of weeds.

A strange cool breeze blew over Callie and made her shiver. There was something different about the house. She had wanted it to be the same happy place where she'd spent many a summer. She wanted it to be full of laughter and the smell of a cherry pie cooling on the windowsill. She wanted the things it had once been, but now she felt like a stranger. Once, her grandmother had stood on the porch and waved as she arrived. Today, something seemed to be pushing her away. She shrugged it off, thinking she hadn't been here in twelve years. It was her own fault if everything seemed different. She should have come more often and seen the house and Mamère in better times.

They walked up five stairs to the broad porch and saw that one of the tall double doors was ajar. "That solves a problem," she said. "I was worried about where I'd find a key."

Don't go inside!

She hesitated – something had just flitted through her mind. She decided she'd listened too much to that rude man back at the gas station. All that talk about strange happenings had made her nervous. That was it. She walked across the veranda toward the door and paused again.

Don't go inside!

There it is again! What's wrong with me? I've walked across this porch hundreds of times. I spent entire summers here with Mamère when I was a child. Why am I feeling so nervous? I have no bad memories of this place. I played all over the house – it was like home to me – a warm, comfortable house instead of the place where I really lived. Why do I dread to set foot inside?

He noticed her trembling. "Are you having second thoughts?"

"No, it's nothing. Too many memories at once, I think."

Mustering courage she didn't understand why she needed, Callie pushed the door open and it gave off a mighty creaking groan. They stepped inside and she felt as if she'd entered a time warp. They stood in a wide main hall that ran completely through the house from front to back. To her left was the beautiful stairway and the door to her great-grandfather Michael's vast library. There was the kitchen on the right, where it had always been. Although she hadn't been here in twelve years, everything flooded back into her mind as though she'd left yesterday.

In a moment, her apprehensions disappeared.

Through dim light filtering through the grimy windows, she saw evidence of trespassers. Two cigarette butts and a soft-drink can had been tossed on the floor near the front door. For some reason, it appeared the intruders hadn't gone far inside. The footprints in the fine layer of dust on the floor extended no more than ten feet from the door. Whoever had come inside stopped there, and that was good news as far as Callie was concerned. The thought of someone vandalizing her Mamère's home made her unhappy.

Mark stood quietly beside her as she turned in this direction and that, lost in the memories of her childhood visits. "Does being here make you sad?" he asked.

"Not as much as I expected. Mamère's only been gone eight months and I'm glad the trespassers didn't venture farther into the house. At least it looks that way. What this place needs is a good scrubbing and a crew of workers to fix it back up."

"You hesitated before coming in. Were you thinking about what the guy back at the store said?"

"About the stories people tell? That didn't bother me – there have been ghost stories about this house for years. Mamère would laugh; she never let it bother her, so it didn't bother me either. Maybe the people who came in were scared away by the looks of the place. You do have to admit it looks spooky with dust and cobwebs everywhere." She kicked a roach clip with her sandal. "It looks like somebody smoked a joint to help cope with the spooks."

She walked him through the first floor and explained about each room. The furniture and wall hangings were draped in sheets. Callie knew Uncle Willard wouldn't have gone to the trouble, so Mamère must have done that sometime before she died.

As she took him through the library, the parlor, a sitting room, music room and dining room, she was even more surprised that whoever came inside had hardly come past the front door. They'd dropped their joints and sodas and left without exploring even the nearest rooms. Wouldn't they have wanted to see what was under the sheets? Wouldn't they have pulled away at least one? It didn't make sense.

What happened? What – or who – scared them away?

Nothing, she answered herself. *Nothing "scared them away." Quit the drama, girl. They had second thoughts. Spooky old house, creaks and groans, all that Hitchcock stuff. They scared themselves away.*

She walked through the rooms, pulling away sheets and looking at the beautiful old furniture that brought back even more memories. Mark commented about what great condition the chairs and tables were in and that they could be valuable antiques.

"Yeah, if my cousins Madeline and Carmine end up inheriting them, this stuff will be out of here in twenty-four hours. There are so many memories here I don't know if I could part with anything."

He asked her if Willard's daughters had spent summers at the house too. She said no – in the first place, they were much older than she and wouldn't have been here when she was anyway, but they also didn't care for their aunt Juliet. They didn't want to spend time with her or do things for her. They never came around, even though they lived just twenty miles away.

"I was the one Juliet loved," she said. "And the feelings were mutual. I loved her too, and I thought she was the most interesting person I'd ever met. She told me tales that were passed down through the generations about the house during the Civil War and afterwards."

She walked to the far end of the dining room and stood in front of a hinged door. It was closed, and Mark stepped up to push it open.

"Stop!" she exclaimed.

He drew back in surprise. "What's wrong?"

"Nothing," she stammered, wondering that same thing herself. "Just give me a moment."

I know what's behind that door – some of my fondest times were spent in there. How many afternoons were Mamère and I in that kitchen while she cooked? She would pass me the bowl and spoon to lick when the cake was ready to go into her ancient cast-iron stove. I remember the smells and I can even recall the songs she hummed while she cooked. It was so much fun to be with her. But now, after all these years, I'm afraid to go in there. There's something scary in there. What's wrong with me? What's making my skin prickle? I love that room!

Mark touched her hand. "Are you feeling okay? Do you want to sit down for a moment?"

"No. It's the memories again. We want things to always stay like they were when we were little. We want things to be perfect, but nothing can stay the same. I think I'm going to see her around the next corner, but she's gone and I've got to get used to it. Come on. I'll show you the kitchen."

Mamère's old stove was still there. So were the same gaudy pink-and-chrome Kelvinator refrigerator and Frigidaire dishwasher. She had proudly told Callie her refrigerator was the first one in the parish to have a built-in ice maker. Today they were antiques that stood out grotesquely in the plantation house. "If this were my place," she told Mark, "I'd restore the kitchen back to how it looked in the 1800s and put modern appliances in the storeroom." She pointed to an adjoining room, which contained an ancient front-loading washer and dryer.

As she walked around, ran her fingers over the countertops and recalled sitting there while Mamère cooked, her earlier fears disappeared.

"I've reminisced enough." She stood and declared it was time to go to the ballroom and see where the hand-drawn map led them. They climbed that broad staircase that Mamère had said Yankee soldiers had used when they briefly were at the house in 1863. She glanced into a couple of the bedrooms and pointed one out as hers – the one Mamère had kept just for Callie when she came every summer. She didn't go in; she'd had enough memories and flashbacks for one afternoon.

"This leads up to the ballroom," she said as they came to a door at the end of the hall. She opened it and peered into a dark, narrow stairwell she hadn't seen in over a decade. She paused for a moment.

The third floor was the magical part of this house. I spent countless hours up there, pretending the enormous

31

room with its dormer windows overlooking the river was my house. Mamère let me do anything I pleased; I would place the old chairs and tables first this way, then that, creating rooms for my dolls and me to live in. This staircase seemed larger then – maybe I was just smaller – and it had always seemed friendly and welcoming. It was the entryway to my kingdom and I always scampered up with delight. Why does it make me so uneasy today? What's making me hesitate to take the first step? There's nothing in the ballroom but wonderful memories. Is it because there's something else – something that's going to frighten me?

"More memories?"

She nodded and forced herself to walk up fifteen steps in the dark. The door at the top wouldn't open.

"It was never locked when I was a kid," she commented.

"Maybe it's just stuck. Let me have a go." They traded places on the narrow stairway and he tried the knob, but it wouldn't budge. "I'll get my tools out of the Jeep and open it," he said, and she commented that since it was locked, maybe all the stuff from years ago was still stored up there. It puzzled her why someone would have locked it. It had to be Mamère Juliet and it must have been years ago; she probably wouldn't have gone up and down this narrow staircase in her later years.

She watched out a second-floor window as he walked through the grass to his Jeep. *I was lucky to find him,* she thought to herself. Without Mark, she wouldn't have had a place to stay, and he'd even paid for her meals.

Mark jimmied the lock and the door creaked open, a sign that it had been ages since someone had been up here. He led the way, and Callie followed close behind. Everywhere they stepped, their shoes made an imprint in the dust. There were no other footprints but theirs.

"Wow," he said, surprised at how big the room was. It was as long and wide as the house itself, and along one side wall there were half a dozen doors.

"Those are storage closets," she explained. "They're full of clothes and stuff from Mamère's time and even further back. I'd put on the dresses and hats and pretend I was the lady of the house, shooing the Yankees off my property during the War!"

"Should I call you Scarlett?" he quipped, and that made her laugh.

There were old hall trees, some discarded chandeliers lying in a corner, lots of furniture and an enormous four-poster bed that Mark couldn't imagine how someone ever managed to haul up the stairs. One end of the room had a slightly raised floor – a bandstand, Callie explained – a throwback to the 1800s when this grand ballroom would have been the venue for many fancy parties.

"I would pretend that there was an orchestra up there," she recalled. "Ladies and gentlemen in flowing gowns and top hats would whirl around the floor while waiters in tuxedoes served mint juleps to guests seated at the other end. My dolls and I danced around the room, and then we sat at a table and sipped our drinks."

She paused and returned to reality. They'd come up here for a reason, not to reminisce about the past. She pulled out Juliet's hand-drawn map and oriented it to the room.

"Everything fits," she said, showing it to him. "I thought it would."

The small room with the red dot inside was behind the third door along the wall. Surprisingly that one was locked too, but Mark had it open in seconds. When she looked inside, she stepped back in surprise. Once this had been an empty closet. Now it was crammed full of cardboard boxes stacked one on top of the other from floor to ceiling, from front to back. There wasn't an inch of room to spare. The contents of the boxes near the front were marked in the same shaky handwriting as on the map. Mamère had put these here, but how? She wasn't frail by any means, but this would have been a serious undertaking for someone her age.

"I remember this closet being empty. She must have hired someone to move all these boxes up here. I guess it was crazy to think I'd open the door and find my inheritance lying on a silver platter." She laughed.

He asked her what she wanted to do, and she decided to tackle the project one box at a time.

With the two of them working, it didn't take long. There were around sixty boxes of varying sizes. Most were recent, such as wine boxes from the liquor store, but the ones at the back were old. Some of those were falling apart and had to be gingerly dealt with.

As they pulled the boxes from the closet, she glanced at the list of contents. They were filled with handbags, shoes, costume jewelry, blouses, scarves and old hats. They once belonged to her Mamère, Callie assumed. As Mark removed them, she examined the much older ones, hoping to find that red dot. She found clothes from a time long, long ago, now decayed and moth-eaten. There were boxes crammed full of papers, and one was filled with nothing but correspondence. She took a letter out – it was addressed to Mrs. Leonore Arceneaux, Beau Rivage Plantation, Point Charmaine, Louisiana, and had been mailed by someone in Philadelphia. It had a very old stamp she'd never seen before, and it was postmarked May 1, 1878.

"How exciting!" she exclaimed, showing it to Mark. "This letter is addressed to Leonore Arceneaux, my grandmother's grandmother. Mamère told me about how she came to own this house. My ancestor Henri built it, and when the South was about to lose the war, he deeded it to his brother John, who lived in Philadelphia. He hoped that the Yankees wouldn't burn a home that belonged to one of their own, and it apparently worked, because Beau Rivage was untouched.

"The idea was that Henri would get the house back when the war ended, but he died before that could happen. John never set foot on the property and neither did Leonore for several years, but eventually she moved here with her child, Michael, Mamère Juliet's father. I guess Leonore and John had split up – I never heard why she was here but he stayed in Philadelphia. When Leonore died, her son inherited the house, and when he died, he left it to my grandmother."

Mark gazed at the letter in his hand and listened intently to her grandmother's story. "Didn't Henri have children that Leonore could give the house back to?" he asked when she was finished.

"Henri had only one child – a girl who died when she was ten years old. There were no other heirs."

"Where are your relatives buried? Your grandmother Juliet, for instance?"

"Her grave is in the Krotz Springs Cemetery. I walked over there yesterday and saw it. As far as my ancestors go, I have no idea where they're buried. Mamère never mentioned it. Maybe their graves are in Krotz Springs too."

"I'd be surprised. Krotz Springs itself dates to the early twentieth century. Your relatives had to have been buried somewhere else because they died long before that. How about other living relatives? Did they come to your grandmother's funeral?"

"I'm the only one left except Uncle Willard and his daughters. I didn't come because I couldn't afford it. Mamère was cremated and Uncle Willard handled everything. There couldn't have been many people there – I never knew her to have any friends."

"Maybe there's a lot of history in these boxes that will tell you about your family. But so far, we haven't hit the jackpot. Where's that red dot?"

They examined the sides, tops and bottoms of each box, but there were no red dots and no clues.

"Let's take a break," she said. "I need some water and my back's aching from sitting on the floor."

"Want to put these boxes back?" he asked, since there were dozens of them scattered around the room.

"I guess so. Whoever ends up with the house isn't going to want a roomful of clutter."

He propped the closet door wide open to make it easier to put the boxes back. She stood, picked up the nearest one and carried it to the closet.

"I'll be damned," she whispered as she pointed to the inside of the door.

Thumbtacked to it was an envelope with a big red dot on the outside.

"All those boxes for nothing," she cried, removing the envelope. She opened it and found several folded papers. She looked carefully at each one, then refolded them and put them in her lap.

She sat on the floor again and asked him to join her. "I want to tell you more about my past and then I'll tell you what these papers are. I should have kept in contact with Mamère over the years, but I didn't want her to know how bad off I was. God knows there were times I wanted to ask her for money, but I was determined not to do it. Part of it was pride, but there was more than that. She had been unbelievably good to me. How did I repay her love and generosity? By breaking off communication with her for the last twelve years of her life. I felt like a total ass, to tell the truth, and the longer I didn't contact her, the more embarrassed I was about it."

She explained how her grandfather – the father of Mamère's child Simon – had disappeared once Juliet became pregnant. Later her own father would do the same thing, leaving her mother destitute. "Despite our poverty, I studied hard and made good grades in high school. Mamère paid my tuition to Virginia State University in Petersburg. I got a journalism degree and went to work for the newspaper there, and I've spent the last six years in that crappy job, making thirty grand a year. I was so broke I couldn't even afford to look for another job because I'd have to travel somewhere for an interview. Then Mamère died – Uncle Willard called to tell me that – and I told him I couldn't come. Eight months later I heard from him again. That was a few days ago, and now here I am holding my inheritance in my hand."

"You've had a hard time," he agreed. "But at least she left you something. Things have to be better now, right?"

She shook her head and bit her lip. "She left me the house, Mark. She left me this old mansion and everything in it Plus forty acres of land."

"God, Callie, that's great news!"

"Really? I don't think so. Now I'm more broke than before. Now I own a big money pit. She thought she was doing me a favor, giving me the house she loved, where she'd lived for her entire life. It should be a wonderful inheritance. But she had no idea what a total failure in life I am. She didn't know I'm so poor I couldn't even pay someone to mow the front lawn. She was passing down the Arceneaux mansion, but she should have given it to Uncle Willard or his kids. At least they could have afforded to keep it up."

He gave her a hand to stand up and they walked out. As she closed the door behind her, she wondered if her earlier fears about this room had to do with how wonderful her past had been, and how much she'd screwed things up since.

Once Mark and Callie were gone, the child walked across the ballroom and closed the closet door that Callie had left open. Her footsteps left no imprint in the dust on the floor.

CHAPTER FIVE

They left Beau Rivage and decided to find a place for coffee – somewhere more inviting than Phil's c-store in Point Charmaine. Mark gave a jocular honk and a wave as they drove past it on the way to River Road. They went five miles to Krotz Springs, a town of maybe a thousand people that still had a few stores. There was a tidy little restaurant, and soon they were enjoying steaming mugs of chicory coffee.

The banker returned her call and advised that Juliet Arceneaux had opened an account in her name. She needed to come in, sign some paperwork and it would be hers.

Maybe this is the good news, Callie thought optimistically. *Maybe she didn't just leave me the house. Of all people, she knew it would take lots of money to keep it up.*

"Can you tell me the balance?"

"Until you sign the paperwork, you aren't officially authorized to access the account. I can only say that it's in the low four figures."

She said she'd come in later today. Afterwards, she asked Mark what he thought low four figures might mean.

"A few thousand dollars," he answered. "High four figures could be something like nine thousand dollars. The lowest of four figures would be a thousand bucks. Sounds like she's left you something under five thousand, if I were guessing."

Wow. Thanks, Mamère. That won't even make a dent in things.

As soon as it flitted through her mind, that thought overwhelmed her with guilt at her ungratefulness. Even though she hadn't bothered to visit her grandmother in twelve years, Mamère Juliet had left her the family's most prized possession – Beau Rivage. Mamère couldn't have known that Callie was destitute. She probably thought the money would help get the upkeep under way. In her granddaughter's situation, it wouldn't help at all.

How could I have made such a mess with my life?

Coming back to reality, she asked Mark, "What do I do now? I inherited the family home, but I can't afford the upkeep. You're in the home-repair business. Of all people, you know that a few thousand dollars won't begin to cover what's needed at Beau Rivage. I'm supposed to be going back in a day or two. I guess with my new bank account I can fly home instead of riding the bus. How do I protect the place while I'm gone? There's no telling when I'll ever get back. I'm not sure why I should come back, for that matter."

"I could watch it for you," he offered, but they both knew that wasn't really a solution. The place was full of furniture and she'd been lucky so far that vandals hadn't stolen everything and destroyed the house. Leaving it abandoned wouldn't work.

"I have an idea," Mark said. "This may be something you'd never consider, but hear me out. There are some real positives about Beau Rivage. As one of the few antebellum homes the Yankees didn't destroy, it's historically significant. The forty acres of Atchafalaya riverfront property might have value someday, like properties up and down the Mississippi.

"Let's consider the negatives. One is that it's remote. If we can find the road from the property to the highway, we can solve that problem. A big problem is that the house is deteriorating, and if someone doesn't fix it soon, it's only going to cost more later. It would be a shame to let that happen. You need to get a work crew out there as soon as possible."

"I appreciate your ideas," she interrupted. "But have you forgotten that one little issue of mine called money? I have a 'low four figures' net worth, Mark. You and I both know how far that'll go to fix up the property. It kills me to see what the place looks like. It was grand. Mamère made sure it always looked perfect, but she had the money to make that happen. Now it's mine; it would be horrible of me to sell the thing my grandmother left me – that place full of her memories and mine. But I can't afford it. What do I do – just let it sit here for a year while I go back to Virginia and win the lottery? Maybe in a year a prince on a white horse will ride up and want to buy it for his castle. Or maybe there'll be some other fairy-tale ending ... some outcome better than Callie Pilantro eventually selling a piece of history to Uncle Willard for a few thousand bucks." She choked on the words, composed herself and continued. "You're the real estate guru. What would you do?"

"If you want to sell it, I'll buy it from you. I'll give you ten thousand dollars for it right now, but I'd advise you not to do it. It'll be worth a lot more when it's fixed up."

"I really appreciate your offer and maybe I should sell right now, but I'm going to wait for a while. I've always heard when you inherit something you should take some time before making hasty decisions. As much as I hate to let it deteriorate even more, I can't let it go until I feel it's the right thing to do."

"Then let's fix it up. We can borrow some money ..."

Her words were harsh. "*We* can borrow some money? No, Mark. *We* can't borrow anything because one of us is flat broke. I have a net worth of twenty dollars plus whatever's in the bank account. No bank's going to lend me money."

"You could put up the land as collateral."

"Are you kidding? You saw the place. What would they loan me – maybe five grand? You know that would be gone in a week if we started fixing up Beau Rivage. Even I know it's going to cost a lot more than that."

"I'll make a deal with you. My bank will loan me money based on other collateral I have. We'll ask for fifty thousand. You give them a mortgage on forty acres, the house and the contents, and we'll sign a promissory note for the money. That'll work."

"How far would fifty grand go?"

"If we concentrated on the first floor, we could have the place looking really good. You and I can do a lot of the work ourselves. When we need more than fifty, we go back and ask for more based on what we've done so far to improve the value of the bank's collateral. I've done it a dozen times on my own properties and it works so long as we spend the money wisely and can show the value we've added. We might even be able to open the first floor to tourists – that would definitely make our borrowing ability better."

"Yeah, but if anything went wrong, I could never pay the money back."

"Don't worry about it. Nothing's going to go wrong. It'll only take a few months to put the place in shape to open it for tourists. You need to think what it might be – a bed and breakfast, or a riverfront museum and tearoom for people who are traveling downriver, or several apartments. Once it's redone, if you decide to put it on the market, I'd like to list it myself. I'll make a commission and you get whatever profit there is after we pay back the bank loan."

"It sounds too easy. It'll never work."

He smiled. "I think you need to have a little faith. I think it really could work. With all due respect, I have a little more knowledge about the real estate business in St. Landry Parish than you do. There are only a few other mansions along the river. We could make this one a showplace without spending a fortune."

"I can't sign a note knowing I might not be able to repay it."

"Okay, how about this? Let's go to the bank and see if they like my proposal. If they do, I'll sign for the fifty grand by myself. You put up the house and land as collateral. If everything went bad – which is almost impossible to imagine – you'd lose Beau Rivage, but the bank would sell it to me since I already have fifty thousand in the deal. I'd sell it and split any profits with you. Even if the deal falls apart, you really haven't lost anything. Not owning the house would put you exactly where you were when you arrived in Opelousas a few days ago."

She was already thinking how much fun it would be to work on restoring the old house she loved, and she was beginning to think working with Mark wouldn't be such a bad idea either. He had been a huge help to her every step of the way, and maybe they might end up as partners in more than just a real estate deal. She pushed that thought away; this wasn't the time to involve her emotions. This needed to be a business deal that made sense, even though she had absolutely nothing to lose by joining forces with him.

"Let's go to Mamère's bank and see how wealthy I am," she said with a grin. "Then I'll go to the bank with you and I'll listen to what they say. I'm not promising anything."

He drove her back to his house. They changed clothes, ate lunch and went downtown. The First National Bank visit took only five minutes. Callie signed some papers and got an online access code. The banker told her that including interest, the current balance of the account was one thousand and twelve dollars.

"I'm rich," she quipped as they walked down the street to the Cotton Belt State Bank. "When I add in the nine bucks in my pocket, I'm Mrs. Bill Gates!"

The vice president who was Mark's loan officer listened to his pitch, pulled up his banking history on his computer and said he needed Mark's current financial statement. "You've repaid every loan on time or ahead of schedule," he continued. "If your net worth hasn't changed from your last statement, we could lend you fifty thousand dollars for twelve months. You'd pay interest monthly and the principal would be due in full at the end."

They left with Mark's promise to email the financial information that afternoon. "My net worth's fine," he told Callie. "They'll loan me the money. Now it's up to you. What do you say?"

"I say I want to sleep on it."

Upstairs in her bedroom she changed back into a T-shirt and shorts, enjoying the smells of the barbecue grill in the backyard wafting through her open window. She looked out and saw Mark cleaning the grate, getting it ready for the hamburgers he was cooking for dinner. *He's really a nice guy*, she thought to herself. *Maybe I should do this. He knows this business, like he said. He wouldn't risk fifty thousand dollars if he didn't think it would work.*

Her cellphone rang. It was a local number, and when she answered, she heard Willard Arceneaux's obnoxious voice. "Callie darlin', I was callin' to see what all you inherited from Juliet. My girls were pretty happy once they realized what she'd done for them. Surely she took care of you too."

His gloating was unmistakable and she was determined not to let him get the best of her. "I'm not sure yet what I have," she answered. "It's kind of complicated."

"Oh, really? The word in town is that you got yourself a piece of property. Doesn't sound too complicated to me."

How in the hell could he already know that? She'd only just found out herself and the only places they'd been were two banks. She realized she was seeing firsthand the connections Willard had in St. Landry Parish.

"I'm not exactly sure yet," she answered.

He seemed eager to rub it in a little more. "The girls came out well. You know Madeline got that claim check from the car repair place. I called over there. When you were a kid visiting Beau Rivage, do you remember what Juliet used to drive around in?"

His words were so condescendingly sickening that she wanted to hang up, but she remained steadfast. "Are you talking about the old convertible?"

"Yep. That old convertible, as you call it, is a Rolls Royce Phantom III that belonged to Juliet's father, Michael. He bought it brand new in 1939, the year before he died. Know what it's worth?"

She didn't say a word.

"It's worth a minimum of two seventy-five. That's thousand, darlin'. Two hundred and seventy-five thousand dollars. Not bad, I'd say! And guess what Carmine got!"

She kept her mouth firmly shut.

"As I suspected, that little key went to a safety-deposit box at the bank. It had treasury bills in it. I doubt you even know what those are, since your momma barely had a dollar to spare. They're issued by the government and they pay interest. These had been in the box a long, long time. They're worth nearly three hundred thousand dollars!"

"Good for them," she muttered.

"Well, just wanted to check in with you. Good luck on that property you got. If you need any help from me, you know my number." He disconnected.

You've already helped, Uncle Willard, she thought with a smile. *You've helped me make up my mind.*

As she walked into the kitchen, Mark handed her a beer, tipped his and clinked bottles. "Cheers!" he said brightly. "Here's to possibilities."

I couldn't have said it better myself!

She told him her decision and they spent a pleasant evening in his backyard. They celebrated with a bottle of wine, then one more for good measure. After dinner, she cancelled her return bus trip. She now knew that she would be here a while. Her apartment rent was due in twenty-six days. Recalling the words of Scarlett O'Hara, she decided she'd deal with that issue later. Anything could happen in twenty-six days.

CHAPTER SIX

Mark and Callie signed the papers, opened a joint bank account and deposited the fifty thousand dollars he had borrowed. As they'd agreed, she had given the bank a mortgage, which would allow it to repossess Beau Rivage if they defaulted, but as Mark had said, even if she lost it, she was no worse off than when she had arrived here.

That first afternoon, he looked inside the outbuildings on the property to assess what was there. When he was finished, he found Callie and said that her grandmother had left her a present.

"Is this one going to cost me too?" she chuckled, but he shook his head.

"Actually, this one's going to help." He took her out to a barn a few hundred yards away, where a 2007 Pontiac four-door sedan sat inside. There was a note on the floorboard that said, "Callie, the keys are where Socks used to hide."

"Socks was my stuffed rabbit!" she cried. "Thanks, Mamère! I'll be right back!" She ran to the house and soon returned with a set of keys and the title to the vehicle, which her grandmother had signed. "These were under the stairs in a box where I pretended Socks lived. Mamère must have remembered that." She made a mental note to buy car insurance and get the title transferred the next time she was in town.

Mark was surprised when the car started immediately. She drove it over to the house and noticed the odometer registered only twenty-three hundred miles, showing how little her grandmother had driven in the past ten years.

"I guess she quit driving the Rolls, put it in storage and got a more practical car. I owe you big-time for this one, Mamère. You have no idea how much I needed this."

"I'll bet there are more surprises in store for you. Every closet in the house is crammed full of stuff, and so are the outbuildings. It'll take months for you to go through everything."

They worked at Beau Rivage from eight to five. Mark started on the essentials – replacing broken doors and windows so the mansion would be secure. He put up No Trespassing signs along the riverbank and at the road, and he had the utilities turned back on. Now the house had water and electricity and there was gas for the kitchen stove. Afraid she was becoming an imposition for Mark, Callie wanted to be able to stay at Beau Rivage as soon as possible, and now she could do that.

As Mark worked outdoors, Callie was inside. One room at a time, she uncovered chairs, tables and paintings, applied stain to windowsills and floorboards that had suffered water damage, dusted and slowly began to return the once-proud sitting areas to the way they'd looked long ago. The things Mamère Juliet had displayed on end tables, buffets and in breakfronts were gone, but she had a hunch she'd find them in the storage closets on the top floor. She'd already seen a box of wrapped objects she knew had come from the drawing room. It made sense they'd be there. Other than Willard's children, there were no heirs, and as far as she knew, Mamère hadn't had any close friends she might have given things away to.

It took a day and a half to finish one room, a parlor on the back side of the house away from the river. She'd cleaned and scrubbed, and it would be her bedroom for now. There were five bedrooms upstairs, but they were concentrating their efforts and money on the ground floor.

On the third night, Callie used her new bedroom at Beau Rivage for the first time. She turned down Mark's offer to stay too. She had to face this, and she'd spent so many nights here as a child that she believed she'd be fine. She was accustomed to the old structure, so its creaks and groans during the night didn't alarm her. Limbs tap-tapped on the roof, the windowpanes rattled, and there were eerie, moaning sounds as the wind whipped down through the chimneys. Rather than fear, the ghostly sounds brought back fond memories as she snuggled under a quilt she'd found in an upstairs closet – one that Mamère had made for her long ago.

Around three in the morning she awoke with a start. Had she heard footsteps in the hallway outside her door? Maybe it had been a dream, but it felt more real than that.

"Is someone there?" she asked, her voice shaking a little.

The only response was the groan of the old front door as a gust of wind shook it. She got up, slid the pocket door open and stuck her head out. Moonbeams poured through the side windows by the back door and lit the hallway with an unearthly glow. There was no one there and she hadn't heard footsteps after all. She told herself that over and over until she fell asleep and woke shortly after six.

Mark arrived around eight and she asked if he'd take a look at the downstairs bathroom. "If I'm going to stay here, it needs some work," she told him, explaining that there was no hot water and the shower didn't drain properly. He made it top priority.

She was on a step stool, washing windows, when Mark tapped her on the shoulder, startling her.

"What is it?" she shouted.

"See for yourself." He pointed to the hallway and Callie turned and was surprised to see a pretty girl around ten years old standing in the hallway a few feet away. She wore a starched frilly blue dress.

"How'd you get in here?" Callie asked.

"I came through the door, of course." The girl was smiling and her voice was quiet and had a melodic undertone.

Mark said, "I saw her when I came out of the bathroom. I spoke to her, but she didn't answer. That's when I came in here to get you."

Feeling a sense of unease, Callie told herself to calm down. This was a child, for goodness' sake.

"Who are you?"

"The girl is Anne-Marie. I come here sometimes."

The girl? Why was she referring to herself in the third person? There was something very odd about her.

"Do you live nearby?"

She smiled and hummed to herself for a bit. Then she pointed at Mark and said, "Who is he?"

"I'm Callie and that's Mark. Juliet was my Mamère and I own the house now. We're working on it so we can ..." She stopped. Why was she telling a little girl all this?

"I know who you are."

"How can you know anything about me? I've never seen you before."

"Because I do," she said with a smile. "I know lots of things."

"Why aren't you in school?" she asked, but Anne-Marie ignored her.

"How long will you be here?" the child asked.

"I don't know. We're going to fix up the place. Who are you, anyway? Where do you live?"

"The house has secrets."

A shiver ran up Callie's spine. "What secrets? What are you talking about?"

The girl hummed and smiled; then she turned and walked down the hall where they couldn't see her anymore.

"Stop!" Callie yelled. "Come back here!"

They both ran to the hallway, but the girl wasn't there. The back door was closed, but the front door – the opposite way from where Anne-Marie had gone – was standing open, just as Callie had left it this morning.

The girl had walked toward the back. Callie looked and saw it was locked.

After looking outside for a few minutes, they returned to the house and sat on the front porch. "She scared me," Callie admitted. "Something about her made me uneasy. She's not ... well, normal, I guess, whatever that means. She said she came in through the door. If that's true, it had to be the front door, because it was the only one open. But she didn't leave that way, right? Help me out here. Where did she go?"

He shook his head. "I'm with you on the uneasy part. She acted really strange and then she disappeared. Do you think –"

She cut him off. "I don't know where you're going with this, but I'm trying to get used to this house. Why did she creep me out so much? Did we see a ghost? Listen to me. Talk about someone who's not normal. Am I crazy?"

"You're not crazy because I saw everything. She didn't look strange to me except that she was dressed oddly, wearing that party dress out here on the river. She didn't speak like a child either. It was like everything she said was carefully thought out. And she wasn't good at answering questions. She was better at asking them. Maybe she's just curious about us. Maybe she lives nearby and came to see what's going on."

"Nobody lives nearby. This place sits on forty acres. As far as I know, there's not another house anywhere close to here except for the ones in the settlement across the river. You don't think she could have crossed over, do you? How could she have crossed the river?"

"She didn't. There's always a strong current on the Atchafalaya. If she had a motorboat, she could do it, but I think we'd have heard her coming or going, and she's pretty young to be handling a boat by herself."

They had to let it go; there was work to be done and they had to return to their tasks. After completing basic repairs on the bathroom to make it functional, Mark left at four; he had a real estate board dinner that evening and said he'd see her first thing tomorrow. As the sun began to set, she finished arranging furniture in the parlor and went to the kitchen to get a beer. They'd used part of the bank loan to buy provisions, and the pantry was well stocked. Except for the ancient stove, the kitchen appliances were all from the nineteen sixties, but they worked.

Callie sat in a rocker on the porch and watched a barge heading south on the river toward the Gulf of Mexico.

The sun was setting, and as usual this time of day, the birds, cicadas and crickets began a frenzied chirping and buzzing. She leaned back, closed her eyes and remembered hearing these same pleasant sounds when Mamère and she would sit out here. When it was dark enough to turn on the lights, she stood, turned to walk inside and saw something in the trees a hundred yards away to her left. Daylight was fading fast, but she could see that it was a figure – a short person – standing in the darkness. She felt a shiver run down her spine.

"Hello? Is someone there? Anne-Marie, is that you?"

It was so dark now that she wondered if she'd seen anyone after all.

She fixed a ham sandwich and thought about it as she ate. Had someone really been there? Was it Anne-Marie? The spectral figure she might have seen had been short and wearing a dark color – maybe blue. Or maybe not.

Come on, Callie. Get a grip. The kid scared you and now you're seeing her everywhere. You're letting your mind play tricks on you. There was no one there.

She checked all the locks twice and pulled the heavy drapes tightly shut in the parlor where she was sleeping. She played a game on her phone and surfed the web until she was tired enough to fall asleep. She awoke sometime during the night to the sound of raindrops softly striking the windows. The sound made her relaxed and comfortable, and she settled back into a dreamless slumber.

After the rain, the morning dawned bright and sunny. Mark arrived around eight and said he intended to work upstairs today, repairing and replacing windows. She told him about the figure she thought she'd seen last night. She admitted it had made her apprehensive.

"You're always welcome to stay at my house," he offered, but she said she was worried about leaving the place at night now that they were putting money into it.

"If someone vandalized the place now, we'd be back at square one," she replied. "I need to stay here. I've got to conquer my fears. I don't even know why I'm doing this.

This place has always been like home to me. Even as a kid I never spent one scared minute in this house."

"How about I move in with you?"

She glanced up with a startled look and he smiled and shook his head.

"That didn't come out like I intended. What I was trying to say is let's fix up another room and I'll stay here too."

"Let me think about it," she said. "We have a lot to do and we can talk about it when we stop for lunch."

He went to the second-floor balcony and began repairing and replacing windows while Callie worked in the music room. Except for the wood-paneled library and dining rooms, every room in the house had wallpaper that was beginning to yellow and fade. Eventually she wanted to remove it and paint instead, but that would have to wait until there was more money. Only one room – the music room where she was working today – would be painted for now, and that was only because the wallpaper was peeling, with strips hanging down in places.

She started on one side of the room and worked her way around. The job was tedious; Mark had brought a tall ladder from his house and she was constantly going up and down, stripping paper off the twelve-foot-high walls. She worked carefully to protect the crown molding around the top that she was sure was original, which would make it nearly two hundred years old.

The mowing crew Mark had arranged to clean up the grounds arrived at the dock in a pontoon boat. Four men unloaded riding mowers and other equipment and went to work. When he and Callie took a coffee break, they sat on the front veranda in the sunshine and enjoyed the smell of freshly mowed grass.

Someone rounded the corner of the house, startling them. It was Willard, dressed in a seersucker suit and a yellow bow tie.

"Mornin'!" he said cordially. "Mind if I join you?"

Callie pointed to another chair and he sat down. "How'd you get here? Did you take the road from Point Charmaine? It's a mess."

"There's more than one way to Beau Rivage. You just have to know where it is."

"Are you talking about the old road from the highway? We couldn't find it," Mark said.

"It's still there. It runs through a canopy of trees and doesn't hold the rain like that sloppy road from Point Charmaine does. You drive on grass all the way. The trees get a little close, but my trusty BMW made it just fine."

I'm sure it did, Callie thought.

Enough faux cordiality. "What do you want, Uncle Willard?"

"I just came to see what kind of folly you all are up to. Everyone in town's talkin' about it, you know. I heard you're workin' on the place, and I suppose you're using this fellow's money," he said, pointing to Mark. "You never had a head for business, honey, and you have no idea how much money it's going to take to even make a dent in this place."

Turning to Mark, he said, "How about you? What's in it for you? Or is it my niece you're interested in?"

Callie exploded. "That's none of your business! If you drove all the way out here to check up on me, then get off my property!"

Forcing a smile, he ignored her. "I saw Juliet's car at the back of the house. You're just happier than a pig in slop, aren't you, darlin'? You think you're gettin' gifts everywhere you look. But your old mamère didn't do you any favors, Calisto. She handed you a pig in a poke. She unloaded the one thing that has burdened the Arceneaux family for two hundred years – this albatross that Henri built. A long time ago it was a grand old mansion sitting proudly on the river, but ever since the Civil War, it's been a struggle for one of our relatives after another. Juliet was smart enough to stash money aside, and she was smart enough to give her fancy car and her investments to my girls instead of you. She wasn't your nice, loving granny. Before this is over, you'll rue the day you ever knew Juliet Arceneaux."

"Shut up and get out! Get out of my house!"

He stood slowly. "I'm goin'. Just one more thing, darlin'. My offer still stands. I'll buy the place from you. I'll give you whatever you and this gentleman have put in it so far. You may walk away from Beau Rivage broke, but hell, that's the same way you got here, right? Think about it before you spend anything else. I'm the only one in the family who can afford to do anything with it, but my offer won't last forever."

After he was gone, she started crying and couldn't stop. Everything inside her – all the feelings, hopes, desires and dreams about a new life – had been dashed back into reality by her wretched uncle. She held her head in her hands and sobbed.

"I wish there was something I could do," Mark said softly.

"You've helped me so much. You've been the only one on my side," she cried. "Willard's right, Mark. How could either one of us ever have thought borrowing fifty thousand dollars was a good idea? It's only been a few days and how much have we spent already? Thousands, I'm sure."

"Around fourteen thousand so far. I've bought most of the materials we'll need and we've also put down utility deposits. It takes a lot of money to fix up a place this big."

"My point exactly," she said, beginning to pull herself together. She wiped her eyes with a napkin. "And to finish, it's going to take a hell of a lot more money than we have. What are we going to do when we run out?"

"Callie, it'll be all right. We already went over this. We're going to open it for tourists or as a B&B, like we told the bank. We don't have to spend a fortune to make it presentable; your grandmother kept it up, so we only have eight months of deterioration to deal with. Keep the faith. We're going to make this work for you!"

He hugged her and she clung to him for an extra moment. It felt good having someone else to talk to.

It's been so long since I haven't felt completely alone.

He spent the night. There was a simple, brief hug as he retired to one side of the broad hallway and she the other. They pulled shut the ten-foot pocket doors and the next thing he realized was that it was morning and he was smelling the delicious aroma of coffee.

He padded to the downstairs bathroom. Although he'd worked on it already, he saw more things to fix as he brushed his teeth, showered and shaved. He joined her in the kitchen and she handed him a mug.

"Morning," she said brightly. "Thanks for staying here last night. I thought about it and I don't think you need to do that anymore. You have your own life and I'm a big girl."

"We'll see how things go," he said. "I'm happy to do anything to help."

Plus, I'm happy to wake up to a cute girl in a T-shirt and shorts who fixed my coffee.

CHAPTER SEVEN

Mark had a real estate closing in Lafayette that afternoon at two and promised to be back before dark with gumbo and étouffée from Prejean's, one of Callie's favorite restaurants. Neither of them mentioned where he'd stay tonight.

He met his client at the title company office, walked him through the closing and left with a commission check. He picked up the food around four and began the hour-long drive back. He had to pass through Opelousas, so he decided to deposit the check before going to Beau Rivage. As he waited in the bank's drive-through line, he saw a fancy silver BMW 700 Series pull in behind him. The door on the driver's side opened and Willard Arceneaux walked up to his Jeep.

"We need to talk, son," he said affably.

Although Callie had serious issues with her uncle, that was her fight, he had thought as he watched them bicker. Although he'd never done business with him, Mark had always gotten along with Willard. Opelousas was a small town and it didn't make sense to alienate influential and important people.

"What's up?" Mark asked.

Willard handed him a card. "Here's my cell number. Call me when you can talk privately. It'll be worth your while. Keep this conversation to yourself." He walked to his car and left.

As Mark drove along Highway 190, he thought about the encounter. Willard Arceneaux wouldn't typically give him the time of day. He'd seen firsthand how Callie and her uncle interacted, and everyone in the area knew the Cajun Crusher was a formidable opponent. Willard was a man who abhorred losing. He'd do anything to win, and Mark didn't think he cared a bit about family. He debated whether he'd call him back and decided it wouldn't hurt to find out what he was up to.

Mark stayed on River Road past the turn to Point Charmaine, driving very slowly until he found what he was looking for – a cutoff that led into the woods. A rusty mailbox with "B.R." on its side was halfway hidden in the undergrowth. He pulled alongside it and took out some junk mail addressed to Juliet Arceneaux. He was in the right place.

He followed a rutted trail until it popped out of the woods a hundred yards from the entrance to Beau Rivage. As Willard had pointed out, once it was cleared, this old entry would be much easier than going through Point Charmaine.

Mark found Callie in the kitchen, holding a glass of wine. "I fixed you one too; it's in the fridge," she said. Her voice sounded cheerful, a tone he hadn't heard much since they'd arrived. He put the sacks of food on the counter and handed her a loaf of freshly baked French bread, which she wrapped in foil and put in the oven to keep warm.

As was becoming a custom, they sat on the front porch to take in the setting sun. Now that the yard was mowed and the bushes trimmed, the wide expanse of lawn looked beautiful, befitting this wonderful old house. She asked him how his day went, and he said the closing was uneventful and he'd stopped by Opelousas to deposit his commission check. He could see her fidgeting as he talked, and he knew that she was waiting to tell him something too.

"Anne-Marie came back today," she said.

"Really? Did she make you nervous?"

"A little at first, but only because she's so strange. She just appears – do you know what I mean? One minute I'm all alone, stripping wallpaper in the music room, and then I get this tingly feeling – you know, like someone's watching me. Today I turned around and there she was; I'd left the front door open since it was a pretty day and I guess she walked right in. I had a dream about her last night. I dreamed she told me the house had a secret and she'd show it to me."

"Really? Well, did she come through on her promise?"

"Yes, she did. She showed me something about Beau Rivage that I never knew."

She took his hand and led him inside. That hadn't happened before; he found it comfortable and he felt a little remorseful that he was keeping his talk with Willard to himself. He decided there was no reason to mention it until he found out what the man wanted.

She stopped at the entrance to the music room. The room was vast – twenty by twenty feet at least – and Callie had been hard at work today. Long strips of the old wallpaper lay strewn about the floor.

"Notice anything different about this room?" she asked.

"Nothing except that you've torn the place apart."

She laughed. "There's something here I never knew about until today." Still holding his hand, she walked him across the room and pointed out a wooden door about half the height and width of a regular one.

"You found this behind the wallpaper?"

"Yes, thanks to Anne-Marie. I said hello when I saw her, but she didn't say anything, as usual. I went back to work and I noticed her running her hands up and down the wallpaper on this wall. I was on the other side of the room, peeling paper. She asked me to look at something and told me to remove the paper right here. This is what was behind it. It must have been covered up for decades. Mamère never mentioned it; I wonder if she even knew it was here."

There was a tiny keyhole but no knob, and it was totally flush with the rest of the wall, which was why it was unnoticeable under the wallpaper.

"Did she show you how to open it?" he asked.

"Yes, and this is weird. Anne-Marie smiled and asked if I wanted to see what was behind it. When I said yes, she pulled out a key on a silver chain around her neck and put it in the keyhole. She opened the door herself, Mark.

She's ten years old, I'm almost thirty and I've never seen that door. How did a little girl know it was there?"

"What's more bizarre is, how did she have the key? Is the door unlocked now?"

"Yes. Take a look!"

She inserted a screwdriver between the door and jamb and it swung open easily. Inside there was a very narrow, very steep staircase that led up to a turn. He followed her into the musty passageway and she fired up the flashlight on her phone. At the turn, there was another set of stairs, another twist at the top and a third set. It was dusty, hot and claustrophobic. They saw gas lamp fixtures protruding from the walls every so often, an indication of how the stairway was illuminated long ago.

There was another door at the top that Anne-Marie had unlocked with the same key. They stepped through into a dark room. Cardboard boxes were all around them.

"Obviously we're on the third floor," he said. "Where exactly are we?"

"We're in another storage closet like the one you and I went through. I had to push hard to get the door open. There were boxes stacked in front of it, which I think is why I never found it when I played up here as a kid. I went through everything – at least I thought I did – but here was a secret I never knew about."

They opened the closet door and stepped into the ballroom. "That stairway's amazing," he said. "We can make it part of the home tour. A hidden staircase adds to the marketing appeal. What do you think it was used for?"

"Anne-Marie wouldn't answer me when I asked her. She just hummed and smiled – you know? She frustrates me when she does that. She's just so strange. She was wearing that same blue dress, and who knows why she isn't in school. I said I thought I saw her in the trees the other night and she shook her head. Then I asked if there were other children around here, and of course you know what she did then."

"She just smiled and hummed."

"Exactly. And then I stuck my head back in the closet for a minute to look at the door again. When I came out, she was gone. She's like a ghost with her appearances and disappearances. It's unnerving. Not scary – that's not the right word for her – but there's something really different that I can't put my finger on."

Down in the kitchen, she warmed up the gumbo and étouffée. He put two place settings at the dining room table and soon they were digging in to the fabulous food and Abita Amber beers. They tried to understand why the secret staircase had been built but got nowhere. Callie said she'd ask Anne-Marie about it again.

"I made up my mind today that I wasn't going to be afraid here," she confided. "I've always been strong and there's no reason to let fear get the best of me. I'm living in a huge old mansion that's full of memories. Anyplace I turn, I see things that remind me of my childhood. I half expect to see Mamère walking down the hall. It wouldn't surprise me a bit. I refuse to be afraid in this house that I loved much more than any real home I ever had. Now it's mine, if I can figure out how to keep it. Regardless, I'm committed to positive thinking."

They went to bed across the hall from each other just like last night. She thought to herself that the topic of whether he'd stay tonight had never come up. He just had, and that was okay with her.

Callie had wound the old grandfather clock that stood in the hallway, and its deep chimes every hour through the night brought back more memories from her childhood. She heard the clock chime one and then she thought she heard something else. She opened her eyes and sat up immediately. Anne-Marie was standing across the room, wearing her blue dress. Too sleepy to feel anything but surprise, Callie asked her what she was doing up in the middle of the night and how she'd gotten into this room with the pocket door still closed.

"I don't like him," she whispered. "He's going to hurt you."

"I know," Callie said. "Uncle Willard wants to take this house from me. But I can handle him."

"I can help you. I can show you more secrets."

Suddenly a rush of cold air swept over her and her skin prickled. She reached down for the quilt and when she looked up, Anne-Marie was gone.

Callie ran to the hallway. "Mark, Mark!" she shouted, and in seconds his door slid open and a bleary-eyed guy in black boxers asked her what was wrong.

"Anne-Marie was in my room! She was talking to me!"

Mark checked all the doors, came back and said, "Callie, go back to bed. You were dreaming. You had an encounter with her today and you're still thinking about it. There's no way she could have gotten in. Everything's locked up just like when we went to bed. See you in the morning."

He was right. She couldn't have gotten in ... unless there were other secrets like the stairway she'd uncovered. Was there another way in? But it didn't really happen at all. A little girl couldn't be out here on the river in the middle of the night, still wearing her clothes from this afternoon. It simply wasn't possible. She really had dreamed it.

She fell asleep at last, and this time it was her turn to wake up and smell the coffee.

CHAPTER EIGHT

Two men sat in the dining room of the Magnolia Country Club in Opelousas. They had a quiet table by the window overlooking the ninth hole. The waiter watched attentively, ready to respond to any request, but kept a respectable distance as the men lunched and conversed in low voices. The tables around them would remain empty until they left; Willard Arceneaux always demanded privacy for his luncheons, and since he also tipped generously, Mr. Arceneaux got whatever he wanted.

"We've been patient with you for several months," the man in the dark suit said. "You made certain representations to us, and to be perfectly frank, my directors are beginning to wonder if you can deliver. We were led to believe we'd be under construction by now. There are other opportunities, you know, and we've wasted precious time relying upon your representations. I can't hold off my directors much longer."

"Now, now, Marvin," he answered, which irritated Marvin White, who had no intention of ever being on a first-name basis with this man. "I hope you didn't mislead your directors. I never gave you firm dates on how quickly all this would happen. I couldn't, because we still have a missing will, you know what I mean? It's going to take a little more time, but how about this – I'll give you a firm date now. If the will doesn't turn up in the next thirty days, then as executor, I'll do what is best for the estate. I'll sign the agreement and you'll have what you want. Will that satisfy you and your board?"

"Thirty days, Mr. Arceneaux. That's a hard deadline and I'm holding you to it. If you don't come through, then my company will withdraw and you'll be required to return our million-dollar deposit."

"There's no problem, Marvin. Leave it to me. By the way, isn't that Dover sole delicious?"

CHAPTER NINE

"Did you move my ladder?" she called to Mark as she prepared to finish the wallpaper-removal project in the music room.

"Nope," he shouted back from upstairs somewhere. He was installing the last of the broken windows on the second floor; the ballroom would be next.

Wonder where I put it? She walked from room to room and finally found it in the library, standing to the left of the fireplace beside one of the bookcases overflowing with dusty volumes. She was puzzled; since the massive library would be the hardest room to clean, she was saving it for last. She hadn't set foot in here since she arrived. But here was her ladder.

Mark must have forgotten that he moved it.

She lugged it down the hall, and within an hour the last of the paper was off. When they took their midmorning break, she asked if he'd like to go to Opelousas with her to buy paint. He said he'd stay and finish the windows. They talked about how many gallons to buy, and she embarked on her first trip in the Pontiac. With the windows rolled down and the wind in her face, she felt alive for the first time in ages. Maybe this was going to work out after all. Mark's enthusiasm and positive attitude were a huge contribution to her own well-being, she admitted, and she wondered where their relationship might be going.

From an upstairs bedroom window, Mark watched her drive away. He pulled out Willard's card and dialed the number. He left a voicemail and went back to work. In a few minutes the lawyer called back.

"I have a business proposition for you," he said abruptly. "How'd you like to make more money at one time than you've had in your entire life?"

Mark answered cautiously. He had no idea what this was about, but something made him nervous. If this was about Callie, he didn't intend to get anywhere near Willard Arceneaux.

"What'd you have in mind?"

"It's not something we can talk about on the phone, son. Are you at Beau Rivage?"

"Yes. Callie went to town for supplies."

"Don't tell her that we spoke," he said smoothly. "The less people who know about a sure thing, the less people can screw it up, know what I mean? Next time you're in town alone, call me and we'll meet." He hung up.

When Callie returned, he helped her carry drop cloths, paint cans, brushes, rollers and pans into the music room. Soon she was on the ladder, painting walls, and when they broke for lunch, he announced all the windowpanes were caulked and securely weatherproofed.

"Looks like you finished just in time," she commented. "It sprinkled on me when I was in town, and someone said we're in for a big storm the next few days. I listened to the radio in the car. There's a Category 2 hurricane forming in the Gulf."

"We'll have to keep an eye out for other leaks," he said, "but at least the windows and doors are secure."

He told her he was starting on the bathrooms next. The nine-thousand-square-foot house had only three – one on the first floor and two upstairs for the five bedrooms. They'd decided to repair those and clean them up. If Callie decided to turn Beau Rivage into a B&B, she would need several more, but that was a decision for later, not for today's limited budget.

He was working under the sink in a Jack and Jill bathroom on the second floor, where he'd seen a small leak. He was wearing a head lamp and had a pair of pliers in one hand and a screwdriver in the other.

"What are you doing?"

Shit! He jerked his head up and banged it on the underside of the sink. "Dammit!" he said, backing out and sitting up. Anne-Marie stood in the hallway two feet away.

"Don't ever do that again!" he snapped. "You scared the hell out of me!"

She smiled and said, "There weren't any bathrooms in this house until 1922."

"How do you know that?"

"I know a lot of things."

"Did Juliet Arceneaux tell you? Did you come here before she died?" He'd been thinking about the girl. She must have been coming here for some time; how else would she have known about the secret staircase?

Anne-Marie smiled and hummed.

"I asked you a question and I want an answer! Did you come see Juliet when she lived here?"

"Don't yell at me," she said quietly. "I don't like it when people yell at me." She smiled again and walked away.

He jumped up as quickly as he could in the cramped space where he was working, but by the time he got to the hallway, she was gone.

"Callie! Is Anne-Marie down there?"

"No. Why?"

"Because she was up here a minute ago. She talked to me." He paused. "She's up here! I can hear her humming! Anne-Marie!" he yelled. "Come here right now!" Suddenly the humming stopped.

A little shaken from his first direct encounter with the strange girl, he went downstairs and told Callie what she'd said about the bathrooms. "Why would a kid be interested in the year that bathrooms were installed in someone else's house, and who told her that? Was she here when your grandmother was alive?"

"Who knows anything about her? I told you she was different, and now you've seen it for yourself."

"I don't like what she's doing. If she has a secret way to get in, I'm sure she pokes around when we're not here."

"Don't be too hard on her. Her sudden appearances are startling, but I don't think she's a threat, do you?"

"I don't think that's it. There's just something that ..."

"That gives you goosebumps? That's what she gives me."

"Yeah, I guess that's what I mean. I'm not afraid of her. It just bugs me how she ignores what you ask her and smiles and hums at you. It's ... like you said earlier. It's unnerving. And frustrating as hell."

"I'm going to ask around about her when I get a chance," Callie said. "Somebody must know something."

By mid-afternoon it was raining off and on, and the sky was filled with low-hanging gray clouds. Two men in a fishing boat pulled up to the dock and offered them some catfish they'd just caught. Mark bought several and told Callie he'd filet and pan-fry them. He asked if she'd run to the grocery store in Krotz Springs and pick up the fixings he needed.

He added, "I'll go myself if you want, but if you don't mind running over there, I can filet these fish and get them prepped. It's not supposed to rain much for another couple of hours, so you can be back here before the storm hits."

She was the small store's only customer. She picked out the things Mark wanted, and she selected a bunch of fresh flowers that she was surprised to see for sale in such a tiny place. As she checked out, she asked the elderly woman behind the counter if there were any children that lived nearby. She replied that the only ones she knew of lived in the settlement on the other side of the river – the place Mark had mentioned earlier.

"How about a girl around ten years old? I saw a child wearing a blue dress – fancy, like for a party."

"A party dress? That sounds strange." The woman changed the subject. "Word is, someone's workin' over at Beau Rivage. Would that be you?"

"Yes. I'm Juliet Arceneaux's granddaughter and she left the house to me."

"That so? Big old house. She really let the place go, I hear."

"I think it fell into disrepair after her death. I'm hoping to fix it up so it's something to be proud of again."

"Hope you have a lot of cash and a lot of nerve," she muttered, handing Callie her change.

"What do you mean by that?"

"Nothin'. Just takes guts to fix up an old house, that's all I meant."

"Did you know my grandmother?"

"Would've been pretty hard to live five miles from her place and not know her. Years ago, she'd drive into town in that Rolls Royce of hers. She was some high-and-mighty lady. She was nice enough, don't get me wrong, but there was no mistaking that we were down here and she was way up there somewhere."

"I loved her. She was a wonderful woman," Callie shot back. The woman's remarks were beginning to irritate her.

"You must have known her better than us common folk did. Like I said, there wasn't anything she ever said or did to me personally. It was more just kinda the way she dressed and walked around, all hoity-toity, if you know what I mean."

"I understand perfectly what you mean," she said, taking her groceries. "After talking with you, I can even understand why she did it. She was a real lady, if that's what you were trying to say. And I guess that would have made her different from the rest of you." She huffed out, vowing to spend her money someplace else. As she drove back, she thought how strange it was that she'd only been here a few days, and so far, she'd marked two local merchants off her list to patronize.

Are they all as mean-spirited and nasty as the guy in Point Charmaine and this old woman?

Mamère had been a kind person. Callie had never heard her say a negative word about anyone. She wasn't going to tolerate gossipy locals talking badly about her.

It was raining a little harder, but after the encounter she just had, Callie decided to make one more stop before going home. After all the negative talk about Mamère Juliet, she went to the cemetery to pay her respects. The place was small and her grandmother's was the only recent grave. She stood under her umbrella in front of a large tombstone that had the simple inscription "Juliet Arceneaux, born 1928, died 2017, aged eighty-nine years. Rest in peace." She took the flowers she'd bought for the house and put them on her grandmother's grave instead.

She placed her hand gently on the wet stone. "I love you."

Callie told Mark about the woman at the store and he laughed it off, telling her to let it go. "The locals can be odd sometimes. They don't care much for strangers. Even though you're a relative and you used to come here in the summers, you're still an outsider. The thing I'm sorry about is that you didn't learn anything about Anne-Marie."

"I'll keep asking. Someone will eventually tell me something."

As he cooked the fish, they discussed their progress. Mark reported that he'd finished minor repairs on one of the upstairs bathrooms and it was ready for a deep cleaning. Tomorrow he'd finish the other, and if the weather permitted, in a few days a crew of painters he hired would power wash and repaint the brick exterior. They hadn't spent much money on outside labor to date, but that was about to change. They would need professionals with the proper equipment for a lot of the repair work.

A plumber and an electrician would arrive soon to make sure everything was up to code and ready for whatever the future held for Beau Rivage. She'd also picked out a few new kitchen appliances. The gargantuan gas range that had sat in this kitchen for over a century would stay, but she wanted a new refrigerator, an ice maker and a commercial wine chiller. If Beau Rivage became a tourist stop someday, all this would be important.

She told Mark that she only had one room on the first floor left to clean. The library was a gloomy, cavernous chamber with floor-to-ceiling bookshelves, an Oriental rug that was fifteen feet square and a chandelier made from antlers. A couch and plush armchairs covered in brown leather were arranged near her great-grandfather Michael's massive desk and chair, which sat in the middle of the room.

"Originally the library was Mamère's father's office," she explained. "She said she kept this room just as it had been when he was alive. He died when Mamère was twelve, and her mother died when she was twenty-one. Shortly after that, Mamère had a son, my father."

"And your grandmother never married?"

"No. My mother said Mamère's lover was a worker on a riverboat that docked here. Mamère was only twenty-one, but her parents were gone, so she was the lady of the house. She must have been quite a beauty, and maybe she was saucy too. I guess the deckhand gave her a present as a token of his affection. Nine months later my father, Simon Pilantro, was born. I guess she gave him the sailor's last name – no one ever said for sure. I'm a Pilantro, but I know a lot about my Arceneaux heritage and nothing about my father's."

"Did she raise Simon here?"

"I don't know that either. She never said a word about his childhood. Thanks to my mother, I know that he ended up in New Orleans, married her, and skipped town when he heard there was a kid on the way. Like father, like son, I guess. Momma raised me and we didn't have a nickel to spare. Every June, Mamère would send bus fare and I'd come up here for three months of heaven. I didn't have anything to worry about while I was here, and I always went back home with some new clothes and a little money to help my momma out."

"Do you ever see your mother these days?"

"She died in 2007 when I was a sophomore in college. I came back to New Orleans for her funeral, and it was a good thing I did. I was the only person in the room except for some preacher who'd never met my mother or me. The funeral home hired him, and he spoke for ten minutes about heaven and God's will and faith and the afterlife, and I snickered right there in the pew. I'd never heard those words used about my mother before and I have no idea if she believed in God."

"That's sad," Mark commented. "Where's she buried?"

"I don't know. I barely had the money to come for the funeral. I couldn't pay the undertaker or the preacher, so I skipped town as soon as the service was over. I got a demand letter from the mortuary, but I threw it away."

"They'd have been paid from her estate," he said. "That's what happens a lot. The undertaker puts a claim in and gets his money that way."

Callie began to laugh. "I don't think you'll ever understand where I came from. I may be sitting here in a mansion – my mansion – but this isn't how my life has ever been. We were one step from living under a bridge. We moved three times a year, every time we got evicted. There was no estate. She didn't leave me anything."

"I'm sorry," he said, taking her hand in his.

She squeezed it. "Thank you, Mark. You've been patient the last three days, listening to all this crazy stuff about me, and I appreciate your being here to help."

"Did your grandmother attend your mother's funeral?"

"No, and I'm not terribly surprised. Mamère was a kind, loving person, but when her illegitimate son left my mother pregnant, for some reason she never reached out to Momma. Maybe she was embarrassed by what he had done. Maybe it brought back memories of the riverboat worker who left her pregnant. I'll never know that part of the story. All I know is Mamère loved me and I loved her."

They ate wonderful fried catfish and hush puppies, and sat on the porch as the rain came down steadily. As darkness fell, she commented on how beautiful the river was, even on a gloomy evening in a rainstorm. Before bed, Mark made the rounds upstairs and down, locked everything up and pronounced the house secure.

"See you tomorrow," she said, reaching up and giving him a peck on the cheek. He smiled, hugged her and went to his room.

As she reached to draw the shade, she looked outside. Through the downpour, she thought she could see someone standing down on the bank by the river. She looked more closely but she'd been mistaken.

No one could have been there. It's pouring rain. I can't keep playing mind games, she told herself as she padded down the hall to the bathroom, brushed her teeth, pulled her door closed and crawled onto the sofa that had become her cozy nest each night.

Shortly after 2 a.m. she was jolted awake by a very loud noise. She jumped up, slid open the door and walked into the hall just as Mark came out of his room. Shaking off sleep, she realized she was standing there in a T-shirt and panties, and there he was in a pair of boxer shorts, but how skimpily they were dressed was the last thing on her mind.

"Did you hear it?"

He nodded. "Wonder where it came from?"

"The wind's coming up and the storm's getting worse. I'll bet a window's broken somewhere."

They checked every door and window from the first floor to the ballroom, but everything was just as it had been.

"I'd have decided it was a dream if you hadn't heard it too," he said as they went back downstairs. When they reached the second-floor landing, they heard the banging noise again. It was coming from somewhere below them.

They rushed down the staircase. When they got to the hall, they looked at each other in astonishment. The front door was standing wide open, the wind banging it back and forth against the wall. Rain was blowing across the porch and into the house. As she rushed over to close it, she looked out toward the river and saw someone standing next to it, far from the house. Even through the storm, they could see the girl was wearing a blue dress and a yellow hat with flowers on it. Callie's first fleeting thought was that she must be drenched. Her next thought was that she recognized her somehow. Once, perhaps long, long ago, she'd seen this child.

"Mark! Come here!" she shouted. She threw open the door and pointed. "Do you see her?"

"See what? I can't even see the river."

"There's a little girl standing on the bank. She's looking toward the house."

He looked more closely and shook his head. "Sorry. It's raining so hard I can't see anything that far away."

"She's right there! Can't you see her?" But when she looked again, she saw nothing. The child was gone.

"Callie, you're still half-asleep. There's no one out there. It's raining like hell. Let's get you back to bed."

"I'm not asleep, dammit! I just climbed three flights of stairs. I saw her."

"Was it Anne-Marie?"

"At this time of night in a rainstorm? How could it have been her?"

How could it not have been?

But it hadn't happened. She knew that. Visibility was getting worse by the minute, and it just wasn't logical that a child – Anne-Marie or not – was out in the storm.

Mark said he couldn't understand how the front door had gotten open. They had just gone upstairs and he was sure it had been closed. He'd locked it before going to bed, and she said she hadn't been out of her room since.

Maybe the lock was loose, she offered. The wind was really whipping around, and maybe it blew the door open.

They were grasping at straws, she thought when she was back in bed. They were trying to think of logical answers for the strange things that were happening. The girl standing by the river was one thing – it might not have happened at all – but that door was another.

She hadn't checked it herself, but Mark said he'd locked it. How did it get open?

She spent the night tossing fitfully as the storm raged and she dreamed of secrets in an old house.

Bad secrets.

CHAPTER TEN

Mark awoke to the intoxicating aroma of bacon cooking on the stove. He walked into the kitchen, gave Callie a brief hug and went for the coffee.

"Smells wonderful in here," he told her. "It's a nice way to start the day, lying in bed while someone fixes breakfast. I could get used to this."

His remark gave her a naughty thought, but she let it go. "I'm glad you're finally calling that old sofa a bed," she retorted. "It's a foot too short for you."

"It's really comfortable, actually." He thought about asking if he could work on the bedrooms so they'd have a more comfortable place to sleep, but he decided against it. He didn't know where this situation with her was going, and for several reasons, he had kept out the thoughts that he was having often now that they were working so closely together. Mentioning the bedroom wasn't a good idea. Not right now.

"It's really dark outside, but it looks like the rain's slowing down," he commented, looking out the window. "Have you heard any news about Hurricane Jack?"

She nodded. "I checked my phone earlier. Jack's expected to make landfall as a Category 2 down around Morgan City late this afternoon. Depending on the path, we're looking at either a few more inches of rain, or a hell of a lot more. I think the lull in the rain right now is the proverbial calm before the storm."

"I'm going to run into town," he said. "I'm sure my crew battened down the hatches on the rentals, but I should check them myself. Same thing for my own house."

"Why don't you just stay in Opelousas until it blows over? You can't take care of things if you're out here in the boondocks, and I'll be perfectly fine now that you've made the house watertight."

"If Jack comes this way, we'll find out how watertight I've made it. Let me see how everything goes in town. I'll check the storm's track on TV and we can decide what I should do late this afternoon. I don't want to leave you by yourself ..."

"Don't think a thing about it," she replied more confidently than she felt. She didn't relish the thought of riding out a storm alone, but she could do anything she put her mind to. Things would work out and he needed to take care of his business.

He went to the porch and glanced up at the ominous, low-hanging storm clouds that were building in the southern sky. Through the gloomy fog, the Spanish moss hanging from the ancient trees framed Beau Rivage like a setting in a scary movie. Today of all days, it was easy to see why the townspeople spun yarns about the mansion being haunted.

She came outside and commented about how nice it was to smell the rain coming. Suddenly she saw a figure in the trees where she earlier thought she'd seen someone.

"Look, Mark! Look over there. Do you see her now?"

The fog and the trees made it difficult to know for certain that someone was there.

"I see her! Anne-Marie!" he yelled as he ran toward the woods. Callie half-expected the figure to disappear, but this time the girl began walking toward Mark. He tried to take her hand, but she pulled it away. He said something and she followed him to the house.

"You're soaked!" Callie said. "How long have you been out there? What are you doing? Did you come through the woods?"

Anne-Marie smiled. "I came to see you. I want to dry off." She walked into the kitchen, picked up a hand towel and ran it through her hair.

"Where do you live, Anne-Marie?" Mark said.

She pointed in the direction from which she'd come.

"In the woods? There aren't any houses over there."

Without answering, she ran the towel through her golden hair a few more times and then walked down the hallway. They followed her into the library. With little light coming through the windows, the room was even more dark and ghostly than usual.

Anne-Marie walked to a huge overstuffed leather couch, dug her hands down beside one of the cushions, and pulled something out.

She handed it to Callie. "I think this is yours."

It was a Raggedy Ann doll with buttons for eyes, wearing a faded gingham dress.

Callie's eyes opened wide in astonishment. "How did you know this was there? I haven't seen this doll in ..."

"Years." Anne-Marie finished the sentence for her.

"I lost this doll one summer and never found it again. How did you know she was there?"

Anne-Marie hummed and said softly, "I knew she was yours."

Mark suddenly grabbed her and shook her hard. "What else do you know? What is it about you? Who are you?"

The girl broke free, stared into his eyes and said menacingly, "Don't ever touch me again. I don't like it when you do that."

Callie jumped in surprise. She hadn't heard this dark, sinister tone from the child, and it startled Mark too. He stepped back, put his arm around Callie and said to Anne-Marie, "Go home. Get out of this house and stop bothering us."

The girl smiled and began to hum as she walked through the open front door, crossed the yard in the rain and disappeared into the trees.

"There's something really weird about her, Mark. She's just a little kid, but she's so strange that she makes me really nervous sometimes."

"I'll admit I'm a little spooked myself. At any rate, she knows to stay away now."

Callie doubted what he had said would make any difference.

Mark left around nine, promising to check in later with a storm update. The rain intensified throughout the morning as she worked in the library. She brought in three floor lamps to get as much light as possible and picked one corner to begin. It would take days to work her way around the room. She intended to take out every single book and dust it. Out of curiosity, she counted how many books were on a single shelf, then multiplied the result by the number of shelves in all the bookcases. She discovered there were more than five thousand volumes, and if the first ones she saw were any indication, they hadn't been dusted in ages.

If Callie ever opened the house to visitors, the library would be a focal point. It was so different – so dark, eerie and forbidding – that people would love it. If there ever was a room in a haunted mansion, this was it, she thought, remembering that she'd rarely spent time in here as a child. It had been scary even then. Mamère had told her that the furniture in this room was original, so it was nearly two hundred years old. Of all the rooms in Beau Rivage, she intended to make this one the most interesting for visitors because she found it eerily fascinating herself.

She worked for two solid hours as the rain came down in sheets. Enormous flashes of lightning were followed by thunderous booms, and soon the lights in the library started flickering on and off. Callie had seen oil lamps throughout the house – probably for this very purpose – and she carried two of them into the library, just in case.

She heard a banging sound and decided one of the shutters on the back of the house must have come loose. In a moment she heard it again, followed by a shout. Someone was at the back door.

She looked through the windowpane on the side of the door and saw Willard huddled under an umbrella. "Let me in!" he shouted. "I'm getting drenched out here!"

He stepped inside and put his umbrella in a stand. He removed his raincoat, folded it inside out so it wouldn't drip everywhere, and put it on the floor by the door.

"Sorry to come without notice," he said. "I tried to call, but your phone isn't working. Probably the storm."

"What do you want?"

"Nice to see you too, darlin'," he replied sarcastically. "I saw your friend in Opelousas this mornin' and I decided to come out and see if you were all right, since he obviously left you out here all by yourself. You may want to stay in town yourself until this blows over. Looks like it could be a real big one."

"I don't have a place to stay in town," she replied, ashamed that she'd been so abrupt with him when he'd come to check on her. "I'm fine here. This is my house, rain or shine."

"You stayed at that fellow's house earlier, from what I hear. I figured you could stay with him again. Looks like you two are becoming good friends, if you know what I mean." He raised his eyebrows suggestively.

"There's nothing going on, if that's what you're insinuating. Not that it's any of your business anyway. I'm fine, but I'm busy. Thank you for stopping by to check on me."

Just then the lights went out, plunging the house into darkness. It startled her, and she was glad not to be alone, even if she was with her despicable uncle.

"I've got lamps in the library," she said, bringing one into the front hall, where Willard was putting on his raincoat.

"Don't forget my offer," he said as he opened the door. "You're going to sink a fortune into this place – his money, not yours – and what'll you have when it's all done? A half-finished house?"

"Get out," she said quietly. "Leave me alone. I know what I'm doing."

He shook his head, walked in the rain to his car, and drove away.

Needing light so she could work, she carried the lamp back to the library. As she put it on a table, a voice said, "I don't like him."

She whirled around, startled. If the lamp had been in her hand, she'd have dropped it. Anne-Marie was sitting on the couch where the doll had been hidden.

"What are you doing back here? Mark told you not to come again."

"I came to see you. I don't like that man."

Realizing the girl had heard them talking, she said, "I don't like him either, but that's not your business. How did you get in the house? And why aren't you wet?"

"I never left. I just waited until he was gone, and then I came to see you."

"That's not true, Anne-Marie. I watched you walk to the woods in the rain. I saw you with my own eyes."

She said nothing.

Callie sat next to her. "We're going to have a talk. Unless you start explaining things, you can't come here anymore. I want to know where you live, why you don't go to school, how you know so much about this house and my grandmother, and why you keep coming here. You're just a girl, but ..." She paused, hesitant to reveal how disturbing everything about the child was. "You're not like other children. You're more serious or something. There's something different about you."

The child smiled.

"Please answer my questions. Where do you live?"

"On the other side of the woods. I care about you. I just want to be sure you're all right."

Suddenly a bolt of lightning shot down from the sky and struck a tree at the edge of the forest. A huge limb fell to the ground and there was an enormous crash of thunder. At that same moment, the lights flickered back on. She ran to the window, saw the downed tree, and said, "How do you know so much about my grandmother?"

There was no reply. She turned – the couch was empty.

She ran into the hall and looked at the front and back doors. Both were closed, and Anne-Marie was nowhere in sight. The child had to be in the house somewhere because Callie hadn't heard her open a door.

"Anne-Marie! Come back here!"

The only sounds were the incessant beating of raindrops and the wind whipping around the corners of the house.

Frustrated, she decided Mark was right. They had to put a stop to her visits.

She scares me, Callie admitted for the first time. *She keeps talking about how she doesn't like Uncle Willard and that she wants to help me, but everything about her disturbs me. She wants to tell me secrets, but the biggest question I have is Anne-Marie herself. I can't let this keep going on.*

She poked around in the downstairs rooms, knowing she wouldn't find the girl, and went back to the library to continue cleaning. When she walked in, she saw the ladder standing to the left of the fireplace.

I was working on the other side. I sat on the couch with Anne-Marie five minutes ago, and I saw the ladder over in the other corner, where I've been working all morning. I didn't move the ladder.

Did I?

First Anne-Marie, then this thing about the moving ladder. She fought off a growing tension in her gut. Was all this really happening? Was she dreaming it, or lapsing into some type of trance? Anne-Marie existed, of course. Mark had seen her too. He had spoken to her, ordered her out of the house. But the ladder – was she moving it herself and not realizing it? How else could it be happening?

Am I losing my mind?

She got her phone, put in her earbuds and played her favorite music with the volume turned way up. That helped keep her mind from wandering to the questions she couldn't answer, and she worked in a frenzy, dusting books and cleaning shelves for two uneventful hours.

She stopped for lunch, thankful that the lights hadn't gone off again. As strong and resourceful as she had acted with Mark, she really hoped he'd be back to spend the night. Beau Rivage, she admitted, was beginning to make her uneasy, and she couldn't explain why. As a child, this had been her refuge – her safe place. She had been excited when she learned it was hers, even with no money to fix it up. Now

81

the dark halls, shadowy rooms and creaks and groans were becoming ominous instead of familiar.

And the mysterious child who appeared and disappeared at will only heightened Callie's apprehension.

CHAPTER ELEVEN

Mark must have tried her number ten times. The storm had interrupted cell service, and without her phone, she couldn't get weather updates, nor could he talk about when he'd be back to the house.

Willard Arceneaux called.

"I expected you to contact me before now," he said harshly.g

"I've been busy at the house. You said to call when I was alone."

"You're alone right now. I saw you in town earlier, and I know where Calisto is. I stopped out at Beau Rivage this mornin' to be sure she was all right. She's not thinking clearly, with her wild ideas about fixing up the place. You and my niece seem to be gettin' on very well these days, but you're part of her problem. You've put her in a jam and it's going to be up to me to get her out of it."

"What are you talking about?"

"Somebody's throwing a lot of money down a rat hole out there. I don't know where it's coming from, but I know one thing – it's damned sure not hers. She's dirt poor, if you don't know that already. So that means it must be your money. The word around town is that you barely have a pot to piss in either. That means you borrowed it, but who would be foolish enough to lend money for that project? It would take a fortune to even make a dent in that place.

"I can help you now, or I can take it all later. It's your choice. If I get involved now, you'll come out looking like a smart, successful real estate guy who knows what he's doing. If I don't, I'll end up with everything when it's all said and done. You'll both be bankrupt, which won't mean anything to her – she's broke already. It'll be bad for you –

you'll lose your business and you'll be a failure. Depending on what line of bull you sold my niece, you may even be looking at fraud charges."

Mark couldn't believe what he was hearing. Everyone in Opelousas knew how ruthless Willard Arceneaux could be, but this sounded like pure extortion. Rather than firing back a response, he decided to hear the man out.

"What are you after?"

"What I'm after is to save the mansion that my dear sister Juliet owned and which has been in my family for over two hundred years. I don't need two amateurs out there throwin' pennies at a project that needs hundred-dollar bills. I hoped Juliet would do the right thing and leave Beau Rivage to my children. But she always had a soft spot for her only granddaughter, the by-product of Juliet's roll in the hay with some common laborer. I want Beau Rivage, and if you know anything about me, you know I always get what I want."

"Why? You have everything. I can't believe you want to restore it. So what's the real reason?"

"Son, it's time to make a decision. I know you probably haven't had to make many, since you don't sell much real estate and you mostly fix up houses for a living. But you're either with me or you're against me. Which will it be?"

Mark hesitated. "What are you asking me to do?"

"You're going to work with me to take the property away from her. We'll be partners, but you don't have to put up any money. You'll never do this project without me. You really don't have a choice unless you're prepared to lose every dime you ever had."

"I can't do that to her. She trusts me ..."

"I'll take that as a no. Call me back if you come to your senses." He hung up.

Willard's threats could affect him personally. His own motive was still a secret; if Willard knew what it was, the lawyer would have used it as leverage. Willard's getting involved with Beau Rivage was a twist in the plans he hadn't anticipated, and he wasn't sure the right way to deal with it. The man had far more assets than Mark did. Furthermore, his connections in St. Landry Parish were legendary. Suddenly everything had changed; now Mark was playing in the big leagues. It wasn't just Callie he had to contend with, it was her uncle too.

Driving around town in the rain, he checked on the four run-down properties he'd bought. They looked fine, and a little water damage wouldn't be a big deal anyway. He dropped by his office, picked up the mail and told Mrs. Collins to go home until the storm passed. He checked his phone and saw the hurricane was a Category 1, set to make landfall around four p.m. ninety miles south of Opelousas. He had experienced the devastation when Hurricane Gustav came onshore at almost the same place in 2008. That one had been a Category 2, but this one could still cause huge problems for people in its path.

He tried Callie's phone again, and then he locked up his office, drove to his house and made sure everything was secure there. Just in case, he grabbed his weather radio and some extra batteries, tossed two cases of water and a twelve-pack of Miller Light in the Jeep, and headed for Beau Rivage.

Three inches of rain had already fallen, and forecasters were predicting seven more for St. Landry Parish. Mark's goal was to go to the house and bring Callie back to town. If they stayed at Beau Rivage and the river overflowed, the grounds could flood and they might be stranded for days. He slowed to check the river as he crossed the cantilever bridge near Krotz Springs. It was raining so hard he could barely see, but it appeared to be getting higher already.

His wipers strained against the driving rain and he was glad there was very little traffic. He was worried that he'd spent too much time in town – he might already be too late to rescue Callie. He needed a contingency plan in case they couldn't get out.

He drove into Krotz Springs, hoping to buy tarps and duct tape at the store. He and Callie had already plowed three-fourths of his loan into the renovations, and he wanted to protect the house. He pulled under the canopy and saw a sign tacked to the door.

Closed for storm. All sold out – no food, no gas.

So much for that idea. He pushed on, doubling back when he missed the turn, and finally located it. The Jeep slid several times on the grassy trail through the woods, but the four-wheel drive made it easy.

As he approached the house, he saw that it was dark. The power must have gone out, and he noticed a flicker through the windowpanes from somewhere inside. He maneuvered the Jeep as close to the veranda as he could, pulled up the hood on his poncho, and ran to the back porch. He unlocked the door, left his soaked poncho, boots and socks just inside, and yelled for her.

There was no answer.

As he walked toward the library, he could see the dancing light was coming from there. He looked inside and saw three oil lamps glowing in the near darkness.

"Callie? Are you in here?"

He heard a whimper and jerked around. She was sitting on the couch wrapped in a blanket, clutching Raggedy Ann to her chest and rocking back and forth. Her cheeks were stained with tears.

Mark rushed to her. "Callie! What's wrong? I'm so sorry I left you. I tried to call ..."

"I'm terrified," she whispered, her body still swaying.

He sat and put his arm around her. "I know. The storm –"

"It's not the storm. It's her."

"Who? Has Anne-Marie been here?"

She pointed to the fireplace. There was something above it he hadn't noticed earlier. It was a full-sized, ornately framed portrait of a woman wearing a floor-length black dress and a wide-brimmed hat. The painting was old; her clothing dated it to the nineteenth century. Her face was stern, her eyes piercing, and she had a clenched jaw that showed a strong, determined spirit. It wasn't intended to be a flattering portrait and something about it caused Mark to shudder.

"Your grandmother?" he asked.

She shook her head and forced herself to stop crying. *"Her* grandmother."

"You mean that's Juliet's grandmother? She looks just like the picture of Juliet I saw. What did you say her name was – Leonore?"

Callie nodded. "She watches me. She does things while I work."

Mark was worried. She had changed completely since he left this morning – something must have frightened her. Suddenly there was a powerful flash of light, a huge cracking sound from somewhere outside, and a fearsome peal of thunder. Another lightning strike followed, much closer this time. He had to see if there was damage to the house, but he was reluctant to leave her.

"I never noticed the picture. Has it been up there the whole time?"

"It was covered up, like all the others. I was up on the ladder. I pulled the cover off and I thought for a minute it was my grandmother's portrait. But the woman's eyes bored right into mine like something menacing. It rattled me so much I nearly fell off the ladder. I tried to work, but she moved things around. She's the one moving the ladder, I've decided. I got so nervous I had to stop working. I've been sitting right here for a long time, just hoping you would come back."

"Let's get out of here. I tried to call you all day and now I'm here and we're going back to town."

She answered in a whisper. "We're not leaving tonight. I can't go. She told me not to."

Come on, Callie. This was getting weird.

"Who told you? Leonore?"

"No. Anne-Marie. I'll be in danger if I leave Beau Rivage tonight."

She's lost touch with reality, he thought, as he searched for comforting words.

"She's just a kid, and that was just talk. She's trying to get to you, Callie, and you can't let her. We have two hours until the storm comes ashore and things could get bad. We've spent a lot of money on this place, and I thought for a while that we might just ride it out here, but you're in no shape to do that tonight. We'll go back to my place until it's over. But we have to leave now before the rain gets any worse."

"You don't understand. They're not going to let us leave. Leonore wants me to stay here too."

"It's a painting. She couldn't tell you anything."

She looked at him blankly and whispered, "You don't understand, do you?"

He gently pulled her up and put his arm around her waist. With him practically carrying her, they walked to the back of the house. He put her on the couch in her temporary bedroom and he put on his socks and boots. He opened the door and saw what had made the huge noise. Several hundred feet away by the entry gate, an enormous tree had been struck by lightning. The tree was so far away and the rain was so heavy that he couldn't assess the damage. He had to check it out.

"I need you to stay here for a minute," he told Callie. "One of the oaks was struck by lightning. I'm going to drive to the gate and see about it. I'll be back in five minutes."

"No!" she shrieked. "No! You can't leave me here alone!"

"Callie, I'm right here. I'm not going more than a quarter of a mile and I'll be back in less than five minutes."

"No," she whimpered, beginning the rocking motion again. "They'll come back."

Despite her protestations, he had to go. He had to see if there was damage. If the tree had fallen across the driveway, he'd have to depend on the four-wheel drive to get them through the sodden fields on either side. He hugged Callie, pulled on his poncho, locked her in and ran to the Jeep. He headed down the tree-lined drive and stopped when he saw where the huge old oak had fallen.

The strike had torn it in two. One huge part of the trunk was lying across the drive, but the other was blocking the entrance gate. The jagged iron fencing was on either side. They weren't going anywhere tonight. When the storm was over, he might be able to pull it out of the way with the Jeep. Otherwise it would take a chain saw, and his was in town.

The Jeep slid crazily on the wet ground as he tore back to the house. He rushed inside, but she wasn't in the parlor.

"Callie!"

He heard a small voice. "She wanted me to come back to the library."

He threw off his wet shoes and ran down the hall. She was sitting on the couch again, holding her doll and clutching a blanket. She had a distant look in her eyes, and he knew she was losing her grip on reality.

"We're not leaving tonight, are we?"

"No. The road is completely blocked."

She nodded. "I told you we couldn't leave."

CHAPTER TWELVE

Thankful for the gas stove, he brewed up some coffee that turned out better than he'd expected. He led her to a chair in the kitchen, set the mug in front of her and took inventory. They could eat their leftovers first, but the pantry had canned goods, pasta, some fresh vegetables and fruit, and the refrigerator had lunch meat and the trimmings to make maybe four sandwiches. He had no idea how long the electricity would be off, but they were well prepared to ride out the hurricane.

With no heat, the house was quickly cooling down. He turned up the burners on the stove, and soon the kitchen was warm and cozy as the flames cast dancing shadows on the walls. One thing they wouldn't run out of was natural gas, so they might spend most of the next forty-eight hours right here in this room.

He found two bags of ice in the freezer and transferred them to a Yeti cooler he'd brought out earlier. He had the water and beer in his Jeep plus three bottles of wine. He'd been through other hurricanes and figured they'd be stranded maybe two days. Once the rain subsided – maybe tomorrow afternoon – he could do an assessment. He was already planning his attack on the downed tree, hoping he could winch it far enough that they could get out the gate.

She looked up from the coffee and said, "I'm sorry. I don't know what came over me."

Glad that she was better, Mark patted her shoulder. "When you're up to it, I want to hear what happened. Right now, I have to get us ready for the storm. Will you be okay while I drive to the barn for a minute?"

"Yes. I'm fine now. Go do what you need to do."

BILL THOMPSON

He drove to the barn, opened its tall double doors and backed the Jeep in. The other day he'd noticed a stack of firewood – more than a cord – that someone had put in the barn to keep it dry. He put as much in the back of the Jeep as he could and took it to the house, leaving it in the hallway by Callie's parlor bedroom. There would be scratches and nicks on the floor, he knew, but they were due for refinishing later anyway.

He made a second trip and soon there was a large stack of wood in the vestibule. Shortly there was a roaring fire. There were four fireplaces downstairs and four up. He didn't intend to light the library fireplace; that room seemed to frighten her. Instead, he built the fire in her bedroom, hoping that she'd sleep tonight with the fire to comfort her.

By four in the afternoon the skies were black, the rain was coming down in torrents and the wind was shrieking like a banshee. Mark checked every door and window once again and then joined Callie in the parlor, where she had curled up on the sofa, her pillow under her head and the quilt pulled up to her neck. He turned on the weather radio. The outer band of Hurricane Jack had taken a significant turn to the west and made landfall southwest of Lafayette. That was good news for them, but the towns on the coast like Morgan City and Patterson had gotten three inches of rain in the past hour. The storm was expected to head northwest, with the eye passing between Lake Charles and Port Arthur, Texas.

"How close will it get to us?" she asked.

"The last-minute turn was a blessing for us, and for people from Baton Rouge to New Orleans. It'll still dump a lot of rain, but the worst will be farther west than they thought." They listened as the announcer urged people in the western coastal parishes to seek shelter and move to high ground immediately.

"We should be okay," he said reassuringly, although their proximity to the river still concerned him. The first floor of Beau Rivage was a couple of feet above ground level and the yard sloped slightly down to the river a hundred yards away. Unless this was a storm of the century – or it changed course again – he and Callie should be fine.

Once he closed all the doors to the parlor, it became a snug retreat. She blew out the oil lamps since the fireplace provided plenty of light. She asked if they'd run out of wood, and he said there was plenty in the barn. There wouldn't be any electricity for a while, but the parlor and the kitchen would be warm.

She lay on the sofa while he sat on the floor next to her. No one spoke for a long time.

"I want to talk about today," she said at last.

"I want to hear about it."

"A couple of hours after you left, Uncle Willard showed up. He said he saw you in town and he was checking on me since you'd left me out here alone. He tried to scare me; he said we were sinking all this money into something that would never work. He said we didn't have enough money, and he's right. We don't. We both know that. He told me to keep his offer in mind. He'd buy the house for enough to pay back your loan. I wouldn't have anything, but at least you wouldn't owe fifty thousand dollars anymore."

"Callie, we've been through this. I thought we agreed we were going to keep going."

"We did, but what do we do when the money runs out? There's only a little more than ten thousand left. What do we do then?"

"Don't worry about it right now. Once we show the bank how we've used the money, I'm sure they'll loan us more. We will have spent the money and improved the worth of the property. That improves the bank's collateral. The more we spend – wisely, of course – the better it's going to get. I'm also putting one of my rent houses on the market; my guys say it'll be ready in two weeks, and it should sell fast for around eighty thousand. I'm willing to put in the profit from that sale as soon as I get it."

"I trust you," she told him, and she meant it. She had struggled with her feelings – he was her business partner, not anything more – but there was much about him that she liked. "On a different subject, I told you Uncle Willard came to try to talk me into selling him the house. After he left, I went back to the library. Anne-Marie was sitting in there on the couch."

"Damn that girl. I told her to leave!"

"I don't even know how she comes and goes. I don't think she uses the doors because I checked them after she left. She must have heard my argument with my uncle, because she said she didn't like him. I asked her some questions, but all I got was that she lived on the other side of the woods. I asked her how she knew Mamère, but then I turned around for a minute and – as usual – she was gone. She spooks me. She's just a child, but she knows this house better than I do."

"It's no wonder that she scares you. From now on, she's going to follow the rules. This is your house, and she's not welcome unless we say so."

"Anyway, that unnerved me, as her appearances always do. I went back to work. My plan was to start at one corner of the library and dust from the top shelves down. I'm going to dust every book in the room. There are three wall hangings that were covered up. I moved the ladder to the fireplace, climbed up and pulled the cloth off Leonore's painting. I already told you what happened after that. I was so frightened I couldn't work any longer. I just sat in there, afraid to look up at her face, waiting for you. I think she talked to me – at least that's what was in my mind – and I could hear Anne-Marie talking too. That's when they told me I couldn't leave tonight."

He chose his words carefully. "Do you still think Leonore spoke to you?"

"It couldn't have happened, could it? Maybe it was the storm, the light from an oil lamp, and the eerie old room. Maybe it had to do with Anne-Marie always disappearing. Leonore is a fierce-looking woman, and I think it all piled up in my mind and I lost it. No, I don't think she spoke to me. But it all seemed so real at the time. Do you know what I mean?"

He nodded and took her hand. "I can't tell you enough how sorry I am. I shouldn't have left this morning. It was selfish of me."

She smiled. "Selfish? It's nice of you to say that, but you were going to batten down the hatches, remember? That's not selfish – that's smart. The good news is that you're back now, and I'm not letting you leave me again!"

Her words made him stop and think. Where was all this headed anyway? He'd had clear intentions when he'd coaxed her into partnering with him on the Beau Rivage project. He'd known exactly where things would end up. But he hadn't planned for what was beginning to unfold between them. He could keep his distance – they were sleeping in separate bedrooms, after all – but what she'd gone through today had affected her deeply. The storm, her fears, his bravado – everything could mesh perfectly in this dark room with a roaring fire. This was a perfect night to take this relationship to an entirely different place.

The wrong place.

Callie saw his face darken and she could have kicked herself for sounding so aggressive. How many times had she done this before – coming on too strong and driving men away? She hadn't even meant the words the way they sounded. She was genuinely grateful that he was back. Being alone in this old house during a hurricane *was* scary. The portrait of Leonore would have been perfect in the Addams family mansion and it had given her the creeps. And there was that other thing – the feeling that Leonore was moving things around as Callie worked in the room. And of course, there was Anne-Marie. There was always Anne-Marie.

How crazy did all that sound? *No wonder Mark's trying to distance himself,* she thought. *I'm talking like I belong in an institution.*

He spoke at last. "Old houses can do things to your mind. This one's affecting you more because you have so much history with this place. When you uncovered that painting, it had to have startled you. You thought it was your grandmother and when I first saw it, I did too. I've seen her once or twice over the years, and that woman really resembled her. That must have spooked you."

"It did. I thought it was Mamère and I smiled when I uncovered it, but when I looked up into that face, I felt something evil. It really unnerved me."

"You can say that again. I felt it too when I saw the portrait. It must have been up there a long time. Do you remember seeing it when you were a child?"

"No, but I wouldn't have been interested in the history of my family back then. I probably looked at it a hundred times when I was in the library, but it didn't make an impression."

She paused. "And I want to say something about a minute ago. I'm sorry that I came on too strongly. I have no control over you. You have other things to do than to spend all your time out here. I really didn't mean it that way."

He smiled and patted her hand. "No worries. You had a traumatic few hours today and I should have stayed here to help you. Anyway, like you said, here I am! Ready for some chow?"

He heated leftovers in a skillet and they drank wine at the kitchen table in the warm glow of the gas burners. The storm howled more fiercely than ever. During a brief break from the intense rain, they looked out and saw the raging river almost at the top of its banks. Mark commented that if the rain kept up, it would overflow at some point during the night.

"Will we be all right?" she asked, and he promised her they were high enough and far enough away to be safe. The lawns might be under water, but they would weather the storm without a problem.

Without electricity or phones, there was nothing to do but go to bed. After her day, she was ready. Around eight he tucked her in, patted her cheek and said, "See you tomorrow." He handed her a flashlight he'd taken from the Jeep and took another with him.

"Don't take this the wrong way," she said, "but you've got this room nice and warm. If you get cold, come back and sleep in here. In fact, why don't we go ahead and pull a couch from the music room in, just in case?"

"I'll be fine. I may check out the house during the night, so I think I'll sleep in my clothes. I'll be warm. See you tomorrow."

She watched as the logs burned low in the fireplace, casting shadows on the walls and ceiling that looked like ghostly figures. *He's right across the hall,* she thought as she closed her eyes.

Something woke her. Was it real, or was she dreaming? In the faint glow from the dying embers, she heard faint footsteps in the room above her. She exhaled in relief. Mark was checking out the house, making sure everything was safe.

It was almost midnight; she'd been asleep for several hours, and outside, the storm raged on. She got up for a moment, noticed how much colder the room had become now that the fire was dying, and walked to the window. She pulled back the curtain, and when a bolt of lightning streaked across the sky, she saw water covering the lawn. The river had overflowed after all, but Mark had said they would be safe.

Callie looked toward the woods, half-expecting to see someone standing there, but the rain and wind were so fierce that it was impossible to see anything that far away. She put on more logs and stirred the embers so they'd catch, and she crawled back into bed. As she closed her eyes, she again heard the faint footsteps from upstairs.

Thank you, Mark.

CHAPTER THIRTEEN

She snapped awake again to another sound. This time it was a light tapping noise and then there was a whisper.

"Callie, are you up?"

"Yes. Come on in."

She pulled up the quilt and smiled as he slid open the pocket door. He was wearing jeans and a windbreaker, and she had a fleeting thought that he wouldn't be a bad thing to wake up to now and then.

He brought more wood into the now-chilly room and restarted the fire. "How'd you sleep?"

"Not bad. The rain woke me up once or twice, and I guess you made rounds during the night."

"Sorry I failed on that promise. I guess I didn't realize how tired I was until I hit the sack. I was asleep in minutes and I didn't wake up until about half an hour ago."

"But I heard your footsteps upstairs. It was just before midnight ..."

"Not me. It must have been old Leonore ..."

She covered her face with her hands and stifled a scream. "Don't say that! It was you! It had to be!"

"Easy, Callie. That was a stupid attempt to make a joke, and it was insensitive of me after what you went through yesterday. Maybe you dreamed you heard something."

"Yeah, maybe I did."

Except I didn't. I was standing up in the room, wide awake. Maybe I'm going crazy.

"Ready for coffee?"

"Sure. Give me a little bathroom time and I'll be there shortly."

He had left an oil lamp in the bathroom for her, and after a brief, cold shower, she joined him in the kitchen.

"The rain's easing up a little," he advised. "Looks like we have a few inches of water covering the yard so far, but nothing that'll cause any lasting damage. The weather guys are saying the eye moved past Lake Charles during the night and it's been downgraded to a tropical storm. We may get four or five more inches today, but by tonight it sounds like things will start getting better."

"What's the plan for today?" she asked.

"Except for no electricity, it's back to work for me. If you want to keep working in the library, I can start a fire in there for you. I'll use one of the lamps and my flashlight to work in the upstairs bathroom. But if you'd rather, I can find things to do down here and stay close by."

"How silly would that be?" she said with only the slightest quiver in her voice. "I'll be fine. You're just a yell away! Build me that fire, and Leonore and I will get back to work!"

Mark started a roaring fire, took his toolbox and a lamp, and went upstairs. He dropped his tools in the bathroom and walked down the hallway to a bedroom that was directly above the parlor where Callie had slept last night. She said she'd heard footsteps on the second floor, and he opened the door. Since no one had begun cleaning yet, the floor had the same layer of dust as everywhere else. And it was smooth – undisturbed. No one had been in this room last night, just as he expected.

This was about scaring Callie.

An hour later, he walked downstairs to check on her. She was on the ladder in the library, and she had finished dusting about a third of the first bookshelf.

"Everything okay?" he asked.

"Thanks to you," she replied, coming down to take a break. "Thanks for covering up the portrait. I don't think I could have worked in here if you hadn't done that."

He looked up and saw that Leonore's picture was draped in black. "I didn't ..." he began, and he saw her chin start to tremble.

"You did cover it up, right?"

He recovered instantly. "Sure. I was going to say I didn't think you wanted her watching you."

She exhaled loudly and squeezed his hand.

I'm beginning to depend on him, she thought to herself as he went back upstairs. *Don't let your feelings mess everything up this time, Callie. After yesterday, he must think you're crazy as hell. Just take things slowly.*

Out of curiosity, she pulled the covers off the two other paintings that hung in the library. The first was sepia-toned and hung in a very old frame. The figure was a distinguished older man in a suit and top hat, and his hand rested on a walking stick with an ornately carved ivory handle in the shape of a skull. A dusty plate at the bottom proclaimed that he was Joseph Arceneaux, the man who'd received the forty acres from the French in 1756. Although the picture had undoubtedly hung here with Leonore's, Callie didn't recall seeing it either. She mentally calculated the "great-greats" and decided that Joseph was her grandfather four times removed.

She felt her skin crawl as she looked at the other portrait. It was a girl about Anne-Marie's age who bore a resemblance to her. The girl had blond hair and was wearing a blue dress that ended just below the knee. Beneath it was a petticoat that made the outfit fuller, and she wore a fancy yellow hat with a band of flowers.

Two nights ago, when the storm began, she thought she'd seen a child standing in the rain down by the river. *This* child, wearing *this* outfit. It couldn't have happened, she had told herself. But here she was.

I thought I recognized her from my past. It was this painting! I must have seen it when I was a little girl, but I didn't remember.

Feeling goosebumps on her arms, she leaned over and studied the plate. She turned as Mark came back in the library and asked, "Is that your grandmother as a child?"

She shook her head. "The plaque says, 'Our beloved daughter and only child,' but there's no name. I'll bet it's

Maria Arceneaux. She was Henri and Caroline's only child and she died young."

"How did she die?"

"I don't know. Mamère never spoke of her, but she left her portrait in the library all these years. If it is Maria, it could be a hundred and fifty years old."

"I wanted to ask if you'd like me to take down Leonore's portrait. It might make you feel more comfortable while you're working in here."

She shook her head. "Thanks, but that's not necessary. Once the storm passes and this place doesn't seem quite so spooky, I think everything's going to be fine. Leonore certainly was a cross-looking woman, but she couldn't have been as nasty as she looked in her painting. Maybe she hadn't eaten her prunes that day! Anyway, with her covered up, I'm fine."

An hour later the lights flickered and then came on for good. They walked to the veranda and saw that the rain had diminished to a steady sprinkle and the skies were getting lighter. There was ankle-deep water from the house to the river, but Mark assured her as soon as the rain stopped, it would recede quickly.

CHAPTER FOURTEEN

The dawn brought a freshness in the air that they hadn't felt in three days. It was sprinkling off and on, but the water that had covered the lawn was gone. The skies were still dark, but there were patches of blue in the western sky. Tropical storm Jack was all finished here. He was headed for Texas.

Nearly ten thousand people along the coast had evacuated to Houston, they learned from the radio. Most were staying in temporary shelters and hoping to return home soon. She was thankful that rain and the power outage had been their only real problems.

"Do you think the road is open between here and Opelousas?" she asked. "I'd love to go buy a big juicy T-bone for tonight, if only there was a chef around to grill it!"

"I'll bet I can find a chef for you, and I'm sure the roads will be fine once you get to River Road. But before anybody goes anywhere, I have to see if I can move that tree trunk without getting help."

"I'm sorry. I had completely forgotten about it. There's no rush if you have other things to do. I don't have to go to town today."

It had to be done sooner or later, so he drove to the gate and parked his Jeep as close to the tree as he could. He unrolled the steel winch line, secured it and started pulling. The tree creaked and groaned as it began to move. Fifteen minutes later the driveway was clear. He had been concerned about the archway over the entrance, but fortunately the tree had missed it.

She had watched from the porch, and when he returned, she gave him two thumbs up.

"I cleared the drive, but why don't you let me go for you?"

"Thanks, but I'm really looking forward to going myself. I need to get away from here for a while. Between the storm and all the crazy stuff going on, I feel like I've been locked in a cage. You're welcome to come too – I'm certainly not saying I need to get away from *you* – but I need a change of scenery."

"I completely understand, and I'll let you have a little peace and quiet." Mark had a project of his own and her announcement that she was going off the property was perfect timing. In case she had problems, he followed her to the highway in his Jeep, and they waved as she pulled onto River Road and headed north.

He took out some stakes and a two-hundred-foot tape, and he carefully measured the length and width of the outside of the house, recording the exact dimensions. Then he moved inside. He wrote down the size of each of the first-floor rooms, the walls in between, and the broad hallway spanning the structure. When he was finished, he had a basic floor plan complete with dimensions.

He sat at the kitchen table and tallied his numbers. He checked his figures, then checked them again. At one point, he went back into the music room and opened the door that led to the hidden staircase. He measured it and compared it to the other calculations he'd made.

He studied the results and jotted notes on the floor plan. What he learned was what he expected: the hidden stairway in the music room wasn't the only anomaly in this house. There were three in all – three places where the total of the interior dimensions didn't tally with the exterior measurements. As cleverly as the staircase had been inserted into the structure of the mansion, he expected the others to be well concealed too. He needed to find two more secrets – one in a library wall and another somewhere in the first-floor hallway.

The process had taken forty-five minutes, and he was keeping an eye on the time. He wanted to measure the other two floors as carefully as he had done the first, and he just managed to finish the project when he heard her drive up. Other than the hidden staircase that opened into the third-floor closet, there were no anomalies above the first floor.

As she walked through the back door, he ran to the kitchen. He quickly gathered the papers strewn about the kitchen table, tossed them in a drawer and closed it just as she walked in.

"Good day so far?" she asked.

"Yeah, wonderful. I've spent the day in heaven, working on bathrooms. I'll have my plumber's license before I'm done! How was town?"

"It was a nice break. The supermarket was better stocked than I expected. I got us some steaks and baking potatoes. It'll be a hearty meal for the plumber and the housekeeper." She laughed.

She went back to work in the library. As soon as she was out of the kitchen, he moved the papers to the portfolio he always kept with him.

They worked all morning and at noon they met in the kitchen for lunch. She put four books on the table that she'd brought from the library. Three were beautifully bound in leather and the other was a very old paperback that was worn and tattered.

"What are those?"

"Everything I see in the library is interesting, and a lot of the books up high are really old. The lower shelves are full of newer ones – probably Mamère's reading material – but I doubt she ever ventured up on a ladder to see what was twelve feet above her. I pulled these four at random. Three beauties and one beast."

"These are first editions. They could be worth a fortune," he commented as he carefully thumbed through them. The hardbacks were nineteenth-century classics by Melville, Whitman and the former slave and abolitionist leader Frederick Douglass. "Are there more like these?"

"Yes. All of them. Most are leather-bound, and now and then there's a stray like this paperback. Since I'm physically dusting every volume, I've seen every author I ever heard about in high school and college, plus a lot whose names aren't familiar."

"Your Mamère left you a hidden treasure. If they're worth what I think they might be, you could sell a few and pay off the bank easily. And you'd still have an entire library left!"

She said that was a good idea. She had no sentimental attachment to the books, and except for a few rows of modern works, there were thousands just like these four.

"What about that ragged one? Why would anyone have kept it?"

He looked at the title. *Tamerlane and Other Poems*, by Edgar Allan Poe. "One of your ancestors might have liked Poe. It's in much worse condition than the others, that's for sure, but it could be worth something too, I guess."

"How do you find out what a book is worth?"

"We can look online. If you decide to sell, I'd start with the antique dealers in New Orleans. Those old stores along Royal Street in the French Quarter would probably get into a bidding war over this brand-new first edition of *Moby-Dick.*" He did a search on his phone and announced, "One of these came up at auction in New York a year ago. It brought nearly thirty-five hundred dollars!"

"Are you kidding? Look up the others!"

His revelation was bittersweet. When she'd first walked through the house as its new owner, she had had the lofty ambition to keep everything just as it was. But as she got into the project, she knew that wasn't possible. It would take money – lots more than she had – to fix this place up properly, regardless of what she ended up doing with it. She'd already told him she was willing to part with some of the books, but it still pained her to sell anything from Beau Rivage.

Let it go. There's five thousand of them. Sell ten – hell, sell fifty and you'll never even miss them. Maybe this is the answer to our money problems.

He continued his online search and learned that the others were valued from two to five thousand dollars each. "The big thing you have going for you is their condition.

106

Most of the ones sold at auction weren't in perfect shape like three of these are. I doubt if anyone ever read these books. I guess one of your ancestors bought them new and put them right on the shelf where they stayed until today. You have some valuable books here. What do you want to do with them?"

"Put them back in the library for now. You have my attention, for sure. I'm going to look more closely as I work to see what other surprises might be on the shelves!'

He climbed the ladder and replaced three of the books in an empty space on the top shelf from which they'd obviously been taken down. He slid the fourth one – the small Poe paperback – into his portfolio. There was something about the title that seemed familiar. He knew something about Poe's early works from his college days. He recalled learning about this very title. He wanted to look at this one more closely.

Out of curiosity, he took down four more hardbacks, brought them into the kitchen and looked up the values, which turned out to be in the same range as the others.

"How many books did you tell me were in there?" he asked.

"Five thousand, give or take."

"I'm going to do some conservative calculating. You've been cleaning the top shelves that contain the oldest books. Let's be conservative with our numbers. Let's say there are four thousand books in all, and fifteen hundred of them are like the ones we've examined so far. Then let's say after commissions and discounting, you'd end up with fifteen hundred dollars apiece." He clicked the numbers into his phone.

"Want to take a guess?"

Callie had a wide, expectant grin. "My head's spinning. Tell me!"

"Two million, two hundred and fifty thousand dollars."

Feeling light-headed, she sank into the chair next to him. "Could that be possible? That's more than the house is worth – right?"

"Way more," he agreed. "Restored completely, I doubt Beau Rivage would fetch more than a million."

That afternoon her work in the library was punctuated by gasps, giggles and singing as Callie looked at the books she dusted and contemplated what she might have inherited. *Thank you, Mamère,* she said aloud over and over. What she had considered a tedious, never-ending chore – cleaning up a roomful of old books – had become an exciting adventure that might be the answer to all her problems.

"Did you move the ladder?" she yelled up the stairs in the middle of the afternoon.

He came out of the kitchen across the hall. "I'm finished upstairs for now. I don't have the ladder. It's in there, isn't it?"

"Yes, but it's on the left side of the fireplace, and I was working on the right side. Are you sure you didn't move it?"

"Not me."

She gave him a bewildered look and asked quietly, "This is the third time it's been over there, and I don't know how it got there. Do you think I could be moving it myself, and forgetting I did it? Am I going crazy?"

He smiled at first, but then he realized she was serious. He put his arm around her. "I have no idea what's happening, but you're fine. You've been put through a lot of stress, but you're just fine. Together we can fight any battle."

Together. That word made her very comfortable. She snuggled closer to him and this time it didn't seem to surprise him.

But she couldn't dismiss the fear and doubt. *If he didn't move the ladder and I didn't move the ladder, then who did?*

He grilled the steak to perfection while she prepared baked potatoes and a salad. A bottle of red wine added to a perfect dinner, and they talked excitedly about the possibilities that she'd found in the library bookcases. The books could not only solve her temporary cash requirements, they could be the means to make Beau Rivage into the showplace she dreamed about.

They washed dishes together, toasted to success and after a good-night hug, they retired, to their separate bedrooms. Callie fell asleep almost immediately but Mark lay awake for over an hour pondering the inconsistency of the measurements inside the house versus out, and doing online research to learn more about Poe's *Tamerlane and Other Poems*.

CHAPTER FIFTEEN

The board of directors of the Cotton Belt State Bank of Opelousas met every third Monday at 9 a.m. Today four men and three women sat around an enormous conference table in the boardroom, a thick stack of reports before them. Dudley Hibbard, the bank's president and chairman of the board, was running the meeting. Dudley was the third Hibbard to run the Cotton Belt. His grandfather had started it in the 1880s, and thanks to conservative leadership and policies, the bank turned a nice profit every year.

Except for Robert Talmadge, the bank's senior vice president and loan officer, the directors were civic leaders – the movers and shakers of Opelousas, whose considerable wealth contributed to the bank's growing asset base.

Problem loans were always discussed by the board, and there were rarely more than one or two, thanks to Talmadge's watchful eye over the institution's ultraconservative lending practices. After five minutes reviewing the problems, he asked if the directors had any further questions about loans.

"How's that real estate fellow Mark Streater doing?" Willard Arceneaux asked, looking over the top of his glasses as they rested on the bridge of his nose. "Are we still loaning him money on his fixer-upper projects?"

"We are," Talmadge replied, explaining that although he was young and still fairly new at what he was doing, Streater appeared to be conservative in his approach to borrowing. He provided quarterly financial statements and everything else the bank required, and he was always on time. He'd never been late even one day, and if he saw anything on the horizon that might concern the bank, he was proactively at Talmadge's desk discussing it.

"Frankly, Mr. Arceneaux, the bank would like to have a hundred Mark Streaters as customers. He only owes us a little over a hundred thousand, and the collateral he's put up is worth four times that much. He never bites off more than he can chew, and I think he has a bright future."

Willard paused, thoughtfully perusing the problem loan report that was still in front of him.

"If that's everything, then we'll move on," Dudley Hibbard said.

"One more question, if I may," Willard interjected. "Did the bank loan Mr. Streater money to fix up Beau Rivage?"

"Technically we loaned the money to a Miss Calisto Pilantro. She mortgaged the house and forty acres, along with its contents, and Mr. Streater signed the note because we required additional collateral."

"You loaned them fifty thousand dollars. Is that correct?"

Robert Talmadge was getting just a bit nervous. Directors never asked anything about the performing loans, and this one was so new the first monthly interest payment hadn't come due yet.

"That's correct, Mr. Arceneaux. Is there something specific about that loan I can explain for you?"

"For those who might not know, Calisto Pilantro is my grandniece, the granddaughter of my sister, Juliet, who owned Beau Rivage until her recent death." The directors nodded in unison; they had all known Juliet. "Ordinarily I'd abstain from discussions about loans that involve relatives, as I know my colleagues in this room would do. But my obligations as a director of this bank override family affairs. I feel compelled to ask you to call that loan."

Dudley Hibbard was aghast. In his years as a banker, nothing like this had ever happened. Board meetings were routine affairs where a group of rich people who'd served for years got together, drank coffee, acted like bankers and collected a director's fee of one thousand dollars per month each. He couldn't remember the last time there had even been a comment about a performing loan other than the "atta boys" his team usually received for the jobs they did.

"May I ask what your concern is, Willard?"

"My niece, to put it bluntly, doesn't have a cent to her name. She hurried down here from Virginia because I told her there was going to be a reading of Juliet's will and she was an heir. Unfortunately, she didn't have the money for bus fare and food. She's family and I felt sorry for her, so I wired her two hundred dollars. She inherited the house, such as it is. I was out there yesterday and I was sorry to see what bad shape it's in.

"When Calisto got to town, she hooked up with Mark Streater somehow, and next thing I knew, I was hearing they'd borrowed fifty thousand dollars. That was a surprise – I wouldn't have thought anyone would loan money to him for that project. Then I heard it was our bank that loaned the money. I was floored, to put it mildly."

He looked at Robert Talmadge, who appeared to be close to having a nervous breakdown. "I'm not blaming you, Robert. Mr. Streater's been a good customer and he has collateral, but every one of us knows what real estate's worth in a fire sale. It'll take a fortune to fix up Beau Rivage, and even if you spent it, all you'd have is a huge old mansion nobody wants. Fifty thousand is a drop in the bucket, and when that money runs out and they're back here, hat in hand for more, what do we do next?

"I've been on this board for twelve years, Dudley. You all know I've never criticized a loan decision, even on the handful that went sour. You folks have always done well. But as a director and shareholder of the Cotton Belt State Bank, I'm telling you we must call this loan."

"He's drawn down most of the fifty thousand already," Talmadge reported dejectedly. "If we call the note there's no chance he can pay it back. He'll have to fire-sale everything he owns, and that'll put him out of business."

"My niece doesn't know a damned thing about business," Willard said abruptly. "Her daddy left town before she was born and he came from a bastard before him. She works for some two-bit newspaper in rural Virginia –

presuming she still has a job – and she should never have let Mark Streater talk her into mortgaging worthless property. What his motive is, I don't know. But I know one thing – this loan is no good for the bank. In fact, I make a motion that we call Mr. Streater's loan and give him thirty days to pay. Let him finish drawing the rest of his fifty thousand – that's only fair and I'm not trying to kick him when he's down – but in thirty days it all has to be paid back."

There was nothing the other directors could do but vote in favor of the motion. None of them knew anything about Callie, and Willard obviously was worried about his own kinfolk borrowing money from the bank. The motion passed with only one nay vote – Dudley Hibbard's. Willard abstained and so did Robert Talmadge, since he'd approved the loan in the first place.

"Okay, Willard," the bank president said. "What do you suggest we do now? If this was a risky deal before, it's a damned sight worse now. I know his financial situation better than anyone in this room except Robert here. He can't pay the money back in thirty days. He'll have to sell property and that takes time. The loan will go into default and we'll probably end up foreclosing the property."

Willard paused as if in deep thought. The others sat expectantly until he said, "You make a good point. The last thing I want is for a relative of mine to put the bank in a bad spot. Here's what I'll do. I'll buy the loan from the bank. If the other directors agree, I'll pay you in full – fifty thousand dollars plus the interest he owes to date – and you'll be out of the deal completely. No more worries about collateral or repayment. If it all goes south, then it's my problem, not yours."

The woman next to him said, "That's a very generous offer, Willard. Blood is thicker than water, and you've proven that today. You're a gentleman and I for one appreciate your willingness to protect both your niece and the bank's assets. I say let Mr. Arceneaux buy the note."

Except for Willard's abstention, this vote was unanimous.

CHAPTER SIXTEEN

On Monday morning at breakfast Mark told her he was going to Opelousas for the day. He'd neglected his own work and he needed to dedicate several hours of catch-up time. She promised she was fine and sent him on his way shortly after eight.

She had finished one twelve-foot bookshelf and had eleven more to go. Some were packed with books; on others, there was bric-a-brac – personal mementos, briar pipes, a statue of a Greek god and so forth. Even with the occasional break in the solid shelves of books, the library cleaning was going to consume several days of her time.

She worked until a little after ten, got a bottle of water and took a break on the front porch, where she could see the river. It was four feet above its normal level, but an occasional boat went by, signaling that things were returning to normal post-hurricane.

When he left the house, instead of turning left on River Road, Mark had gone in the other direction. A few miles south, he got on Interstate 10 east, and he was in New Orleans by 10:30. He visited two galleries in the French Quarter and received confirmation about the incredible news he'd learned last night when he researched the paperback he'd brought with him.

Tamerlane and Other Poems was Poe's first book and had been published in the mid-1820s. The first dealer Mark visited – a man named Parsons – spent some time on the internet, reviewing many of the same sites Mark himself had visited last night after Callie turned in. The small paperbound book had originally received no acclaim from critics, and less than a hundred were ever published. Today, one was in the British Museum and eleven more were in the hands of smaller institutions or collectors, mostly in Europe.

"Condition is normally a significant issue when considering the value of books," Parsons said, "but in this case, so few copies exist that condition becomes secondary to rarity. There appear to be none of these books ever found that are in pristine condition, and only seven have both the front and back cover. I'd say you have made an astonishing discovery. This may turn out to be the most valuable object I've ever personally handled."

The man pressed Mark as to how he came into possession of the volume, but he declined to answer. Instead he asked, "How valuable could this book be, once it's authenticated?"

"In 2009 Christie's sold one at auction that fetched over six hundred thousand dollars."

Astonished, Mark kept his face impassive. He'd missed that story on the web. He knew it was important, but this was a priceless rarity, and he had no doubt it was the real thing, given the dozens of other first editions he'd seen in the Arceneaux library.

When she showed him the four books yesterday in the kitchen, he'd immediately homed in on this one. The others were by famous and respected authors, but he knew from his college days that although the eccentric author's early works could hardly be given away during Poe's lifetime, they became valuable later.

Mr. Parsons advised that the book would need authentication from a team of experts, and he recommended a firm in Boston that specialized in rare books. Mark thanked him and said he'd be in touch. He left without providing contact information, even though the dealer had requested it.

More careful with the book now that he knew what it was worth, he walked three blocks to Chartres Street and visited a second dealer. The man was far less forthcoming about the book, saying it was perhaps a first edition but more likely a forgery. "Originals like this don't just turn up," he said condescendingly. "People don't just walk into my shop and offer something that's incredibly rare. I'm not saying it doesn't happen; I'm saying it's almost beyond imagination. But perhaps you do have something here. It will take time to find out. Where did you get it?"

Mark ignored him. "What's it worth, in your opinion?"

"What would I give you for it today? Seventy thousand dollars. I'd be taking a gamble that it's authentic, and if it is, I'd make a decent profit. That's today's offer. If you'd leave it with me and I had it authenticated, we could find out for sure what you have here. If it's the real deal, I'd offer you three hundred thousand."

"If it were real, I wouldn't sell it for anything close to that. I've had much higher offers."

"Then with all due respect, you should accept one of them. I don't know who you are, and I don't know where this book came from. Without a lot more information about you – and an authentication, of course – I don't want anything to do with it."

––––––

Callie called Mark's office around 2:30, and Mrs. Collins reported that she hadn't seen Mark all day. That worried Callie for a moment, but when she thought about it, it made perfect sense. When he'd left this morning, he said he was going to catch up on his own work. She interpreted that to mean he was going to the office, but he didn't do his work behind a desk. He was out in the field where the crews were working on his rental properties. She tried his cellphone and he picked up immediately. She asked how everything was going in town and when he thought he'd be back.

"I'm wrapping things up," he said, glancing at his watch and calculating that he'd be off the interstate highway in forty-five minutes. "I have two errands left – I've got to stop by the bank and then run over to the Eunice house and check the progress. I should be back there in an hour."

She drove to the Point Charmaine store and filled the Pontiac with gas. She'd vowed not to come here again, but it was convenient and close. She went inside to pay.

"Driving Miss Juliet's car, I see," he said, running her debit card.

"Yes, I found it in the barn."

"What else have you found?"

After the brusque brush-off when she and Mark were last here, she was surprised at his more cordial attitude today. He seemed genuinely interested in Beau Rivage this time. *Probably searching for gossip fodder,* she thought.

"The same wonderful old house I knew when I spent my summers here growing up. The renovations are really coming along."

He harrumphed and replied, "I hear tell it's going to take a lot more money to fix it up than you folks have."

Her eyes blazed and she held back the urge to tell him to mind his own business. She had decided to ask him something herself, and confrontation wouldn't get her answers.

"We'll see," she replied cordially. "Now I have a question for you. There's a child who comes to the house now and then. Her name is Anne-Marie. She's maybe ten years old with blond hair, and she always wears a dress. Any idea who she might be?"

"She came to your house? Why didn't you ask her yourself?" he snapped back gruffly.

Stay calm. "She's different. She doesn't talk very much and she never stays more than a few minutes. I was just hoping you might know where she lives."

"Ain't no families with kids on this side of the river except the Dupres."

She paused, waiting for him to continue, but it was obvious she was going to have to drag every iota of information out of him. "And can you tell me where the Dupres live?"

"In a shanty on the other side of the woods north of Beau Rivage."

"I had no idea there was a house over there."

"There isn't supposed to be. They're squatters; they've lived there for a few years now. Their shack may even be on your property, so you may be their landlady. They come in here now and then to buy a soda. They always have a couple of kids in tow, way younger than ten and dark-headed, so it's probably got nothin' to do with the one you saw. Other than that, ain't nobody around here with kids. Who'd want to raise a family out here in the boondocks?"

He had been far chattier last time. She thanked him and asked if he could give her directions to their house.

"How should I know? I ain't ever been there. It's somewhere off River Road, I guess. There's probably a turnoff north of your place that's hidden in the trees."

Callie drove past the road to Beau Rivage and slowed down, watching the left shoulder and trying to spot a turnoff. Where the woods ended, there were tire tracks heading off west toward the river through a field of unmowed grass. She turned and went almost a mile, constantly worried because the ground was still soggy. If this trail led nowhere and she couldn't turn around, she could get stuck. At least she could call Mark to bring the Jeep, she thought.

When she rounded a bend, she came to a muddy yard with a rusty pickup in it. There was a large pit bull chained to a post and an unpainted hovel that had sheet metal nailed over the windows. The dog began to bark furiously and tugged at his chain. She stayed in the car, hoping someone would come out.

The door opened and a man in his late thirties stepped out. His face was unshaven, he was shirtless and wearing a pair of ragged shorts, and there was a huge gob of tobacco in one cheek. He held a shotgun that was aimed at her.

"Get out of here. No trespassers allowed," he said when she rolled down the window.

"I'm Callie Pilantro," she said. "Mr. Dupre? I'd like to talk to you for a moment."

"Are you the law?"

"No. I own Beau Rivage. My grandmother was Juliet Arceneaux."

That gave him something to think about. He lowered the shotgun and said, "What do you want with us?"

"I need to ask you a few questions. May I get out?"

"It's a free country."

"Is your dog friendly?"

He laughed and spat tobacco on the ground. "Does he look friendly? You can get out. I'll corral him." He grabbed the chain and jerked the dog's neck back roughly. "Be good now, Spike. Unless we find out she ain't who she says she is," he said, grinning at Callie.

She didn't want to talk to this redneck any more than she had to. "Is your wife at home?"

"Molly! Come out here! A woman from Beau Rivage wants to talk to you!"

A tired-looking woman who had been peeking through the doorway stepped outside, along with two ragged children under six. She was younger than her husband; the kids stood behind her and peeked around her faded skirt.

"I'm Callie Pilantro. I inherited Beau Rivage from my grandmother and I'm fixing it up."

The woman stared blankly at her.

"I was wondering if you have another child, a daughter around ten or eleven years old."

Stony silence and blank eyes revealed nothing.

"She don't talk much," the man said with a sneer. "I'm the chatty one and she won't say nothin' until I tell her to. Why did you come here?"

"I just said I'm looking for a blond-headed girl." She already knew the chances that Anne-Marie lived in this squalid environment were slim, but she was already here, so she might as well get it over with. "She comes to Beau Rivage now and then."

"No child of ours goes over there. It's a mile through the woods. Why would she do that anyway?"

Bingo! "So you do have another child?"

"I didn't say that. I'm gettin' a little tired of answerin' questions, know what I mean?" He loosened his grip on the chain just a little and Spike lunged savagely toward her. She hoped she was out of range, but she didn't want to take the chance.

"May I see her?"

"Nope."

"Mr. ... uh, Dupre. Is that right?"

"None of your business."

She had nothing to lose by going for it. "Here's the deal. It looks to me like your house sits on my property. As long as we act like civilized people, it doesn't bother me that you're living over here on the north side of my woods. May I see your other daughter, neighbor?"

He turned to his wife and snarled, "Take her in the house and make it quick."

The doorway was so low that Callie had to duck to enter. The ceiling was barely six feet high and the room felt confining. The walls were the same rough boards that were nailed to the outside – there was nothing covering the inside walls at all. There were puddles of water on the wood floor, left over from the hurricane. The place was incredibly dark, dingy and sparsely furnished. Callie followed the woman through the front room and a miserable kitchen. She saw two doors on the opposite wall. One was open and led to what could be the parents' bedroom. She averted her eyes; she didn't need to look in there.

The other door opened into a room maybe ten feet square with three mattresses on the floor. All the children must sleep in this one tiny room, Callie thought. The windows in the other rooms were still boarded up from the storm, but this one had a large dirt-streaked window that was wide open. A blond girl wearing that familiar blue dress sat in front of it, looking out, with her back to them. It might be her, but unless Callie saw her face, she couldn't be certain.

"Anne-Marie?"

The woman turned sharply and glared at Callie. She was surprised; it was the first indication that she was tuned in to anything that was going on.

"Why did you call her that?" the woman croaked in a gravelly smoker's voice that sounded too old for her. The child sat motionless, staring out the window.

"She comes to Beau Rivage."

"No, she don't. You're a liar. I'm gettin' my husband." The woman stalked out.

This situation was making Callie very uncomfortable, but she only had a moment with the girl.

"Anne-Marie, look at me."

The child stared out the window as if she hadn't heard.

"It is you, isn't it?"

Just then the man burst into the room. "What the hell do you think you're doin'?" he shouted. "You scared my wife. Now get the hell out of my house."

Callie turned to follow him out. She looked back and saw that the child was facing her now. The child smiled, turned away and stared the window.

Back outside, she told the man that his daughter had come to the house several times. "She looked at me as I was leaving. I saw her face. Her name is Anne-Marie, isn't it?"

Her question infuriated him. "Listen to me, lady. I was stupid to let you go in the house. You saw her, so you can tell somethin' about her ain't right. She ain't said a word in six years. She looks out the window all day until the wife makes her eat. She ain't set foot outside the house in as long as I can remember. I don't know what you think you're doin' here, but you've made a big mistake. She ain't the girl you're lookin' for. You don't scare me with your threats about my squattin' on your land. Get off my property and don't come back." He released the dog. "Sic her, Spike!"

I'll bring the sheriff next time, you jerk, she thought to herself as she outran the pit bull, jumped into the car and locked the doors. She backed up in the muddy yard and gained enough traction to head back toward the highway.

Callie was relieved to see the Jeep parked at the house when she pulled in. She was physically and mentally exhausted; the experience with the strange family had been disturbing. Was the child really Anne-Marie? Callie had been in the same room with her. How could she not be? But if her father was telling the truth, that was impossible.

She gave Mark a recap and asked what he thought about her visit to the shanty.

"Are you absolutely certain it was Anne-Marie?"

"I tell you, it looked exactly like her. It was her, unless she has a twin sister. It was so weird over there. The place was nasty, the parents and the little kids were dirty, and she was the only person who looked ... well, normal. She looked as clean and fresh as she does when she's here. She was even wearing the blue dress. If her parents are telling the truth, it sounds like she's autistic. But how could that be possible? How can she not talk or go outside of her own house, while at the same time she comes over here and talks to us?"

"It can't be her. It's just not logical if the father's telling the truth. Either you were mistaken when you saw her, or she really does have a twin."

She had forgotten about calling Mark's office earlier today. She had intended to mention it, but she decided to let it go. She didn't want him to think she was keeping tabs on him. She thought he was going to the office, but he didn't. No big deal. It was his life, and he didn't owe her an explanation for his whereabouts.

Just then, they heard a horn honking. She walked through the house, looked outside and said, "I consider my day complete. It's Uncle Willard."

CHAPTER SEVENTEEN

Willard saw Callie standing in the doorway and waved as he walked to the porch.

"I have some news for you that's best delivered in person."

"This is not a good time," she said. "Both of us have been running errands all day and we just got home."

"This can't wait. There's a clock ticking, and you and your friend need to know about it."

He followed her into the parlor. "We can sit in here. Mark, Uncle Willard needs to talk to us."

She pulled her quilt and pillow off the couch and he fluffed the cushion before he sat.

"Is this where you all are sleepin'?"

She didn't answer.

"Hello, Mr. Arceneaux," Mark said, offering his hand. "What brings you out here so late in the afternoon?"

"Some distressing news, actually. Somethin' that involves you both. Your bank has decided they don't want your loan anymore. Maybe it was the collateral – after all, this old house isn't worth much in its present condition and fifty grand will hardly make a dent in it. Maybe it was something else they were uneasy about."

Mark was astonished, but Callie's face reflected fear. "How do you know about this, and what does it mean for us?" she asked. She turned to Mark. "Why didn't your friend at the bank call you?"

Willard interrupted. "This all just happened at a bank board meeting this morning. When the directors meet, we always review the loans."

"*We?* Are you on the board of Mark's bank?"

"I am, darlin', and I wouldn't refer to it as *Mark's* bank. I've been a shareholder and a director of the Cotton Belt for many years. There was a lot of talk about this loan; I can't say much because everything's confidential in a bank board meeting. There was some concern that Mr. Streater talked you into mortgaging the property because he knew you didn't have any business sense. I stood up for you, of course, being as how you're family and all."

He told Mark that the board wasn't happy with the loan officer's decision to extend credit and had voted to give Mark thirty days to repay the loan in full.

"How did you vote?" Callie asked, beginning to understand.

"I abstained, of course. This loan involved family and it wouldn't have been right for me to vote."

"How *would* you have voted?"

He looked at his watch and his tone of voice hardened. "I don't have much time, so let's cut to the chase. I talked to you privately the other day, Mr. Streater. I tried to be reasonable and help you, but you never called me back. I didn't want to see you all default on a bank loan. That would ruin your credit, Mr. Streater, and yours too, Calisto, if you had any in the first place. So I took the note and mortgage off the bank's hands. You no longer owe the Cotton Belt fifty thousand dollars."

Callie looked at Mark, puzzled. "I don't understand what he's saying ..."

Mark said, "I get it. You own the note and mortgage now – am I correct?"

"You absolutely are correct." He winked at Callie and drawled, "Smart man you got here."

"I haven't got anyone," she snapped. "Why don't you cut the crap? What's the deal? We have thirty days to pay you?"

"You poor girl. You sure don't know much about business. Your friend here signed a demand note. That means if the holder – which now is me – feels uncomfortable for any reason, he can demand repayment with no notice at all. If Mr. Streater couldn't pay the note in full for some reason, then you'd lose the house and land because you foolishly let him talk you into signing a mortgage. I've told you all along you were in over your heads. If Juliet had a lick of sense, she'd have left the house to my children. At least they have the financial resources to take care of it."

Callie was seething. She stood and shouted, "Tell us what you want and get the hell out of my house!"

He smiled. "Won't be your house much longer, Calisto. You have two choices. Deed the house over to me by the end of the week. If you do, I'll tear up the note and you won't owe fifty thousand dollars."

"There's not a chance in hell that's going to happen!"

"Then Mr. Streater owes me fifty grand plus interest in five days, darlin'. It's as simple as that. Oh, and don't think about takin' anything out of the house. The contents will all be mine once you default on the mortgage. Here's my demand notice. Fifty thousand, two hundred and twenty-three dollars is exactly what you owe. The deadline's Friday at 5 p.m. I wouldn't suggest being late."

"You planned all along to steal the house from me, didn't you? Don't talk to me about family! You're despicable!"

Willard walked out. In a moment, they heard him start the BMW, and then he was gone.

They sat silently in the parlor. It was beginning to get dark and the room was draped in shadows. They heard a voice from the hallway.

"I don't like him. He's going to hurt you."

"Anne-Marie!" Callie shouted as they both jumped up and ran to where they'd heard her. "I want to talk to you!"

But she wasn't there. They called her name over and over, but the old house was silent.

"Am I losing my mind? Please tell me you heard her talking."

"I did," Mark replied. "But where is she? How does she disappear and reappear? What is it about her anyway?"

She didn't reveal exactly how she felt. As odd as Anne-Marie was, there was something Callie was beginning to find comforting – a feeling that the girl belonged here.

It was after midnight when they turned in. They had talked for hours about their very limited options.

"We could sell some of the books," she suggested.

"There isn't time. We could fire-sell them for a few hundred dollars each, but to offer what they really might be worth, any reputable dealer's going to demand an appraisal and authentication. I'd bet that'll take weeks."

"How about we offer them to Uncle Willard? We could look them up online and offer him a hundred thousand dollars' worth."

"Why would he do that? It's clear now that he's only interested in one thing – taking the property. If we default, he gets all the books, not just a few. He'd never take your offer."

She remembered that Willard said he'd talked privately to Mark. "Was that the truth? Did you have a conversation with him?"

"I did," he admitted. "I didn't tell you because I knew it wouldn't help family relations, and there was nothing to it anyway. He wanted me to partner with him to force you out. I told him absolutely not."

"He said you didn't call him back."

"I told him no and he said to call if I came to my senses. I didn't call back."

She felt betrayed and angry. "You should have told me when it happened. I thought we were ..."

His reply was sharp and harsh. "What, Callie? What do you think we are? We're business partners in a deal that's going south fast. I wasn't obligated to tell you about a conversation with your uncle and an offer that I was never going to consider. It simply wasn't relevant. What he wanted to do didn't matter. I wasn't going to go against you. This bickering isn't going to help us solve our problem."

"What he wanted matters now, doesn't it?" she said. She was hurt by his acerbic words but knew she shouldn't be. He was nothing but her partner, like he said. There was nothing else between them. He wasn't obligated to tell her anything ... even about why he wasn't at his office yesterday when she thought that was where he was going.

She walked to the kitchen, poured some wine and brought it back to the parlor.

"Sure, I'd like one too," he said sarcastically, getting a glass for himself and coming back.

He sat down across from her. "Callie, we can let this thing tear us apart, or we can work together. I didn't do what your uncle asked because I was confident we could handle this on our own. And we could have if Willard hadn't pulled the rug out from under us. He planned this all along. I'm sure you see that, and I'm sorry it's your relative we're talking about, but he's screwed you – and me too. We have five days to come up with fifty thousand dollars plus the interest. There's twelve thousand still in the bank account. If we stop working at Beau Rivage, we only have around forty thousand to come up with, not fifty."

She didn't want to fight, especially now. *This isn't personal,* she told herself. If there was any way to keep the house, she had to work with him. Without Mark, she was back to square one in the being-broke-all-the-time game.

"What do you suggest we do?" she said at last.

"Let's sleep on it. Try to put the negative thoughts out of your head. All they'll do is clutter your mind and keep you from focusing. Think of every possibility and I will too. Tomorrow at breakfast we'll compare notes and come up with a plan."

He carried his wineglass across the hall to his temporary bedroom and took off his clothes. He walked down the hall to the bathroom wearing his T-shirt and boxers, and ran into Callie coming out, wearing the same thing.

He took her in his arms and gave her a long hug. "It's going to be all right," he said soothingly. "Working together, we'll figure everything out."

She snuggled down under the quilt and fell asleep thinking about the hug and wishing it had lasted longer. She had such conflicted feelings about him. He could be difficult one minute and wonderful the next. She was putting too many restrictions on him and she needed to give him room. She wanted to see where this might go.

For the first time since she'd been in the house, she slept straight through the night without waking.

Mark was puttering around the kitchen when she padded in.

"Morning," he said with a smile.

"You opened the front door!" she noticed, looking across the lawn to the now-serene Atchafalaya River. "It smells wonderful outside, and it looks like we're in for a gorgeous day!"

"I'm convinced this is going to be *your* gorgeous day." He handed her a mug of coffee and they sat on the porch.

"Did you come up with any brilliant ideas?" he asked, and she said she hadn't. Instead, she'd gotten her best night of rest in days, and there had been no tossing, turning or thinking.

"That's great. It's important to have a clear head today. I've thought of a few things we might do. Some are more realistic than others, but don't call me crazy until you've heard my ideas. I could raise the money to pay your uncle. If I give him the money, he has no choice but to release the note and mortgage. He's counting on the fact that I can't get my hands on more money, and he may be right. Anyway, that's idea number one."

"How would you get more money?"

"The four houses I own are in various stages of repair. When they're finished, I'll put them on the market. I've borrowed money on each one to fund the renovations. If they were all ready and they sold today, I'm certain I could pay both Willard and my bank loans and have a hundred grand in my pocket. I'd have to find someone wealthy who believes in me, who agrees that the properties have the value I say they have, and who'd loan me fifty thousand dollars. The bank has the first mortgages; this new lender would have to take seconds, but the right person would do it. The big problem is Willard's influence in this part of Louisiana. If he put his mind to it, he might scare off anyone I might find."

"Do you have anyone in mind?"

"Not offhand," he admitted.

"At least it's an idea. What else did you come up with?"

"My second idea is far-fetched and way more difficult. We'd have to find someone who sees the value of Beau Rivage as a destination, like we do. If we turn it into a bed-and-breakfast, or a riverfront tourist attraction and museum, or a tea room and event center, the house and land will be much more valuable. You also own forty acres of riverfront property. If it were on the Mississippi, the land would be worth a fortune, but it's still an attractive piece of frontage along a great river. I can maybe see Beau Rivage as the centerpiece and clubhouse for an exclusive gated community of upscale homes."

"Find someone who shares our vision. I like that idea."

"Me too, but I have only five days to market that vision to someone outside of Opelousas. I wouldn't even waste my time in St. Landry Parish because of Willard. I'd go to Lafayette or Baton Rouge or New Orleans. The problem is, I know what real estate investors will want to see. They'll want a business plan with projections, an appraisal on the house and acreage, comparable sales to demonstrate what other properties have sold for, and a sales pitch that's convincing. Putting that together would take weeks, and we have five days. The only way that idea would work is if either one of us knows someone somewhere who has faith in us and would take a second mortgage. They'd be loaning the money on a wing and a prayer, and I doubt that'll happen, frankly."

"Yeah, that one sounds tough, but let's give it more thought. Is that it?"

"No," he said. "There's one more and I think this is the easiest, even though it may not be what you'd like to do. This one involves selling some of the things in the house. It's full of nineteenth-century antiques that a gallery would bid on. We could call a dealer and have him come out here. Those guys can give you a bid on the spot and pay immediately. I don't know what kind of value there is in old furniture, but surely there's something."

"I'd be more inclined to sell the books. We already know some of them may be worth a lot of money."

"Right, but there's a difference between selling a book and selling a dining room table. With the table, a trained professional like the ones in the French Quarter can examine it right here and be one hundred percent certain of what they have in front of them. They know the signs that tell them if it's a valuable antique or a cheap reproduction. Your things are extraordinary and you know yourself how long they've been in the house, so I wouldn't be worried about their age.

"A book is different. A dealer can examine it, see what shape it's in and check auction values, but only a handful of dealers would know instantly if it's the real deal. If you found one, he might offer you a lowball figure up front, but with proper authentication – which takes time – he'd pay double or triple his initial offer. I could help you unload some of the books, but it would be just that – dumping them at fire-sale prices. Some dealer will end up very happy, you might end up with fifty thousand, which I'd have to borrow from you to pay Willard, and you might have sold some priceless things for pennies on the dollar. I don't recommend doing it that way, but if we got desperate, it might raise enough money to get us out of this jam."

"I'm desperate, but Uncle Willard warned us not to take anything out of the house because it's all mortgaged. Can we really sell anything?"

"Technically, we'd be violating the loan agreement, but so long as I pay him the money in full by next Friday, it makes no difference because the possessions aren't his anymore. If for some reason I can't pay him in full, then he takes over and everything had better still be here. It's a catch-22, but my advice is to go for it. He can't know every single thing that's in the house. He wouldn't miss a book here and there. The furniture would be a different story; for all we know he may have taken an inventory after your Mamère's death. He may have taken pictures or shot a video in anticipation of this very possibility. Regardless, desperate times call for desperate measures. If you decide the books or the furniture are our best shot, I say go for it and to hell with the consequences. He's not going to throw us in jail for selling off some books or a table."

Callie wondered about that last statement. She had no idea what her uncle was capable of. He was a ruthless attorney comfortable with a fight, and a master at forcing large insurance companies to agree to his terms. How far would he go to hurt his own niece? She had no idea, and she was afraid she might find out.

He said those ideas were all he had and apologized that none might be good enough.

"Mark, thank you so much. It doesn't matter if they'll work. You've given me hope, and I appreciate your taking time to think of answers for us. Let's list them in order of possibility. I'd say the furniture is first, the books second, your fixer-upper houses third, and the Beau Rivage riverfront concept fourth. What do you think?"

"I agree."

"Okay, here's the plan. Let's send the painters home, keep what money's left in our bank account, and work on selling some furniture and some books at the same time. I'll take the books to New Orleans tomorrow and you can call a few antiques dealers and have them come look at the furniture. I'll pick some pieces that I can live without."

"I'll take the books if you want to stay here," he said. "It's over a two-hour drive each way."

"You're sweet to offer, but monotonous driving's what I need to clear my head. We looked at those four old books earlier and you put them back on the shelf. Would you please get them, and bring me six more that you think look interesting. That'll give me ten to show to potential buyers."

He told her he'd call an antique shop in Baton Rouge where a college friend worked. He said this guy might come look at furniture on very short notice, but he doubted the big dealers in New Orleans would.

With so little chance of success, she was surprised that he wasn't trying everything he could. "The big dealers must get calls all the time when estates are being divvied up by feuding family members. I'll bet they can respond on extremely short notice. Just give one or two a try, please."

"I'll see what I can arrange." That sounded like a halfhearted response to Callie.

Why isn't he on the same page as I am? After all, it's his fifty thousand dollars that's at risk.

Deciding she was overanalyzing his response after all the help he'd given her, she let it go.

CHAPTER EIGHTEEN

It was after four when Callie returned to Beau Rivage. It had been a long day; she hadn't done a five-hour drive in a long, long time and her legs and arms were aching. She'd been furious when she left New Orleans, but she forced herself to calm down. She wanted to confront him face-to-face and she wanted to have her thoughts collected when she did.

Mark's Jeep wasn't in the backyard. She didn't know where he was, but she didn't call either. He'd be back eventually. She went into the library, climbed the ladder to a certain shelf, searched through the books and came back down. She poured a glass of wine and walked to the veranda to relax and enjoy the solitude as best she could.

He called about thirty minutes later, explaining that there was a problem at one of his projects and he had been waiting two hours for a plumber. Since it was getting dark and he wasn't sure how long the repairs would take, he said he was staying in town tonight and he'd see her in the morning.

"What did the book dealers in New Orleans say?" he asked.

Now she had to confront him by phone, like it or not. This couldn't wait until tomorrow.

"Where's the little paperback book we looked at – the one by Edgar Allan Poe? You put ten books in the sack like I asked, but that one wasn't there. I specifically asked you for it because I thought it might be worth a lot. I was disappointed to get all the way there and discover I didn't have it. Where is it, Mark? Do you have it?"

"I'm really sorry. I remember now that I took down the three leather-bound volumes we had looked at and then

I just kept reaching for more. I forgot all about the paperback. If it's that important to you, I'll take it to New Orleans tomorrow morning."

"Where is it?"

"It's up on the shelf."

"No, it isn't, Mark. Where did you put it? There's an empty spot where the other three used to be, and I can see where you got the others, but that one isn't there. I want to know where it is."

"God, Callie. I'm not sure. If it's such a big deal, I can drop everything and come out there to look for it. Can't it wait until tomorrow?"

Her earlier decision to be calm and civil with him hadn't lasted for long. There was nothing to be gained by pushing this, she told herself. She trusted him and she was sure there was nothing underhanded about his not giving her the book. Or that she couldn't find it now.

"Tomorrow's fine. I'm sorry I sounded like a bitch. I've had a long day and I'm tired. I'm having a glass of wine to unwind. The day in New Orleans was interesting and I'll tell you about it when I see you. How many furniture appraisers did you line up?"

"Only one."

No surprise there, she thought. He'd resisted her suggestion, but maybe he just wanted his friend to get the first shot.

"I called three in New Orleans. They work by appointment only, and they're booked solid for two weeks," he continued. "My friend's company works that way too, but he pulled strings and the owner will be here tomorrow at ten. I'll come out there around nine."

She went back into the library and looked some more. She searched in various places around the room, but the little paperback book simply wasn't there. Finally, she gave up. She'd get to the bottom of it tomorrow.

She returned to the porch and noticed someone standing by the river. It was her!

"Anne-Marie! Anne-Marie, I need to talk to you!"

She ran across the yard, expecting to see the figure vanish like before, but the child stood there smiling at her.

"What are you doing here?"

"I came to see if you were all right."

"Of course I am. Why wouldn't I be?"

"Because of him."

"Anne-Marie, please answer some questions. You must help me. Why wouldn't you say anything when I was at your house the day before yesterday? Your mother and father told me you never go leave and you never speak. But that's not true, is it? Here you are."

"She never speaks and she never leaves the house."

"What's your sister's name?"

She smiled and hummed.

"I've had a long day and this is beginning to get on my nerves," Callie said sternly. "I like you, and I like having you here, but every time I ask you a direct question, you won't answer. That must stop right now. I went to your house yesterday. I don't understand who the other girl is, but I know about you. Your parents act like they don't know that you come over here. Start talking, or I'm going to take you home and confront them right now!"

She stopped smiling and said, "You shouldn't talk that way to me. I'm trying to help you." She turned and began to walk toward the woods.

Callie grabbed her arm and Anne-Marie stared into her eyes. "You shouldn't touch me like that. Adults who hurt children are bad people."

Her words struck Callie like the stinging barbs of an insect and she released her and stepped back. Freed from Callie's grip, the girl ran toward the trees.

Callie ran after her. The child had a decent head start and she was out of sight before Callie reached the tree line. It was late afternoon and the woods were already getting dark and gloomy. She saw a path that headed into the thick forest and she ran along it, hoping to find Anne-Marie before dark.

She stopped several times to call her name and listen, but she heard nothing except the rustling of leaves from a breeze stirring the treetops. She followed the trail for nearly ten minutes until the woods abruptly ended two hundred feet from the shanty.

In the half-light, she could see smoke rising from a tin pipe in the roof. The old car was in the yard and Spike was on his chain. He picked up her scent and began barking furiously. There was no sign of Anne-Marie, but in a moment her father came into the yard and yelled at the dog, who was tugging furiously on his chain. She stepped back into the trees and watched. If he turned that dog loose, she'd be in serious trouble.

Callie began to run back through the woods. Panting heavily, she stopped along the way and listened, but the dog wasn't following. She slowed her pace and took slow, deep breaths. Around a bend, she saw a faint side path she hadn't noticed earlier. Nightfall was coming soon, but she decided to see where it went. If it led very far, she'd come back in the daytime.

The trail twisted and turned and eventually led to something that astonished her. In front of her was a very old, ornate wrought-iron arch with two rusty gates and a low fence encircling a plot of ground. On top of the arch was the word "ARCENEAUX" in metal letters and she could see gravestones behind the fence. It was the family cemetery, and she had never known it was here on the property.

She was running out of daylight, so she stepped inside the gate and used her phone to take pictures of the first three stones she saw. The etched words had faded over the years, but she hoped she could enhance the photos and read them.

She ran along the path until she was back in her own grassy yard. The sun was setting and there was a full moon in the sky that played across the water. She stopped for a moment to gaze at the house and think how special this place really was. She would do anything to keep Willard from getting it. She'd sell anything in the house. The furniture and books were just things, after all. They were important and maybe valuable, and some pieces held priceless memories for her, but the important thing was keeping Mamère's house.

She built a fire in the parlor, made a salad and ate it on the floor in front of the fireplace. She tweaked the pictures on her phone until she could make out all the words on two of the markers and a few on the third.

The first stone was tall and narrow. It bore the name of Henri Arceneaux, who was born July 1, 1796, and died August 4, 1865. His inscription read, "A brave defender of his beloved South." She looked up the dates of the Civil War. Henri had died just three months after it ended.

Next to Henri's tombstone was a smaller one with a carved stone lamb. "It's a child's grave," she whispered. The words were almost faded away, but she could make out "Our beloved daughter and only child. Born July 17, 1853, died July 17, 1863. Rest in the arms of Jesus."

Even without a name, Callie knew the stone was Maria's. The picture in the library was hers too; the plaque beneath it had the same inscription as the tombstone. It was the marker for a girl who had died on her tenth birthday, at the height of the Civil War. She quickly searched her phone and found that the child's date of death was at the time that Union soldiers were battling Confederates right here in St. Landry Parish.

She flipped to the third picture, the stone on the other side of the child's. As much as she tried, all she could see was part of one word – the letters CAR, and "d. 1877." Despite the limited information, she was almost certain whose grave this was because of the date of death. This would be Henri's wife, Caroline, an ancestor about whom Callie knew almost nothing. Mamère Juliet hadn't ever discussed her, and Callie hoped she could find out more some other way.

CHAPTER NINETEEN

Sometime during the night Callie woke to a scraping noise. Telling herself this house was a place of memories, not a house of fear, she took her flashlight and bravely walked through every room on the first floor. Nothing was out of place, but just as she was ready to return to bed, she had a thought. She walked back to the library and saw the ladder standing to the left of the fireplace. There was no question this time. It had been on the other side because she'd been looking for the Poe book over there.

It must be me who's moving it. Who else? I guess my mind is so filled with worry about money that I'm doing things that don't even register.

But I didn't move it. I know I didn't.

She returned to bed and forced herself to think positive thoughts. It worked, and she awoke as the sun was rising. Although they'd decided to stop working on the house, she had time to kill until the antiques dealer came at ten. Right now, she'd keep working in the library. The books might end up solving their money problem.

She moved the ladder back and climbed to the top of the bookcase she'd last been cleaning. After her visit to the dealers in New Orleans yesterday, she had a new appreciation for these old books. There could be a treasure trove here after all.

She heard Mark come in around nine, and she stopped working so they could talk. She saw him go into the sitting room for a moment. When he came out, she asked him to join her in the kitchen.

"I'm sorry I was so abrupt with you on the phone, but it pissed me off that you sent me down there without everything I asked for. I know you didn't do it on purpose, but that book was important for me to show the dealers."

"I'm sorry too. It's around here somewhere. I just need to remember where I put it. I'll look for it now."

"No. We only have an hour until your guy comes. I want to tell you about the dealers I saw yesterday." She handed him three business cards, explaining that these were the well-established galleries she'd visited. Glancing at them, he saw that one of them was the Chartres Street dealer who had made him an on-the-spot offer of seventy thousand dollars for the Poe paperback.

"All the dealers agreed that those ten books are extremely rare. One – the one I liked the best – commented that they were obviously accumulated long ago by a collector who could afford them but likewise had an eye for value. I told him that Henri Arceneaux was a wealthy merchant before the Civil War and his nephew, my great-grandfather Michael, was a prosperous cotton merchant who had homes in New Orleans and at Beau Rivage. Both had probably been involved in stocking the library with all these wonderful books."

She had become excited when he offered what could be the perfect solution to their problem. "As you predicted, he said they would have to be authenticated. But from his experience, he was certain they were all originals. I told him exactly how much money I needed –"

"You what?" he exclaimed. "You gave away your bargaining position?"

She bristled a little but kept it to herself. "Let me finish. I told him I was in a bind and needed fifty thousand dollars by the end of this week. He said he believed they were extremely rare. If they're authentic, he wants exclusive rights because he thinks they'll bring a lot of money at auction. I left them there and he's going to do some research. If he's satisfied, he'll give me fifty thousand on Wednesday. I'll sign a contract and consign them to his next auction. Whatever they bring, I get sixty percent and he gets forty. He's taking a risk, because I get to keep the fifty thousand regardless. If they aren't real, then it's his loss. He has ten old books he paid too much money for. He jumped at the deal, Mark. He thinks they're genuine. I just wish I had brought the Poe book too. It might have sweetened the deal."

Mark's face was masked in thought. He frowned and rubbed his chin.

"Why aren't you excited? I think this is a perfect solution! I sell ten books, but I have five thousand more. The dealer is reputable, so he's not going to cheat me. There's no downside."

"What if he isn't everything you think he is? Did you do any research on his background? Just because he can afford the rent in the French Quarter doesn't mean he's on the up-and-up."

She glared at him. "I'm amazed. Is this a man thing? Do you think the little lady isn't smart enough to make a good deal? Are you jealous that I figured it out and you didn't? I'm about to lose this house, Mark. And you're about to lose fifty grand. You should be worshipping at my feet right now instead of acting like a jackass about the deal I made."

She glanced up. Anne-Marie was standing in the hallway just outside the library.

"How long have you been there?" Callie exclaimed.

Mark rose quickly and ran to the girl. She didn't flinch as he put his face inches from hers. "Were you eavesdropping on us again? I told you you're not welcome here. Now get out of this house and don't come back."

The child walked to Callie, looked directly in her eyes and whispered, "I don't like him. He's going to hurt you, *chérie*."

"Him? Mark?" She paused a moment and gasped. "What did you just call me?"

"What's going on?" he bellowed. "Get out of here, you little sneak!"

She didn't move; his tirade didn't seem to ruffle her at all. She merely looked at Callie.

He stormed back into the library as Callie yelled, "Enough, Mark! Leave her alone! This is my house and I'll decide who comes and who doesn't."

He glared at her with an expression she'd never seen before. His face was beet red and he looked as if he was about to explode. "I guess you have everything figured out. You don't need me. I'll cancel the furniture bidder I arranged. You obviously don't need me to help."

"Let him come," she snapped. "He's supposed to be here in fifteen minutes anyway and I want to hear what he says."

"Why? It's not your idea, so it won't fly anyway." He stalked out of the room, and in a moment, she heard the back door slam and the sound of the Jeep's engine.

Callie ran to the door, opened it and saw him driving out the front gate.

When she turned around, Anne-Marie was gone. She ran to the library and confirmed what she'd expected to see. The ladder had been moved again.

What's happening? The ladder's the least of my questions now. She called me chérie. It's been twelve years since someone called me that. That was Mamère's pet name for me.

Another car was approaching. As much as she wanted to be alone, she had to talk to the dealer and get this over with. Mark had asked him to come all the way out, and it wouldn't be fair not to hear what he had to say.

She opened the door, but instead of the dealer, there stood Mark.

"I'm sorry. The girl's getting to me, I guess. May I come in?"

Saying nothing, she walked down the hallway. He followed her.

"We have to work together, Callie. We can get past all this if we stick together."

"I believed that too until a few minutes ago. I guess it was another example of how foolish and inexperienced I am, as Uncle Willard would say, but I've considered you part of my solution. Now I don't know what to think. You blew me away."

Part of my solution. Those words had come out before she thought about what she was saying. Was she

144

talking about the house, or was she admitting she'd almost invited him into her heart?

He said, "All this has changed because I told that spooky kid to get out of our house?"

"It's not your house, to be perfectly frank about it. I appreciate everything you've done for me. I would have lost Beau Rivage and been back in Virginia right now if it weren't for you. But I'm not sure you're who I thought you were. I thought you were going to hurt Anne-Marie a few minutes ago. I don't want to think you're capable of something like that."

"I promise you I'm not. That wasn't how I am. I told you, she's really beginning to irritate me. She refuses to do what I tell her, and she has a way of coming and going that defies reality. She won't answer anything you ask her. It's always that damned smile and her humming. You can't tell me she's not getting under your skin too."

Just then there was a knock on the door. She glanced through the side window and saw a man dressed in a suit and tie standing on the porch.

"We'll continue this discussion later. Let's get this over with."

The man looked at three overstuffed chairs, the sofa that Callie had been sleeping on, and the dining room table and twelve chairs. He measured, took pictures, made notes and commented about how well they had been maintained. He assured Callie that given their ages, each of these had value, so it would come down to how much. He explained that a quick sale usually didn't result in the best deal for the seller. Consigning the furniture to an auction would be much more satisfactory for her, but he would call this afternoon with a cash offer. If she accepted, he would wire the funds and pick up the furniture tomorrow.

"I know you're happy about the book deal you made," Mark said after the man left, "and I should have been more enthusiastic about how well you worked it out. It's just that ..."

"What, Mark? It's just what? I'd like to know, because right now I think you're a lot like Uncle Willard, and that's not the opinion you want me to have. He's a chauvinistic, condescending jerk. Are you one too?"

"No. You know me ..."

"I *don't* know you. Until two weeks ago, I hadn't seen you since high school. You were my friend back then, but that doesn't mean I know who you are inside."

"Callie, until you came along, I felt like I was drifting – that I was on a treadmill that was taking me nowhere. I was glad to hear from you, and I've been happier these past few days with you than I've been in years. I was beginning to think there might be something between us."

"Yeah," she admitted. "So was I. But your outburst against a little girl made me think there's a side of you I don't want to know."

"I promise you it was nothing but pent-up frustration. You have to admit that her comings and goings are disconcerting."

"That's true, and I want to believe you, but you're going to have to prove it to me by how you act from now on. We've spent enough time on this for now. I was inclined to do the book deal if the offer was right, but now I'm going to wait for the furniture bid. For once, we have plenty of time. Today's Monday. We'll hear from the furniture man tomorrow, and Mr. Darlington, the book dealer, is going to get back to me on Wednesday. Either way, presuming things work, we can meet Uncle Willard's Friday deadline. I'm cautiously optimistic that without giving up many of the things in this house I love, this is all going to work out."

She had asked him about the ladder in the library earlier. She told him now that the ladder had changed places several more times, always ending up just to the left of the fireplace no matter where she had left it. He said he was mystified. The only other regular visitor to the house had been Anne-Marie, and she wasn't big enough to move a twelve-foot ladder by herself.

"Go look for the Poe book," she said at last. "With all the other odd things going on around here, I don't want it to go missing."

He puttered around the first floor for a few minutes and came out of the sitting room where he slept, the tattered paperback in his hand. "I found it. I remember now that I took it to bed the other night after we looked at it. I was going to research it on the internet, but I guess I fell asleep first."

"Where was it? I looked everywhere in that room."

"It had slipped between the cushions of the couch."

She admitted that she hadn't looked there, but she was still unsure about Mark after seeing his alarming dark side.

She put the book on the table and said she wanted to show him something. She led him into the woods and down the path she'd found. She took the turn and came to the family cemetery.

"This is amazing! How did you find this?"

"I followed Anne-Marie yesterday, but I lost her. The main path goes all the way to her house, but on the way back, I saw the side path and followed it here."

Today in the half-light through the thick growth of trees, she saw that there were more stones, two of which looked much newer than the others.

"Michael and Anne Arceneaux," she whispered, reading the inscriptions. "These were my grandmother's parents." According to the stones, he had lived from 1872 until 1940 and she from 1894 until 1949. "These seem to be the most recent," she commented, wondering why Uncle Willard hadn't buried Mamère Juliet here.

"There are two markers that are toppled," he said. "Let's try to stand them up." One was very old and massive, so they tackled the smaller, easier one first. With some effort they tugged it upright. She brushed away the dirt and began to cry.

"Whose is it?" he asked.

It was a simple stone with a simple inscription. Robin Pilantro. Died April 20, 2007. Rest in peace.

She brushed away the tears. "That's my mother. I told you I came to her funeral, but I skipped out and didn't go to the gravesite. She and I had drifted apart the last few years she was alive and I never asked where she was buried.

I guess my grandmother arranged this. That was nice of her, because Momma never cared one bit about the Arceneaux family."

"We didn't talk about your dad. Is he alive?"

"Simon? Who cares? I certainly don't. His sperm's all that ties me to him. He disappeared before I was born."

"There's only one stone left – the big one. Want to give me a hand?"

Although they tried, it was far too heavy for them to lift. He told her he would get a come-along – a hand-operated winch – and they'd raise it later.

"Whose stone do you think it is?" he asked.

"I won't even hazard a guess. There's so much history here. It makes me sad, finding this place where my ancestors are buried and never knowing it existed. Mamère never brought me here, never talked about it, never gave me a clue there was a family cemetery. I played in these woods as a child, but somehow I missed this place – it was too deep in the trees, I guess. This plot is one more reason I can't let this place go. Willard may be family, but he'll never have the memories that I have. I can't let him take the house, Mark."

He put his arm around her and she drew close to him. It felt good to have him holding her, even though the conflicting feelings about who and what he was still niggled at her mind. They walked back to the house hand in hand without saying a word.

She stood in the woods and watched them.

CHAPTER TWENTY

That afternoon Mark went into town to buy a winch and check on his houses. Callie needed a change of routine; she'd labored up on the ladder for several days, so for the rest of today she decided to look through the second-floor bedrooms. Buoyed by the possibility that she might soon have an answer to her financial problems, she was back on track to make Beau Rivage something special for visitors to see. The closets might be interesting – maybe there would be furniture or antiques she could display once the downstairs refurb was completed. She had hardly set foot up here since they started working, and she was excited to take another walk through the memories of this old house.

Each of the bedrooms was quite large by modern standards, at least fifteen feet square, with a sitting area at one end. Even though bathrooms had been installed in the twentieth century, Juliet had left washstands, basins and chamber pots in the rooms as examples of how the house might have looked in its early years.

Callie took a chair from one room, an end table and some antique vases and sculptures from another, and placed them in the hall. She'd get Mark to help her take them downstairs later. Those two bedrooms had been easy to go through – the next ones would be the hardest because one was her grandmother's and the other had been hers.

She opened the door, pulled back the heavy draperies and let the afternoon sunlight stream into Juliet's bedroom. Callie wiped away a tear as she turned in every direction, seeing things everywhere that flooded her mind with wonderful memories that only a child can have. Here was a beautifully carved walking stick Mamère had used occasionally when her legs bothered her. Over there was a chaise longue, a long, low-backed settee with one arm that Callie had slept on once or twice when a storm scared her and she fled to Mamère's bedroom.

There was a patchwork quilt spread on the tall four-poster bed – a quilt Mamère had told her had been made by her mother, Anne. It had been on this bed when Anne brought her newborn baby home to Beau Rivage in 1928, and it was still here ninety years later.

When she opened the closet door, she saw a dozen floor-length dresses, each with long sleeves and frills at the cuffs. They had high collars and buttons down the front. Most were black, although there were a few in other colors. These were Mamère's everyday wear, so different from the casual look today. Callie recalled thinking how Mamère always looked like a real Southern lady, ready to go to afternoon tea or on a carriage ride. She pulled the hanging clothes aside to look at a stack of boxes behind them. Some were round and others square, and each held a big fancy hat. Callie put one on, remembering how she'd played dress-up with these hats. She would prance around the room like a queen and look at herself in Mamère's tall mirror that stood on the floor in one corner. She glanced across the room and was comforted to see it was still there.

"Do you want to see something special?"

The voice startled Callie so much that she dropped the box she was holding. She had thought she was alone, but there stood Anne-Marie.

"I locked all the doors. I want to know how you got in the house, Anne-Marie. I don't approve of what Mark said to you, but I have to agree that you can't stay unless you're willing to talk to me."

"Do you want to see something special?"

Everything about the girl was peculiar, including her penchant for answering questions with questions. Callie was determined not to let her go today until she knew more about what she was all about.

"Yes," Callie said. "Show me something special."

She led Callie to the stairway at the end of the hall and up to the ballroom. She opened one of the closet doors and pointed to a dusty old wooden toy box that had cardboard boxes stacked on top. Callie moved them and dragged the large wooden box out. It surprised her that she didn't remember it; she thought she'd seen everything in every closet during her summers at Beau Rivage. This ballroom had been her magical kingdom and she'd played here for endless hours.

Callie thought Anne-Marie would open the box, but the girl smiled and waited.

"Am I supposed to open it?"

"Yes."

It was filled to the brim with antique toys. There were wooden blocks and a wagon, a ball-catcher on a stick, dolls with fancy dresses and braided hair, a drum, a set of dominoes, card games, marbles, jacks and pick-up sticks.

Careful to keep Anne-Marie in her line of sight, she looked at the dusty toys and said, "Whose were these?"

"Hers."

"Whose?"

"Hers. The other girl. She and I play with them sometimes."

"No, you don't. No one has played with these toys in years. Look at the dust on them. Look at the prints I made just picking one up. Nobody's opened this box in a very long time. Who do these toys belong to?"

Anne-Marie frowned. "Her."

Callie turned to her and said, "I like you, but I'm not going to let you come anymore unless you do what I ask. I'm going to ask you some things and I want you to answer me. I've seen a girl standing down by the river. It looked like you, but it wasn't, was it?"

"No."

"Who was it?"

"The other girl."

"Your twin sister?"

Anne-Marie smiled and began to hum.

"This is what I'm talking about," Callie said calmly. "You won't answer my questions, somehow you know a lot about this house, you come and go day or night even though you're no older than ten or eleven, and there's something very mysterious about you."

Anne-Marie smiled.

"Who did these toys belong to?"

"Maria."

Maria? Callie's eyes widened and she gasped. "Maria Arceneaux?"

Could that be true? Aside from Mamère, Maria was the only child Callie knew about who had lived in this house. Could these old toys really have been hers?

Anne-Marie smiled.

"Do you play with Maria?"

"Sometimes I play with her up here. She loves her things in the toy box."

Now we're getting somewhere, Callie thought. That was the most information the girl had offered since Callie had met her.

"Is it Maria Arceneaux that you play with? You can tell me."

She nodded.

"You're going to have to help me understand how. She's been ... well, she hasn't lived in this house for a very long time."

"She still lives here. She never left."

But Maria died a hundred and fifty years ago.

"So you and Maria come up here and play with the toys, even though it looks like they haven't been touched in years. Is that right?"

Anne-Marie smiled and hummed to herself.

"Is Maria the girl I've seen down by the river?"

She nodded. "She's scared down there. She likes to be up here."

Callie proceeded carefully. So far this was going well. "Now tell me something else. Was the girl I saw at your house the other day your twin sister?"

"I don't like that man. He's going to hurt you."

"Are you talking about Mark or my uncle Willard?"

"You must be very careful."

"Anne-Marie, do you have a twin sister? Answer yes or no, right now."

Surprising Callie, the girl turned sharply and ran down the stairs. Callie rose from the floor as quickly as she could and followed her, but by the time she reached the second-floor hallway, the girl had disappeared. She looked on the ground floor, checked to see that all the doors were still locked, and then went back to the ballroom. For nearly an hour she sat on the floor, holding one toy after another as if having them in her hands would explain what was happening. She had a lot to tell Mark, but she realized how crazy it would all sound.

A new, more disturbing thought crept into her mind. The toys in front of her really *were* covered in a layer of dust. The lid to the box really *hadn't* been opened in years. And once again, Anne-Marie had appeared inside the house with all the doors locked. Then she had disappeared again without opening them.

Did that episode with Anne-Marie really happen?
Am I going insane?

Mark found her in the parlor, sitting on the sofa. She was wrapped in her quilt and was hugging her knees to her chest. He rushed over and put an arm around her.

"Callie! Callie, what's wrong? What happened?"

"She came. She showed me some toys. She answered questions. She scares me. I promised not to let my mind run wild, but the more I try to figure her out, the more bizarre and frightening it becomes. I don't think she's real."

"Oh, she's real all right. I'll go to her house. I'll tell her father we don't want her coming over here anymore."

She looked at him blankly. "You don't understand. Going to her house isn't going to make any difference because her parents don't have any control over her. Somehow she comes and goes as she pleases. She knows a secret way into this house, and she knows every nook and cranny of it. It's not Anne-Marie that I'm afraid of anymore. I'm terrified that I'm losing my mind."

He walked her into the kitchen and poured two glasses of wine. She told him everything that had happened and said it was so weird that she was beginning to have doubts about her sanity.

Mark consoled her. "She's definitely real, because I've seen her too. I've talked to her and I know how strange she is. I believe you. I believe that she was here today and that everything happened just like you said it did."

"I'm glad you didn't think I was crazy before, because once you hear what I think we're dealing with, I'm afraid you're going to have me committed."

He smiled, glad to see her perking up and beginning to be herself again. "I promise not to have you committed. Tell me your ideas."

"Okay, here goes, and remember, all this is simply my theory. I think she has a twin sister who is the girl we saw at the house. Remember the other day when I told you she said that Anne-Marie never talks? I think she's speaking of her autistic twin – the girl who sits in the window at her house. If the twin is Anne-Marie, then what's the name of the girl we know? I have no idea, so I'm going to keep calling her Anne-Marie.

"Like many twins, Anne-Marie and her autistic sister have some sort of paranormal connection. Anne-Marie's a savant too – she's highly intelligent and I believe she possesses supernatural abilities. That's how she can get into the house when all the doors are locked and why she acts so peculiar when she's asked a question. She also smiles and hums a lot – autistic people sometimes do that, so it may be something she has picked up from her twin."

She paused and said, "Get out the straightjacket. Here comes the zinger part of my theory. Do you remember that I told you about Henri's daughter, Maria, who died as a child?"

He nodded.

"Anne-Marie said the girl we see down by the river is Maria. I think Maria's spirit takes over Anne-Marie's body now and then. I think somehow she *becomes* Maria. That's how she knows so much about the house. It was *her* house a long time ago. The toys were *her* toys. Anne-Marie hasn't really played with the toys lately; it's obvious that no one has. Instead, she's projecting an event in Maria's life. It was Maria who played with the toys, not Anne-Marie. And it was a hundred and fifty years ago, not recently."

She stopped and looked at him. "So tell me - what do you think about my theory?"

He was deep in thought for a long time. At last he said, "It's no crazier than every other ghost story about houses in the bayou. Who knows what's possible in this world? I'm not putting you in a straightjacket. I want to help find out exactly what we're dealing with."

CHAPTER TWENTY-ONE

The next morning at ten the three of them sat in the music room to hear the Baton Rouge antique dealer's offer.

He congratulated Callie on the pieces. "It's always a surprise and a pleasure to find high-quality period furniture in these antebellum mansions. Yours are in the best shape of any I've seen in years. Obviously, Miss Arceneaux cared for them very much. All that said, if you've walked the streets of the French Quarter, you can see that there are hundreds of beautiful things for sale. Many heirs can't afford to keep up the old homes, and it sadly comes down to nephews and nieces selling off the furniture, silver and china they don't care about to get the money they'd rather have.

"For the past five or six years, there's been a surplus of fine antique furniture and household objects. You were kind enough to let me see three chairs, a sofa and the dining room set. If I put those pieces on my showroom floor in Baton Rouge, you should expect a year to dispose of them, and after my commission, you would receive perhaps nine thousand dollars. I could make you an offer today, but my advice is that if you intend to renovate this beautiful place and open it to the public, these pieces should stay right here."

She thanked him for his time and his advice. "I'm glad we have the books," she said to Mark when he was gone. "That's our solution. I decided before the man came today that if his bid was too low, I wouldn't wait for the book dealer's bid. I'm taking the Poe book and a few others back to New Orleans today to show to Mr. Darlington and maybe a few other dealers. Maybe I can get a bidding war started."

He immediately offered to go instead, saying he needed to do a little business there anyway. She explained that the book deal was critical now. It might mean keeping the house or losing it, and she was going to do it herself. "Nothing against you," she said with a pat on his arm. "If this is going to be something good, I want to be there in person. God knows I could use some good news."

Mark watched her leave, worried that she might take the book to the same dealer he'd shown it to a week ago.

If she does, he'll tell her I was there. I must be ready if she confronts me when she gets back. I've got to come up with a reason why I lied to her.

The truth – at least a portion of it – would be the easiest response, he decided after some thought. He remembered the early works of Poe from college, he thought this one might be very valuable, and he wanted to surprise her with what might be a solution to all her problems. It hadn't worked out that way because the dealer didn't believe it could be authentic. If he had believed it, everything might have turned out perfectly for her, and that would have been his big surprise.

That was a good story. Good enough, hopefully, because it was the best he could do.

He went to the Jeep, got out his notepad and tape, and began searching for the two hidden areas he'd learned about when he measured the other day.

After trying to match his drawing to the actual walls, he realized that it wouldn't be easy to find a hidden space. He'd look for the library anomaly last; with all the bookcases, that one could be tough to find. The one in the hallway should have been simple, but after thirty minutes he was frustrated. The house had thick interior and exterior walls, and the secret space could be in any one of them. Decades of plastering and replastering hadn't helped either.

The small hidden door in the music room had been covered by wallpaper, and the entrance to this one could be covered up too. If it was, it might be impossible to find without tearing out walls. He emptied each closet and examined its ceiling, walls and floor. After a couple of hours and a lunch break, he knew this couldn't be where the space was.

He looked closely at the fifteen-inch-wide decorative wooden corner posts that ran from floor to ceiling in every ground floor room and the hallways. He concentrated on the posts along interior walls because the exterior was brick and he figured it would have been harder to build in a hidden space.

After three hours of fruitless effort, he came to a post in the dining room that was slightly different than the others. Most extended into the walls – that is, the walls were built after the corner posts were erected. But this one was affixed to the outside of the wall instead of through it. He tried one thing after another to make the panels move, but nothing happened. He was certain that he'd found something, but he couldn't figure out how to get inside it.

He couldn't risk removing the wood panels because Callie would see the damage, but there was one thing he could do. He got on his hands and knees and used a hammer and screwdriver to remove the decorative molding on the column's base. He smiled when he found something interesting behind it – an old piece of metal that slid back and forth. He moved it an inch and was almost hit by the front panel of the column, which suddenly came loose from the side pieces. He pushed his hands up and stopped it from falling forward and crashing onto the floor. Whoever knew this was here must have been prepared to catch the panel when the lever unlocked it, Mark thought.

The gap immediately behind the column was only thirteen inches, but it widened considerably inside the wall, and it ran for several feet, farther than he could see in the dark space. Dust and dirt were everywhere and he could see the ancient boards from Beau Rivage's construction in 1835. He directed his flashlight into the gap and saw a wooden box lying on the floor about eight feet away. It was too far for him to reach without removing the rest of the column and expanding the entrance. The end of the box he could see was about two feet square, just right to fit snugly in the space. Since it was so far back, he couldn't see how long it was.

There was nothing more he could do for today, although he was curious to know what might be in a box that must have been inside the wall for decades. It was almost five and Callie might be home soon. He had to put things back for now.

He inserted the front panel and closed the lever. As he replaced the bottom molding, he heard something, turned and saw Anne-Marie studying him closely.

"You little ...!" He jumped up and she ran down the hallway. She bounded up the stairs two at a time and he scrambled after her. She darted into one of the bedrooms with him right behind her.

The drapes were pulled tightly shut, making the room gloomy and dark, but he could see that other than a closet door, there was no way out. He had her trapped at last. He closed the door and turned on the overhead light. The dim bulb revealed he was standing in a child's bedroom – a girl's, to be exact. There were dolls nestled between frilly pillows on the bed. Everything looked dated, as if it were an exhibit in a museum, but nothing was frayed or yellowed. There was dust, just as there had been in every other room in the house, but other than that, it appeared someone had lovingly maintained this room for many years.

He looked for Anne-Marie. "I just want to talk to you," he said soothingly. "If you'll come out, I have something to say to you. It's all good, I promise. You just surprised me downstairs. I'm sorry if I scared you."

There wasn't a sound in the room and he saw several places where a little girl could hide. He opened the closet door and saw lacy dresses hanging there. All arranged in a neat row, there were toys, a rocking horse and a child's table and chair, but there was no Anne-Marie.

"Mark? Mark, are you here?"

Dammit, Callie's home! His flashlight, measuring tape and tools were still on the floor in the hall. Anne-Marie had interrupted him and he hadn't finished putting everything back. Thanks to her, everything he was hoping for had changed now.

Dammit! The floor plan I drew is down there too! Things were going from bad to worse.

160

He opened the bedroom door and called down to her. "Up here! I'll be down in a second!"

Any hope that he could hide his work was dashed when he descended the stairs and found her in the dining room, studying his hand-drawn floor plan.

"What's this?" she asked guardedly.

There was no way out of this now, thanks to that damned child.

"After Anne-Marie showed you the hidden staircase, I decided to measure the exterior and interior dimensions and see if everything matched. It wouldn't be perfect, because these old walls are thicker in some places than others. There are places where the measurements are off and I'm hoping that means more secret spaces. These old houses all have them; it's just a matter of finding them."

"Interesting," she replied. "Any luck?"

He glanced at the baseboard he'd replaced and was glad he'd had time for that. "I was knocking with the hammer on the walls but so far I've struck out."

"It'd be exciting to find something. Are you going to keep looking?"

"I'm done for today. I'll keep searching when I have a little extra time now and then."

She told him she was tired from the drive but had news to share. He put away his tools and tape measure, poured two glasses of wine and met her on the veranda. All he could think about was if she had gone to the dealer who'd already seen the Poe book. She seemed in a good mood – if she'd visited his shop, she wouldn't have been, so maybe things were okay.

She sat next to him, sipped her wine and told him the first shop she went to – the Darlington Gallery whose owner had liked her other ten books – was breathless when she showed him the paperback.

"It's worth a fortune, Mark," she told him excitedly. "It's worth hundreds of thousands of dollars. He's certain it's authentic and it's one of only a handful that still exist. He didn't want me to take it to anyone else and he made me an offer on the spot that I had to accept."

That got Mark off the hook. She didn't take it to other shops, so there would be no awkward questions about his secret trip to New Orleans.

"That's great news! What did you end up doing?"

"I already told you he offered me fifty thousand for the ten books I left the other day, and today he said the other six I brought today were worth around thirty thousand. I didn't accept it though. I brought everything home but the paperback. It's good to know what the things in the library may be worth, just so I don't make a mistake and let something go too cheaply later, but after today I don't need to sell off things so quickly. I left the Poe volume with him and he's going to send it to the British Museum for authentication."

"Wow, that's exciting! But what about Willard –"

"Hang on – I haven't gotten to the best part yet! Mr. Darlington paid me a consignment fee so he'd have exclusive rights to it. Once it's authenticated, he'll put it up for auction – maybe in New York, he said – and I'll get seventy-five percent of the net proceeds after expenses. He gets the other twenty-five and then it's done."

"Were you satisfied with your consignment fee?" he asked, hoping it was enough to get them out of hock.

"Ecstatic. Take a look." She took a check from her billfold and handed it to him. It was for ninety thousand dollars, and it was payable to her.

"So you accepted what he offered without going to any other dealers?"

He does this every time, she thought. *Damn cocky men.*

"I hope you agree that he made a fair offer. I can pay Willard and have money left over and I get most of the money when the book sells. Maybe it was stupid, but I was so shocked and pleased at his proposal that I jumped on it. I signed a contract with him. Are you still saying I should have shopped around?"

"Not at all. It was your decision. As you said, you have ninety thousand and you'll get even more when it sells. I think you did a great job."

"I'm happy for you," he said, raising his glass to clink against hers. "It looks like everything's falling into place."

That book should have been mine. Like everything else.

CHAPTER TWENTY-TWO

Searching for information to unravel the puzzle that was becoming more and more complex, Callie called the St. Landry Parish Historical Society in Opelousas. The child's tombstone in the family plot was inscribed with two dates, and she hoped one of those would help her understand what was happening at Beau Rivage.

She didn't tell the person who answered the phone who she was or why she wanted information. The clerk said she'd try to help, but explained that birth and death records during the Civil War were often incomplete. "There was a lot of scrambling around in this parish, what with the Union soldiers in our area," she explained. "If someone died outside of town, sometimes the information got to Opelousas, and sometimes it didn't. But I'll do what I can to help you, dear."

She put Callie on hold and came back a few minutes later, saying that Callie just might be in luck. "You're looking for information on deaths in St. Landry Parish on July 17, 1863. This may not be what you're looking for, but according to the parish records, there were two deaths that day." She paused a moment and said, "Let's see, now here's something interesting. Both died at Beau Rivage Plantation on the Atchafalaya River."

That *was* a surprise. "Who were they?"

The woman paused to read the entries and said, "It can't be a coincidence that two people died at the same place, but given who they were, it's a mystery to me what it's all about. One was a twenty-two-year-old Union soldier named Joseph Souter, who was from Taunton, Massachusetts. He was a private first class in the Massachusetts 41st Infantry.

His death puzzles me. There were no skirmishes in the area at that time. The big battles in St. Landry Parish would be later in 1863, but this one single soldier died on a plantation from a gunshot wound."

A gunshot wound? Instead of answers, Callie found herself with more questions.

"Is there anything else about him?"

"That's it. The other one is a child, the daughter of Henri and Caroline Arceneaux. That was the family that owned Beau Rivage, in case you didn't know that. She was ten years old. Oh yes, I remember now who she was. She died on her tenth birthday."

"How?"

"She drowned, poor child. This story became a kind of local legend. I've worked here for thirty years and I've heard things about her tragic death. She drowned at her home on her birthday. How sad that must have been."

"Is that all – the Union soldier and Maria Arceneaux?"

"Yes, only those two. But the name on the child's death record isn't Maria."

That surprised Callie. "What's the name?"

"Anne-Marie. Anne-Marie Arceneaux."

CHAPTER TWENTY-THREE

Mark offered to take the check to town and deposit it for her, but Callie said she wanted to come along too. She'd never had that much money in her entire life, and now it looked as though that might only be the beginning of her good fortune.

I trust him, she said to herself. *But if I trust him, why do I want to deposit the check myself? Because of his boorish, chauvinistic attitude. That's the reason.*

When they got to the bank, the teller asked Callie to endorse the check and provide the bank account number into which the money would be deposited. She hadn't thought about that. Her only bank account was back in Virginia.

Mark suggested she use their joint house account, since it was technically house business and more than half of the funds would be gone in a couple of days anyway, once he paid Willard. She had a little trepidation about leaving forty thousand dollars in the account, but now – standing here at a teller's window at the Cotton Belt State Bank – wasn't the time to have a discussion with him about it.

She endorsed the check and the clerk prepared a deposit slip.

"The funds will be available immediately, correct?" Mark asked, and the teller said she'd have to ask an officer. She left the window and Callie asked what he meant.

Since the check was a company check on the dealer's account, it was for a large sum and it was drawn on an out-of-town bank, Mark said the bank might put a hold on the funds until the check cleared.

"Why didn't we talk about this before I went to New Orleans?" she snapped. "How should he have paid me – in cash?"

"You didn't ask for my advice, if you'll recall," he replied evenly. "To answer your question, he could have paid you with a cashier's check, or he could have wire transferred the funds here. Either way, your money would have been immediately available. It shouldn't be a big deal. Let's see what they say."

The teller handed Callie the check and asked her and Mark to go to a cubicle across the lobby. The same officer who'd loaned Mark the fifty thousand dollars was waiting for them. He explained that per the bank's policy, the funds would not be available for seven days.

"Seven days?" she exclaimed. "That means next week. Our deadline's Friday."

"We're paying off my loan with part of this money," Mark explained. "I'm sure you know – as we just learned – that Willard Arceneaux owns the note now. He's given us until Friday to pay. Given his standing with the bank, I'm sure you could make an exception so he can get his money on time."

"Please have a seat while I talk to Mr. Talmadge," the man said, and he went into another office. In a moment, someone else also went inside.

"That's Dudley Hibbard, the president of the bank," Mark said. "They must have taken this one all the way to the top."

The loan officer returned in a moment and apologized that they couldn't make an exception. Mark and Callie stood in the lobby and talked things over.

"We're fortunate that it's Wednesday and not Thursday," he said. "We can call your man in New Orleans and have him overnight a cashier's check to you. It'll be here tomorrow and you'll be set to go."

She called the gallery and Mr. Darlington explained that although he would be happy to help any way he could, he had given her a company check. He had no prior customer relationship with her; in fact, he'd never seen her before yesterday, so he couldn't advance more funds while she still had the check. If she wanted to bring it back, he'd swap it for a cashier's check, but that was the only way he could do it. She told him she'd be there as soon as she could.

"Back and forth to New Orleans twice in two days is too much for anybody," Mark said. "I'll go this time. I'll drop you at Beau Rivage and head out. I'll be back before dark."

At first, she wasn't going to do it that way, because there was too much that she had learned but didn't understand right now. She decided to let him go – the check would be payable to her, after all, and the only thing he could do with it was bring it back to her.

While he was away, she couldn't concentrate on anything but getting Uncle Willard paid off, so she returned to the one mindless job that had kept her occupied for what seemed like an eternity. She went back to dusting books and cleaning shelves. As euphoric as she should have been, she was experiencing an overwhelming sadness over what she'd gotten herself into and a sense of dread that something was going to go wrong.

At the top of the ladder, she asked herself, *What are Mark and I thinking? We're ecstatic that we can pay Uncle Willard, but once that's done, we still don't have the money to make this place beautiful again. What do I do next – keep selling off the books? Or maybe it'll be the furnishings next. Is that why my grandmother left me all this, so I could sell everything to strangers?*

She climbed down, dropped onto the couch and began to whisper.

Mamère, I'm truly sorry that I've let you down. You thought you did a good thing for me by giving me this old place you loved so much. Every door I open brings back more wonderful memories, and I treasure the hours I've spent working here. I had to sell some books to get enough money to pay our bank note that Uncle Willard owns now. He's making things hard, but Mark and I figured out a solution.

I'm sorry that I had to sell some of Henri's books. I'm sorry I allowed a man in here to look at your furniture. After we pay Uncle Willard, I'll have nearly forty thousand dollars, Mamère. That's nothing compared to what we're going to need. I don't want to keep selling things. Even the books – ones I'd never actually looked at before – tore at my heart when I had to part with them.

I guess Uncle Willard was right. You should have left the house to Madeline and Carmine. They have plenty of money, even though I don't think their hearts are here at Beau Rivage like mine is. I just wanted to tell you how I feel. I don't see any way out for us but to sell the property. Uncle Willard says he'll buy it, but I don't think he'll treat me fairly, even though we're family. You of all people know how he is.

She laughed at the thought.

You've helped me, Mamère. You've given my life a purpose and handed me a challenge that I think I've handled pretty well. But right now, I don't see a future. So if you have any other way you can help me, now would be a really good time to let me know.

"The house has secrets."

Callie screamed and leapt from the couch. Was this Mamère giving her the help she asked for?

But it was Anne-Marie, standing in the doorway, smiling.

"God, you scared me! How long have you been there?"

She didn't say anything.

Callie said, "I had a dream that night after I first saw you. I dreamed that you were telling me the house had a secret and you'd show it to me. The very next day, you showed me the hidden staircase in the music room. Now Mark's found something in a wall that he hasn't shown me yet. Is it another secret?"

She said nothing.

"Did Mamère send you? Is that why you keep coming here? Is that what this is all about?"

Anne-Marie began to hum softly.

"The girl who drowned. She wasn't Maria. Her name was Anne-Marie. Is that you? Please help me understand all this."

That instant the back door opened. She stepped into the hall and waved at Mark, who was home a little earlier than he'd expected. Realizing she should never have looked away, she whirled back, but the child was gone.

"Did you see Anne-Marie when you came in?" she asked. "She was standing right here a moment ago."

"No. What did she want now?"

"Nothing, really. Just another of her strange appearances." After how Mark had reacted the other day, she didn't go into it, nor did she reveal how apprehensive she was about Beau Rivage and her future here.

"Did the trip go well?"

"Perfectly. I gave him his check, he sent his assistant out to get a cashier's check, and I was back on the road in twenty minutes."

"Great! Show it to me!"

"I don't have it. I thought you wanted me to deposit it."

"But it was made payable to me, right? How were you able to deposit it?"

"We already told my loan officer where the proceeds were going, so he let me endorse it for deposit only and it's safely in the bank, ready to pay Willard before the deadline."

His propensity to do the opposite of what she expected was becoming upsetting. She thought for a moment, then went with her gut instinct and confronted him.

"I trust you, Mark, but that's a lot of money. I want to call the bank and confirm the money's in the house account."

The surprise on his face was clear; the steely look in his eyes was a little harder to discern, but it was there nonetheless.

"I'd do the same thing," he responded evenly. "No problem. I've got the loan officer on speed dial." He placed the call and handed her the phone.

She listened for a moment and handed it back. "It's a recording. It's after five. They're closed."

"Callie, listen to me. I know I did stupid things earlier that shook your confidence in me and made you uncomfortable. That's not who I am. I tried to explain about Anne-Marie and I hope you can forgive me for making a huge mistake. I promise you this – that money's in the bank. Why wouldn't I have put it there? If Willard's not paid back on time, I lose fifty thousand dollars, don't forget. I know your stake is much higher because you signed a mortgage, but I couldn't survive a hit like that. I'd be bankrupt."

There was nothing more to do tonight than trust that everything would work out. She assured him she wasn't worried, even though the money was all she could think about. She was quiet throughout dinner, went to her room early and barely slept a wink.

The next morning, he asked her how she intended to pay Willard. She had planned to write a check from the joint account where the money had been deposited, but Mark wisely reminded her that there was no reason to assume Willard would take a personal check. He said she should get a cashier's check.

They went to the bank at ten. Still apprehensive about his having deposited her funds without her approval, she held her breath as she asked for a cashier's check. She was overwhelmed with relief when the teller slid a withdrawal slip across the counter and asked her to sign it. Fifty thousand, two hundred and twenty-three dollars. Just like it was supposed to be.

"Can you tell me what the balance will be after this money comes out?"

The clerk said there was just under fifty-two thousand dollars left in the account. That would be the twelve thousand still there from the loan, plus almost forty more from the cashier's check. Mark had done everything right, and she'd spent a fretful night worrying about him and her money for nothing. They had a cashier's check and they were ready to pay Willard a day early.

They went to her uncle's office and sat in the same waiting room where this saga had begun nearly a month ago. As they waited for Willard's secretary, she thought how much had changed since that day when the will was read.

Shortly a lady walked across the room and advised that Mr. Arceneaux was in an important meeting and had asked not to be disturbed.

"We'll wait," Callie said. "We have a business transaction with him that I want settled today."

"I wouldn't suggest waiting, Miss Pilantro," she said. "This could last several hours. I'll slip a note in and ask when he can see you." She left and was back in minutes.

"He's in conference all day. He says he will see you tomorrow as he advised earlier. Be here at four p.m."

"That won't work," she said. "Our deadline is at five, and if anything goes wrong, it doesn't give us any time to make it right. It's only ten thirty now. He can see us today. I know he can. Will you speak to him again, please?"

She knew it was a futile request. This was his game, making them sweat until the very last minute. Mark assured her that with a cashier's check in hand, nothing could go wrong.

He stayed in town while she went back to Beau Rivage. She went from one project to another, unable to concentrate on anything but a growing dread that something was going to go wrong. Her uncle was clever – far more than she and Mark – and he had something up his sleeve. He had to know they'd bought a cashier's check, since he seemed to know everything that happened at the Cotton Belt State Bank.

Mark came back around six with a pizza. They ate with few words between them, and she spent a night getting almost no sleep. The only positive thing was that Anne-Marie hadn't shown up unexpectedly to alarm her.

The next morning it was more of the same. Mindless work, no thoughts except scary thoughts, and nervous fidgeting for hours on end. By one p.m. she could fight it no longer. She told Mark she was going back to wait in Willard's office.

"Okay," he replied. "Give me five minutes."

"I can do it myself. He may not see me until four, and all I need to do is hand it over. There's no need to waste both our afternoons."

"Let me come for moral support. Maybe he won't push you around if someone else is there."

"Have you forgotten who we're going to see?" she quipped. "If you come too, he'll push both of us around. Okay, come on. Let's go."

As she had assumed, he made them wait until five minutes after four. When they entered his office, he led them to a conference table at one end.

"Honey, I've prepared a deed and a bill of sale," he said affably. "All you have to do is sign them and everything will be taken care of. The property and contents will be mine, and Mr. Streater here will be off the hook. I'll give you plenty of time to vacate, of course. How about Tuesday? That should be enough time."

"I have the money, Uncle Willard. Cotton Belt is your bank. I'm sure you've already heard that I have it."

"I know you presented a company check that the bank wouldn't give you immediate funds for, and I know that Mr. Streater deposited a cashier's check for ninety thousand dollars into a joint account belonging to you both yesterday afternoon. Don't let that surprise you, my dear. I know everything that goes on at the bank. But none of that has anything to do with the transaction between you and me. What are you proposing?"

"I'm not proposing anything. I'm paying your note plus interest. Fifty thousand, two hundred and twenty-three dollars - the exact amount on that letter you gave us five days ago." She slid the check across the table and he didn't give it a glance.

"Well, I'm sorry, Calisto, but that's not an acceptable form of payment."

She looked at Mark, and the blank expression on his face showed he didn't understand either.

Willard laughed mirthlessly and said, "Ah, the innocence of those with no business expertise. Here's a copy of the note you signed, Mr. Streater." He tossed a piece of paper their way. "See the paragraph I've highlighted? It says the note may only be paid in a form acceptable to the lender. The lender, in case you still don't understand, used to be the

Cotton Belt State Bank. I bought the note from them, so the lender is now me, and what you've given me is not an acceptable form of payment."

Mark spoke up now. "I'm afraid I don't understand, Mr. Arceneaux. Are you saying a cashier's check from your own bank isn't acceptable to you?"

"Now there's a bright boy," he replied with a smile. "That's exactly right."

"Then do you want cash?" Mark looked at his watch. "There's still time –"

"No. Cash isn't an acceptable form of payment either."

Callie stared at him, bewildered. Mark did too.

"Then what would constitute an acceptable form of payment?"

"Nothin'. There's nothin' you can give me that I'll accept."

Callie exploded. "You can't do that! We're doing exactly what we were supposed to do – paying off the note. You have to accept our money!"

"I do? With all respect, who's the lawyer in the room, darlin'? A contract is a binding agreement in a court of law. Is this your signature, Mr. Streater?"

"You know it is."

"Maybe before you sign something important, you should understand what it means. I'd venture a guess that you didn't read one word of it, even though it's a binding contract. The man at the bank put it in front of you, told you where to sign, and you did. That's how lawyers make money, son. Now you two listen to me. Calisto, you can sign these papers, deed everything to me, and we can remain on the same cordial terms as always."

She shot him the bird, but he ignored her.

"If you foolishly decide not to do that, then I'm afraid you leave me no choice under the law but to have the sheriff come out and forcibly remove you from what will be my property –" he paused and looked at his watch for effect "– in exactly thirty-two minutes."

"Come on, Mark," she said. "We're going to find a lawyer."

"Hope you have some gas in that old car," Willard replied sharply. "No lawyer within a hundred miles is going to take a case against me. It's a fact and you'd better get used to it. I've spent over forty years building my practice and my reputation, and there's nobody who'll go up against Willard Arceneaux. Make a few calls and find out for yourself, but you'd better hurry. You're flat out of time, darlin'."

He shoved the papers and a pen across the table. "I'm leaving now. I have better things to do with my time. Sign the damned papers and get out of my office."

He walked out, and two minutes later Mark and Callie left too. The documents lay on the table, unsigned.

CHAPTER TWENTY-FOUR

They sat in Mark's Jeep in the parking garage next to Willard's building.

"He can't do this to us, can he?" she asked.

"It can't be legal, if that's what you mean, but I guess if you interpret the words as they're written, he could tell us he wants the loan paid with the bark of a tree from Brazil and that would be what we'd have to do. That's not the intent, of course; in a world like this, all people want is to get their money back. I've never heard of anybody refusing to accept an on-time payment and seizing the property instead."

"If it isn't legal, how can he do it? What can we do to stop him?"

"When I said it wasn't legal, I wasn't necessarily referring to what's legal in St. Landry Parish. Your uncle has won every personal injury case he's handled for the past twenty years. With his money, he's cultivated friendships and made deals that give him an advantage in court. I don't know it for sure, but I bet his claim that no one will take our case is probably right."

Callie wouldn't accept that fate without giving it a try. She told Mark to sit tight, because next they'd be going to meet their new attorney. She called a law firm in the small town of Ville Platte just up the highway from Opelousas. She briefly explained the situation to a partner and asked if he would represent her. At first he agreed to do it, but when she told him who her adversary was, he backed off, saying he had helped Willard on a case not long ago and it would be a conflict of interest to accept hers.

It took two more calls to learn that his threat hadn't been an empty one. Nobody was willing to take on the Cajun Crusher.

"Can't we represent ourselves?" she asked Mark. "People do that, don't they?"

"We need advice as to how we can stop him from kicking you out on Tuesday. Short of hiring a lawyer, there's no way we can even know what our rights are."

"How about talking to a judge?"

"I'm way out of my league here. I don't know if judges talk to people who are planning to sue somebody. It could be improper for them to do it."

He left the garage, turned into the street, and she saw a painted sign on an office window.

"Stop, Mark! Find a parking place. Look at that sign – Legal Aid of Southern Louisiana. Let's see what they do."

Compared to the Arceneaux Law Firm's waiting room, this one was downright shabby. There were mismatched chairs, a play area in one corner with some broken toys, and a scarred coffee table with well-worn magazines on it. They told a girl behind a bulletproof glass barrier that they wanted to see a lawyer.

As they waited, she whispered, "If this nasty place was my new doctor's waiting room, I'd be out of here by now!"

He smiled and nodded.

Soon they were ushered down a narrow hallway into an office that was only large enough for a desk and three chairs. There was nothing hanging on the walls and the person in front of them looked as though he'd just graduated from high school.

He introduced himself and said there was a series of forms they needed to complete and sign. "We'll need a statement of financial condition," he added, "but don't worry about that. If you need help, we'll help you regardless of your ability to pay."

"Paying the fee isn't our problem," Callie began. "Can I tell you what we're up against?"

"It doesn't work that way," he answered soothingly. "First you have to complete the paperwork and then we do an assessment. In a few days, you'll come back here and that's when we can talk about your issue."

"We don't have time for that!"

"Are you being evicted?"

Mark raised his hand and said, "Give me two minutes to explain why we're here. Then you can tell us if we need to spend time filling out papers or if we need to go a different direction."

The young man agreed, and without revealing who their adversary was, Mark gave him a very abbreviated version of what they were up against. When he was finished, the lawyer said, "This place can't help you with something as involved as that. We help struggling families, single parents in custody fights and issues like that. This is a contracts issue – way out of our league."

"How long have you been an attorney?" Mark asked.

"Two years. I graduated from LSU and came here so I could pay the bills while I look for a firm to hook up with. Why do you ask?"

"What do you know about contract law?"

"I took the course."

"That's more than we know. For now, you're all we have and it's after five on Friday afternoon. Would you let us buy you a beer and discuss this with you? We'll pay you a hundred bucks for your time whether you help us or not."

"Why not? I'm off at five anyway."

They went down the block to a tavern, picked a quiet booth and ordered beers.

"Do you know who Willard Arceneaux is?" Callie asked.

"Are you kidding? Everyone knows who he is."

"He's my uncle and he's going to kick me out of my house on Tuesday because of this." She showed him the promissory note Mark had signed, pointing to the words Willard had highlighted. "I had a cashier's check for him today and he said it wasn't acceptable. I offered cash and he turned that down too. He told us nothing was acceptable, so we were screwed. My question is this – legally, are we?"

He read the paragraph closely and said, "I've been out of law school two years. I've never tried a case in court and so far, I've never even represented a client, unless you

179

count the work I'm doing through legal services. So you have to take what I say with the understanding that I don't know much except what I learned in school. This is egregious – it's crazy. I've never heard of anything like this, and in my opinion it's a total misinterpretation of the words and the intent of this document."

"Our thoughts exactly," she said. Even though this kid was green, he had been to law school and he had confirmed that Willard couldn't do this. "So how do we stop him?"

"Simple answer, you need a temporary restraining order. You go before a judge and convince him to issue an order that prevents Mr. Arceneaux from doing anything until there can be a hearing."

"Can we hire you to draw up what we need?" Mark asked.

"You can hire me and I can prepare the document. That's the easy part. The hard part is finding a judge who will agree with you."

"But you just said it's egregious and crazy."

"It absolutely is and any judge in the state would agree with me."

"I'm afraid I'm not following you," Callie interjected. "Let's just find one and get it done."

"Unless we can prove a judge wouldn't treat you fairly, we have to pick one who's in the same parish where the acts occurred. That means here in St. Landry Parish. Please don't quote me on this since I'll be needing a job someday soon, but we are going to be forced to pick one of Willard Arceneaux's judges. Do you see what the problem is?"

Callie shook her head and Mark explained, "As much as we want to think judges are above reproach, the reality is that your uncle has an almost perfect win-loss record not just in this parish, but in most of the others in southern Louisiana. What do you think our chances are to get a judge who'll grant a restraining order against good old Willard on short notice, pissing off an extremely influential and powerful man who has always been their friend around election time?

I'm not saying there aren't fine, upstanding jurists out there who'd choose right over might. I just don't know if we have time to ferret them out."

She looked at the lawyer. "Do you agree with that?"

"I couldn't have said it better myself."

"We can't just let him win without even trying to fight! Will you prepare the papers for us and see if a judge will sign them?"

He turned his beer bottle round and round as he sat quietly. "What's a lawyer for if he won't take a stand for what's right? I don't have a real job anyway, so I can't lose it. I may end up practicing law in Illinois to escape the wrath of Mr. Arceneaux, but yes, I'll do it. I can't promise you anything. We already talked about that. If you want my opinion, I think this is a waste of time, but if I were in your shoes, I'd be doing the same thing."

"I don't think I ever properly introduced myself," he said, extending his hand across the table. "Leonard Weinstein. Call me Lanny. Now that I'm your attorney, I guess you deserve to know who's representing you."

Since Lanny didn't own a laptop and the one he used at the legal aid office was locked up for the weekend, Mark offered to meet him at his office the next morning at seven. It was a Saturday, and the plan was that he'd draft the temporary restraining order and they'd drive it to the home of Franklin Freed, a judge in town for whom Lanny had clerked one summer during law school. Judge Freed was not only their best chance, he was the only judge Lanny knew, so he might also be their only chance.

At nine thirty the three of them stood on Judge Freed's front porch and rang the doorbell. He came to the door wearing an LSU sweatshirt and jeans, recognized Lanny at once and invited them in. Lanny explained why they were there. When he handed the paper to the judge, they watched him raise his eyebrows.

"Willard Arceneaux? You're going elephant hunting, aren't you, Lanny?"

"It shouldn't matter who it is, Judge. Doing the right thing is what matters. I learned that when I clerked for you."

Freed smiled and reread the document. "I need to give this some thought," he said eventually. "Tuesday's your deadline, correct?"

"Yes, sir," Callie replied. "We really need your help."

"That's a fact," he said, "but I'm not sure this is the way to go about it. Let me have a little time to mull this over, Lanny. Give me your number and I'll call you this afternoon."

As he walked them to the door, he said, "You know, you all don't have the most experienced attorney handling your case, and I understand the reason why. But from the time I spent working with him, there's nobody more honest and principled than Lanny is. However this turns out, you have a very ethical lawyer representing you."

"What does he have to think about?" Mark asked when they were in the car.

"We may never know," Lanny replied. "I've always respected Judge Freed and I hope he'll do the right thing."

The judge took the legal document into his kitchen and put it on the table. He poured himself a cup of coffee, picked up the receiver and dialed a number.

"They've hired a lawyer," he said.

CHAPTER TWENTY-FIVE

"I appreciate your call, Franklin. It's always been good to count you as a friend, and I'm glad to have you on my side now."

"I didn't say that. Don't put words in my mouth, Willard, and this call never happened. This is serious business, and if what they told me is true, I can't understand for the life of me why you're doing this to your own niece. I called to get your side of the story because they're seeking a restraining order. Is it true that you actually refused their attempt to pay you in cash?"

"It's a family matter," he replied smoothly. "The girl doesn't have a pot or a window. My sister, Juliet, must have been suffering from dementia in her final months, because she left the property and furnishings to Calisto, her illegitimate granddaughter. She had to know there was no way that girl could raise the money to properly restore the mansion. Hell, Franklin, I loaned her two hundred dollars so she could take the bus down here for the reading of Juliet's will. That's how indigent she is."

"But none of that makes any difference, and you know it," the judge replied. "What can you tell me about this that would make me deny their request for a TRO against you?"

"You and I have been friends – close friends – for many years. How many cigars have we smoked together at my fishing cabin on the lake? How many Christmas dinners have we eaten at your house or mine? How many times have I contributed the legal limit – and then some – to your election campaigns without batting an eye? I would consider it a personal favor if you'd just let them go on their way. I'm making Mr. Streater whole, Franklin. He won't owe me anything and I won't mess up his credit. My grandniece can go on back to Virginia none the worse for her little sojourn in Louisiana."

"There's nothing special about your imposing a payment deadline of Tuesday," Freed said. "In the interest of fairness, I'm inclined to sign the order and set the matter for a hearing. That's when you can argue your case against their lawyer, who's fresh out of LSU law and never had a client before, just so you know."

Willard had to restrain himself and keep his words calm. "Maybe I didn't make myself clear. I'd appreciate it if you didn't sign the order." Then he hung up on the judge.

Judge Freed had always considered himself a good man. There were people – Leonard Weinstein among them – who considered him a fair, honest jurist. But in the murky quagmire that was politics in Louisiana, especially in Cajun country, there were others who knew that some judges could be bought and sold by influential men. The law down here wasn't necessarily fair to everyone. It was sometimes fairer to good friends with lots of money.

He'd done a lot of soul-searching in recent months. He was seventy-one years old and looking forward to retirement. He enjoyed his friends, the cigars, the fishing and the company, but he had taken an oath years ago to uphold the law fairly and honestly. He hadn't always honored that oath, he admitted to himself, and if Willard Arceneaux could present an argument that would explain why he should prevail against his niece, then Franklin would rule in his favor.

At two p.m., he called Lanny and said he had signed the temporary restraining order and Callie was required to put her ninety-thousand-dollar check into an escrow account at her bank where it would be held until a hearing in ten days. The young lawyer had only a short time to prepare.

———

As they drove back to Beau Rivage, Callie asked Mark if he'd done any more research on potential hidden spaces inside the house. He'd already found the opening behind the hall column but he realized there was no way he could examine what was inside it without her knowing. The house project was a joint effort, and she was rarely away for more than an hour or so. If he was going to see it himself, he had to include her.

"I've looked at my drawings a dozen times, and there's a place in the hall I'd like to examine. It may be nothing, but it doesn't seem to fit the way it should. As soon as I get time –"

"*Time?* Are you kidding? I was going to ask if we could raise the fallen tombstone this afternoon, but this is way more exciting. Let's do it as soon we get there! I'm dying to see if you're on to something!"

She watched with eager anticipation as he removed the molding from the base of the column. He pointed to the metal lever at the bottom, questioning what it was as if he'd never seen it before. Already knowing that the front panel would fall the second he flipped the lever, he asked her to be ready for what might happen next.

"We don't know what this lever is for, but if it releases this tall piece of lumber, it may come crashing down. Think you can catch it if you need to?"

She stood in front of it with her hands ready. "Let 'er rip!"

It came off as smoothly as the last time. She set it aside as he played his light through the opening.

"There's something inside!"

"My God, Mark! It's a box, isn't it?"

"Looks like one to me. Since you're smaller, it might be easier for you to get in. Once you reach the wider part, you can walk on back and see what it is."

"Good thing I haven't eaten today." She laughed as she sidestepped into the opening between the walls and shuffled back to where the box lay. "It's about five feet long," she reported.

"What is it?"

"I don't know. It's made of rough, unpainted wood. Let me try to move it." She gripped the end and tugged on it, but it didn't budge.

"This thing's not going to be easy to move. It's heavy, and given where it sits, there's no way to get any leverage on it."

"I bought a winch to raise the grave marker. We can use it for this too."

She didn't want to stay in the cramped space while he went to the Jeep, so she crawled back into the hallway and drank a bottle of water. He brought in the gear, and after a few minutes of tinkering, he proclaimed the winch ready for use. He removed the two side panels of the hall column, making the opening as wide as the space inside. Now the box would slide out.

He sent her back in the narrow space with a grappling hook attached to a nylon rope. She tossed it to the far end of the box and tried to snag it into the wood. It took four tries, but at last the hook's barbs were securely imbedded. She climbed out and he went to work.

He attached the other end of the rope to the winch. He began to ratchet it, tightening the rope until there was no slack. He pulled the lever again carefully, hoping not to dislodge the hook, and the box slid forward a couple of inches.

Soon it was sitting in the hallway. They looked at it closely; it was made of untreated boards fastened with square nails. He pointed them out to Callie, explaining that hand-forged square nails made it certain that this box was made in the 1800s.

"Ready to see what secrets lie within?" he said with a spooky laugh.

"Yes, Dracula. Let's see what's been hidden inside the wall for over a hundred years!"

He used a pry bar to remove the nails that held the top in place. "What do *you* think's inside?" he asked as he worked. "It has to weigh more than a hundred pounds. Think it's full of gold?"

"Wouldn't that be nice?" she said quietly, wondering if Mamère had led them to this box and if it held the solution to all her problems.

"Showtime," he said. "Here we go."

He lifted the wooden top and they looked down at what was inside.

"Oh, my God," she said, putting her hands to her face in shock.

"Why is that hidden inside a wall of this house?"

They stood in silence for a moment or two, gazing into the box. It held a five-foot-long rose-colored bronze casket with a window in the top. They brushed away a thin coat of dust; through the glass they could see the face of a blond-haired child who looked as if she'd fallen asleep yesterday. The tightly sealed vault had kept her body from deteriorating.

"Any idea who she is?" he asked.

Callie stared into the dead girl's face and stated the obvious. "She looks exactly like Anne-Marie."

There was no question in her mind who it was, but this was a new twist that she wanted to process when she was alone. There were so many things coming together so quickly, and now wasn't the time to discuss them with him.

"I can't imagine why she's buried in the wall," she continued. "I presume that she was a relative of mine, but then again, she could be someone else entirely. Are you certain she's been in there for more than a hundred years? She looks as though she could have died a year ago."

"I could be wrong, but from the looks of the box, I'll bet she's been in there a long, long time." He held up one of the nails he'd pried out and said, "Why would someone put a new casket in an old box and use nails I've only ever seen in a museum?"

He pointed to three latches on the side of the casket and said, "Do you want to open it?"

"No. The air could be bad for her. We can let someone who knows about this stuff help us with that later. First off, we need to find out who she was."

Mark asked, "What do we do with her? Should we call the authorities?"

"Let's don't do that just yet. You just said you think this body has been in there for decades. Let's put her back for now. We can call the sheriff if that's what we decide. No one will know when we found the casket unless we tell them. Close the hidden space and let's go to the cemetery. Maybe the tombstone will help us understand all this."

They put the casket back in the wall and sealed it up. Now there was no way a person could tell something was hidden behind the column. They walked to the cemetery, where he set up the winch and made easy work of the toppled stone.

Leonore S. Arceneaux. Born in Philadelphia 1837. Died at Beau Rivage Plantation 1892. Wife of John and beloved mother of Michael. Resting in the arms of Jesus.

Apparently lost in thought, Mark stared at the tombstone. Callie glanced at him; the marker seemed to be having quite an effect on him.

"Do you know something about her?"

He shook his head. "I ... I just got caught up in the moment. Too many dead people in one day."

"I said earlier that she was my Mamère Juliet's grandmother. She's the stern one in the library, you know. I had thought this might be her stone; almost all the other relatives are either buried right here or somewhere else I know about. Finding my great-great-grandmother Leonore's tombstone is the last piece of the puzzle."

Since it was impossible to know exactly where her grave was, they propped Leonore's headstone against a tree. Callie bowed her head for a moment to honor her relative, and then they walked back to the house.

From a place deep in the woods, she watched them.

CHAPTER TWENTY-SIX

"Mark, can you come look at something? I'm in the library."

He stepped into the room and saw her standing by the ladder. "I was beginning to think I was becoming incredibly forgetful until now. I have walked in here half a dozen times and found the ladder right here, when I left it somewhere else. I worked in here yesterday, and when I finished, I deliberately took the ladder down and put it on the floor behind the couch. Now look where it is!"

There it stood, to the left of the fireplace.

"If you're asking, I didn't move it."

She held herself tightly. "I know that. Neither of us is moving it, so who is? Is someone trying to scare us? If they are, they're beginning to do a pretty good job. Now I feel nervous every time I step into this room."

Mark knew something Callie didn't. From his measurements, he knew there was a hidden area somewhere to the left of the fireplace, just as there had been one where the casket was hidden. He didn't know exactly where it was or how big, but there was an anomaly, and it was somewhere in the area where the ladder kept showing up. Could there be a connection? He had no idea.

"I don't think there's anything to be afraid of. Who's the only person who gains from scaring us away? Your uncle. He's the one who's trying to take the house away from you. But he's an old man. I can't picture him sneaking through the woods, hiding in the bushes and creeping into the house, and then leaving again unnoticed. So we have to rule him out. Eliminate him and there's only one other person who's around constantly – Anne-Marie. She apparently can come and go as she pleases, although it beats me how she gets in when the doors are locked. She might be strong enough to move the ladder, but I'd think she'd make a lot of noise if she did it. If it is her, what's the purpose? She talks to you all the time. Why can't she just tell you what this is all about?"

"She rarely talks. She smiles and hums most of the time and almost never speaks first or answers questions. She's odd, but I don't feel afraid when she's around. It's more the opposite; I think maybe she's trying to help me."

Mark shook his head. "She's strange, all right, and I don't think her creepy appearances and disappearances are helpful. I think she's intruding in our space –"

Callie cut him off. "I get it. I know your opinion of her. But it's my house and I have this funny feeling about her. She knows things about this place. She knew where the hidden stairwell is. I have no idea why, but Mamère must have shown her the secrets. I don't know, Mark. I love this place and I want to make it grand like it was once before, but someone – or something – is trying to keep me from doing it. You can see that too – right?"

"I guess it's a man thing, but I look more at the facts instead of the weird stuff. Willard's out to sabotage you. The ladder moves when no one's in the room. Anne-Marie pops in whenever she wants. The house has a hidden staircase, and a little girl's casket was hidden inside a wall. Those are facts, and since they are, then there's a logical explanation for each one of them. I think old houses can be eerie and spooky. Everyone's seen movies about haunted houses and evil forces, but I don't believe in ghosts or spirits or extrasensory perception. Is something strange going on at Beau Rivage? Absolutely. Is there a rational explanation? Yes. We just have to find out what it is."

She looked past him into the hallway. He turned and said, "Speak of the devil. You're back."

Anne-Marie said nothing and there was no smile this time.

"I'm glad you're here. You're going to answer some questions, little girl," he said.

She walked to Callie's side and took her hand.

"Don't be afraid," Anne-Marie said softly. "There's a book you must find."

"What are you talking about?" Mark shouted.

"Back off, Mark!" she screamed back. "I've told you before to let her alone!"

She squeezed the girl's hand. "Anne-Marie, I'm only afraid because strange things are happening in this house. You know much more than you're telling me. Please tell me about Maria. Please help me."

"I *am* helping you."

"How? You won't even answer my questions."

"I told you there's a book you must find."

Mark swept his arm around the room. "What's she supposed to do, look through all five thousand until she finds a certain one? How's she even going to know which one to look for?"

"I don't like him." She dropped Callie's hand and walked into the hall.

"Where do you think you're going?" he shouted, running after her. He saw the front door shut and he bolted through it. He was seconds behind her, but she was gone. Frustrated again about the girl, he went back to the library.

"Damn that kid."

Callie was furious. "There's something she's trying to tell me – something I need to know. I want you to leave her alone. Don't talk to her again and don't get aggressive with her. Do you understand?"

"Okay, okay. Ease up a little. She's getting you all worked up, but don't take it out on me. I'm going into town to check on some things. Do you need anything?"

Callie was surprised at his sudden switch from offense to defense. There was much about this man she didn't know, and sometimes she wasn't sure she should have let him this far into her life. But what would she have done without him? He had befriended her, helped her financially and emotionally, and she was sitting here in Louisiana, still broke but at least with a glimmer of hope. *This is all part of life,* she told herself. *There are ups and downs in every relationship, whether it's business or personal.* This one was strictly business, and she realized now that it had to remain that way.

Once he was gone, she concentrated on the message that Anne-Marie had conveyed. She had to talk to the girl, but Mark was beginning to be more of a problem than a help when it came to her unexpected visits. It would have been so easy if Anne-Marie spoke directly, but Callie knew by now that wasn't going to happen. Mark had to stop interfering.

The words that Anne-Marie repeated so often disturbed Callie. "I don't like him. He's going to hurt you." Who was she talking about? Sometimes she thought it was Willard, but when Mark screamed at the child or was harsh to her, she wondered if Anne-Marie was talking about him instead. If she was, did she know something about him that Callie should be afraid of? Was he truly capable of hurting her?

That didn't make sense. How could this child know more about Mark Streater than she did?

Anne-Marie's curious way of communicating was one of the things that unsettled Callie most, although she never felt one iota of fear when the child was around. Fear and doubt came later, when she walked through the old mansion and tried to figure out how the girl could come and go without impediment. The dread swept through her mind when she admitted Anne-Marie knew a great deal about this old mansion – far more than Callie herself had ever learned from Mamère Juliet. Callie had inherited the house and everything in it. What exactly did that last part mean? What else was in this house besides what she could see?

And there was a little fear when Mark was around, she had to admit. He was so good to her sometimes, but other times he was like a different person.

Who is Anne-Marie? Why does she come around here? Is she really the girl in the shanty on the other side of the woods? These questions and a dozen others raced through her head as she stood in the middle of the library and slowly turned in a circle, trying to consider every aspect of the huge room and its soaring bookshelves as though it were her first time to see them.

There's something I'm missing. She says I must find a book, but I don't know its name, who wrote it or what it has to do with me. Asking me to find a book in this vast library is like searching for a needle in a haystack. I don't even know where to start.

Suddenly she stopped her circular progression and smiled. At last she understood. She *did* know where to begin her search after all.

Anne-Marie kept saying she was helping me, but I didn't understand. I was missing the clue that was right in front of me. She really is helping me. Over and over, she's showed me exactly where to look.

She's the one who's moving the ladder.

Every time she puts it in the same place, just to the left of the fireplace, in front of a bookshelf I haven't gotten around to cleaning yet. And every time I move it back, because until now I didn't understand. I don't have to look at five thousand books. The one I need is so high in this one shelf that I need the ladder to find it. When I see it, I'll know it's the right one.

She went into the kitchen and got a bottle of water. Excited that she might be on the verge of solving one of the house's mysteries, she was ready to climb that ladder. Her phone rang; the number wasn't familiar, but she answered.

"Callie, it's Lanny Weinstein. I need to see you and Mark immediately. There's been a development in the matter with your uncle."

"Mark's not here. He's in Opelousas. What's happening?"

"Mr. Arceneaux has filed a motion asking Judge Freed to recuse himself from our case."

"Can you explain exactly what that means?"

"He's claiming that the judge can't be impartial with regards to our restraining order. Usually it means there's a conflict of interest. Find Mark and come in as soon as you can. If you can't reach him, come by yourself. This is critical. I'll meet you at the Starbucks down the block from the Legal Aid office."

"I'll be there in half an hour," she promised. She locked up the house, and once she was on River Road, she tried Mark's phone. He always answered, but not this time. She assumed he was still angry, and she thought about going alone to the meeting, but despite the roller-coaster relationship she and Mark were in, he had experience in business and she wanted his input. She left a message asking him to join her at the coffee shop.

Mark and Lanny were at the table when she arrived. She joined them as Lanny was explaining that Willard had filed a motion requesting the judge remove himself from the case. He had received a copy of the motion this morning and he said that in this sort of issue, a ruling always came very quickly.

"Is there anything we can do?"

"Not about the recusal request. Unless one of you has had prior dealings with Judge Freed, this is not about us. That's the reason why I wanted to get us together, so we could talk about it. Callie, you're new here, so I'm going to assume you didn't even know Judge Freed until the other day."

She nodded.

"Mark, what about you? You've been in business in this parish for several years. Have you ever been a party to a matter that came before him?"

"Yes, twice. You know how people sue and get sued now and then when you're in business. I filed a mechanic's lien against a homeowner who refused to pay me what he owed after my guys finished his job. The judge ruled in my favor and that was that. The other lawsuit was one an ex-partner of mine filed against me. Foolishly, we'd entered into a handshake agreement to buy and repair a house and then flip it. I was supposed to get seventy percent of the profits because he contributed the house and I put up the money, which was more than the house was worth. Once we were finished, we sold the house and made thirty thousand. I was entitled to seventy percent of it – twenty-one thousand – but he offered me fifteen, take it or leave it.

"How'd that one turn out?"

"It was a valuable lesson, that's all I can say. Judge Freed asked to see anything we had in writing, which we didn't. He listened to our testimonies – my ex-partner lied the entire time – and he ruled that without a contract, a fifty-fifty split was reasonable. Ever since, I do my deals with a signature instead of a handshake. And I don't have partners when I can help it."

Lanny said, "Nothing about either one sounds like something that would affect his ability to give a fair decision on the TRO. It must be something else – something between the judge and Mr. Arceneaux."

Callie snorted. "You think? From what I hear, there's not a judge in southern Louisiana who's not indebted to my uncle one way or another."

"Everybody's heard those stories, but nothing's ever been proven. Remember, Judge Freed took our case almost without hesitation. If he had a true conflict, he'd never have done that."

Mark said, "So what happens next?"

"In a day or so the judge will rule on Mr. Arceneaux's request. If he denies it, then the hearing will happen on the day the judge set it, and he'll preside. If he recuses himself, another judge will be appointed before the hearing."

"Who most likely will also be under the influence of Uncle Willard."

Lanny nodded. "Although I've hardly begun my legal career, I'm not naive about how things go down here. I want to have faith in the legal system. I want to believe that men like Franklin Freed are honorable and upstanding, because that's what makes things fair. I sound like I'm on a soapbox, but I'm going to hope for the best. If we get a new judge, we'll just have to deal with it. I'll call you as soon as I hear."

———

Franklin Freed held the phone to his ear as he sat by the fire in his living room, reading a book.

"You're going to regret this, Franklin. You're finished."

The judge sighed. "You and I have been friends a long, long time. I've bent the rules for you and I've accepted gifts from you. I tried to tell myself it was the way politics works in Louisiana, but I always knew it wasn't right. I've made a decision. I'm retiring. This request for a restraining order will be the last order of business for this old judge. If you want to tell the world what a miserable excuse for a jurist I've been, then bring it on. That's your prerogative. Just remember it'll bring you down too. You're older than I am, Willard. I don't think you want to spend the rest of your time and money fighting the insurance companies who lost lawsuits in my courtroom. Every one of them hates you, and you know every one of them would be thrilled to see you disbarred. It won't matter to me, because my career will be over.

"Think about it long and hard, Willard. Have a good evening." He put down the receiver.

———

Although she had important things to deal with, such as climbing the ladder to find one certain book and a dead body hidden inside the wall, she couldn't focus enough to start on either. First she had to know what Judge Freed was going to do. Everything else had to wait until she knew if there was even a chance she could keep this house.

Every time her phone rang, she rushed to grab it, hoping it was Lanny. Thankfully it didn't take long before his name popped up on caller ID.

"This may be a first in St. Landry Parish," he announced gleefully. "Willard didn't get what he wanted. The judge refused to recuse himself. Our hearing is on, and he'll be our judge."

CHAPTER TWENTY-SEVEN

"Order in the court! All rise for the Honorable Judge Franklin Freed."

The handful of people stood as Judge Freed strode into the room, his black robe flowing behind him. He walked up a couple of stairs to the bench and seated himself. A court reporter waited next to him for the proceedings to begin.

"The only order of business is the request by Mark Streater and Calisto Pilantro for a permanent restraining order enjoining Willard Arceneaux from foreclosure." He looked at Callie and Mark and said, "Miss Pilantro and Mr. Streater, are you represented by counsel?"

Lanny rose. "They are, Your Honor. My name is Leonard Weinstein."

"And, Mr. Arceneaux, are you represented by counsel?"

Willard stood. "No, Your Honor. I will represent myself."

"Please approach the bench," the judge said. Callie and Mark watched as they conferred in whispers.

Lanny leaned to them and said quietly, "The judge is explaining to Willard that he's entitled to counsel even though he's an attorney, and that he in fact should retain counsel. This keeps him from seeking a mistrial later. We learned in law school that representing yourself is an insane idea."

"That's why Willard's doing it," Callie remarked.

Willard returned to the table across the aisle from them and sat down.

The judge swore everyone in and said, "Mr. Weinstein, you may begin."

They told Lanny he had done an admirable job of presenting the facts. He seemed confident and self-assured and spoke assertively, gesturing toward Willard now and then as he made a point. When he finished, the judge called upon Willard, who introduced two papers into evidence – the note Mark had signed and an assignment whereby the bank sold the note to Willard. He pointed out that the language in the note clearly allowed the holder to refuse payment if it was in an unacceptable form.

The judge made a point of studying the document, even though Lanny advised them that he'd undoubtedly looked at it a hundred times as he prepared for this hearing.

"Mr. Arceneaux, can you tell the court what form of payment Miss Pilantro offered you in order to repay the fifty thousand dollars plus interest?"

"Yes, Your Honor. She offered a cashier's check and then offered to pay cash, although she did not have cash with her."

"Upon what bank was the cashier's check drawn?"

"On the Cotton Belt State Bank, Your Honor."

"Are you either a director or a shareholder of that bank?"

"I am both, Judge. I'm pretty sure you know that." He chuckled and Judge Freed frowned.

"Can you explain why a cashier's check drawn on a bank in which you are an investor was not acceptable to you as a form of payment? Was there something about the check itself, or were you worried about the bank's ability to make good on the funds?"

"No, sir. I merely preferred an alternative form of payment."

"You had given Miss Pilantro a deadline, is that correct?"

Willard acknowledged that, and said the deadline had not yet passed when she met him to pay the note. He also granted that there was plenty of time for her to have gone back to the bank, gotten cash instead, and returned to his office.

"If Miss Pilantro had brought cash to your office, would you have accepted it in full payment of the note?"

"I don't know, Your Honor. She didn't bring cash."

The judge looked at his old friend and shook his head. Willard was getting himself backed into a corner, and this time Judge Freed wasn't going to help him out.

"Did you specifically tell Miss Pilantro that cash would not be acceptable? In fact, did you tell her that there was nothing at all that you would deem acceptable?"

"I don't recall, Your Honor."

"I remind you that you're under oath, Mr. Arceneaux. Did you tell Miss Pilantro there was nothing that she could do to satisfy you, and that you were going to forcibly remove her from the property four days afterwards?"

"Here's the problem, Judge. Calisto sold mortgaged property to raise the money so she could pay me. She sold some books, and under the terms of the papers she signed at the bank – and which they transferred to me – she was illegally selling property that would belong to me if she defaulted, which she did."

Callie shouted, "Are you kidding?"

Lanny put his hand on her knee to calm her down, and the judge rapped his gavel.

"Order!" he said sternly. "Mr. Arceneaux, you're introducing a new issue into this matter which I consider irrelevant. If Miss Pilantro sold some of the contents to raise money – and I remind you there has been no testimony to that effect – and the net result of that sale was that she paid you in full, what would be your objection to her having done so?"

"Listen here, Franklin ..." He paused as he realized he'd made a mistake. "I'm sorry, Your Honor. Miss Pilantro illegally conveyed mortgaged property, regardless of the purpose."

"Was the true intent behind your purchasing the note and mortgage to seize control of the property that rightfully belonged to Miss Pilantro?"

Willard burst into an angry tirade. "What the hell are you doing?" he yelled at the judge. He pointed at Callie and Mark. "These people don't deserve a restraining order. I acted completely within the letter of the law ..."

"If not the intent," Judge Freed interjected. "If you're finished ranting, I'll make my ruling."

Ten minutes later they stood on the steps of the courthouse and congratulated Lanny Weinstein for winning his first court case. The money in escrow would be paid over to Willard, and Callie's dealings with her uncle would be finished at last.

They heard the doors slam open as Willard came out. He walked past them and said, "This isn't over yet. You have no idea what you've gotten yourself into. And you, little fella –" he pointed at Lanny "– you'd better start looking for a job out West somewhere. No law firm in the South will touch you after this!" He stormed off in a huff.

"Is he threatening us?" Callie asked, alarmed at his venomous words and his outraged behavior.

Lanny pulled his cellphone from his pocket. "Knowing him, I'm not surprised. That's why my phone's been recording ever since we came out here."

CHAPTER TWENTY-EIGHT

Callie awoke in the middle of the night to the sound of raindrops softly striking the windowpanes. She rose, went to the window and pulled back the shades. Low, gray clouds hung in the sky and she could hear rumbles of thunder off in the distance.

She walked down the hall to get a bottle of water. As she passed the music room, something inside caught her eye. There was a child sitting on the floor by the fireplace.

Oh, my God! It's her – the girl inside the casket!

She uttered a cry and heard that familiar voice.

"I was just wondering about her."

Callie snapped on the light. It was Anne-Marie and she didn't move.

"It's three o'clock in the morning! You scared me to death! What are you doing here?"

"I was thinking about the girl in the wall."

"You knew she was there, didn't you?"

Nothing.

"Do you know who she is?"

Anne-Marie turned slowly, looked Callie in the eyes and smiled.

"She's Maria Arceneaux, isn't she? How long has her casket been in the wall?"

"Her daddy never got over it. He killed that soldier. Shot him dead, right there in the kitchen."

"Who? Who are you talking about?"

"Find the book and you will understand."

"What book? Help me."

"I *am* helping you. Find the book."

Turning her bizarre thoughts into words acted as a catharsis. She had no idea what was happening in this house, but Anne-Marie was the key to finding the secret.

"Did you know that girl a long time ago, Anne-Marie? Is she you?"

She smiled and shook her head. "How could she be me? That's not possible! She's dead. I'm right here, and she's in the wall, in her coffin!"

"Why can't you show me where the book is?"

"Because you have to find it yourself."

She began to hum.

"How can you come over here in the middle of the night in the rain? What if your parents look for you and you're not there?"

She smiled.

"What's the girl's name, Anne-Marie? Just tell me that. Tell me she's Maria."

"Sometimes we play with the toys in her bedroom. That man chased me up there."

"Who chased you? What are you talking about?"

"I don't like him."

"Who chased you – was it Mark? What are you talking about?"

She arranged the pleats in her dress and hummed.

Callie had given a lot of thought to the children who'd lived at Beau Rivage in the 1800s. There weren't many; all had been Arceneaux offspring and except for one, all had lived into adulthood. There was only one she knew of who died young.

"Is that Maria in the casket?" she asked.

Anne-Marie smiled and hummed.

Callie sat down on the couch. She held her head in her hands and began to cry. "I don't understand any of this. Why do you keep coming here? Why do you taunt me with tidbits of information that make no sense? Why won't you tell me the secrets?"

She raised her head and realized that she was alone.

———

It was raining much harder when she awoke. She went into the kitchen, where Mark handed her a cup of coffee and said, "Good morning. How'd you sleep?"

"Fine. How about you?" She wondered if he'd heard her talking to Anne-Marie, but she didn't bring it up, and neither did he.

Mark answered, "Good too, I think. Listening to rain always helps me sleep, but I woke up thinking about the coffin. We can't just leave it in the wall. Shouldn't we do something?"

"I don't know if there's something legally we have to do. Do we start with the sheriff, or the coroner, or a funeral home, or what? I don't have any experience with finding bodies inside walls. Hopefully you don't either!"

He shook his head. "I wish we knew who she was and when she died. You can see through the glass that her dress is lacy and frilly in an old-fashioned way. Anne-Marie wears the same kind of dress. So maybe the body isn't so old after all. If it's recent, then it could complicate things a lot. What if she was murdered, for instance, and someone stuck her in the wall?"

Callie shook her head. "You don't murder somebody and then buy a casket for them. Somebody who loved her put her in the wall. It sounds odd, but I feel comfortable with her casket here in the house. Let's leave her until I can find out who she was." She didn't intend to reveal her thoughts this time. She'd sounded crazy enough in the past.

"How can you find out?"

"There are parish records in Opelousas, and there's that wonderful historical museum in New Orleans. Somewhere I'll find my family's documents. This house has never been owned by anyone except Arceneaux descendants, and eventually I'll figure out who she is."

"Are you thinking this could be Maria?"

She was careful. "That's the logical conclusion, but Maria's gravestone is in the family plot. This must be someone else – another girl who died very young. But is that possible? Did two children die here?"

He shrugged and gave up on the subject for now. "What's on the agenda around here for today? I need to go into town and check on my guys for a few hours if you don't need me."

"I'll be fine. I'm really looking forward to today. Anne-Marie said there were secrets in the house, and I'm going exploring. You found the hidden place behind the column, but there has to be something else."

He already knew there was at least one more space somewhere in the library, but he didn't mention it. He wanted to see it for himself.

"I'll stay and help. I can go to town later. Two heads are better than one!"

"Go do your own thing," she insisted. "I've bothered you enough, and I want to tackle this project myself. If I find something and need help, I'll tell you when you come back."

She could hardly wait for him to drive through the gate and off to town. She ran into the library, and this time she was thrilled to find the ladder moved again. She climbed up. She had her dust cloth – she might as well clean the books while she looked for a certain one. She had to trust that she'd know it when she found it; Anne-Marie certainly hadn't given her any clues to go on.

As the others had been, most of these books were bound in rich leather. She thumbed through a few, marveling at how bright and crisp the illustrations were in these very old volumes. She dusted Shakespeare, Pliny, Cicero and Milton right alongside the American greats – Benjamin Franklin, Horatio Alger and Mark Twain among them. There seemed to be no pattern to the collection; the genres ran the gamut from politics to religion to spicy novels and great literature. The only commonality appeared to be that most had expensive bindings.

Finishing one, she moved to the shelf below. The work was monotonous, and balancing high on the ladder was hard on her back. Her mind wandered; she imagined Henri Arceneaux buying books from some shop in New Orleans and lovingly placing them in his library. She knew that Mamère Juliet's father, Michael, was wealthy too. He'd had a mansion on St. Charles Avenue in the Garden District, and she imagined him adding to the collection in this room every time he and his wife came out by carriage for the weekend.

She glanced to her right and saw Leonore's stern-faced portrait hanging three feet from her.

"Did you enjoy the books too, great-great-grand-mère Leonore?" Callie asked out loud. "I hardly know anything about you or your husband, but this was your house after the Civil War. Your son, Michael, was born here. Did he play in this room? Did your husband use it for his office too, smoking cigars and drinking brandy while he read a book he'd pulled from this very shelf?"

The next book she took out was a smaller one. It had no title or author's name on the spine. She opened the cover, looked at the first page and began to feel dizzy. Her head started spinning and she gripped the side of the ladder with one hand, clutching the little book to her chest. One careful step at a time, she climbed down and sat on the couch. Feeling a little better, she walked into the kitchen, drank some water and sat at the table.

She flipped through the book and saw that most of it was filled with handwritten words clearly written by a few different people. The back few pages were blank. On the inside back cover, there was an envelope that held a very old skeleton key.

She read the title page.

The Arceneaux Chronicles.

The story of a French family who settled in Acadian America.

She smiled and looked behind her. As she had expected, Anne-Marie was there, and she was smiling too.

This time Callie didn't speak to her – she knew Anne-Marie would be gone in a moment anyway. As supernatural as the child's appearances were, Callie felt a warm sense of comfort and relief. She knew why Anne-Marie had come; it was because Callie had found the book.

It was a journal – a story begun by one member of the family and continued by others for nearly two hundred years. The year 1834 was written at the top of the first page.

She flipped through a few more and saw that there was a notation at the top for succeeding years. She thought that would make it easier to find something specific later if necessary.

The handwriting was bold, with swirling flourishes at the end of sentences as people did in those days. The first entry – January 1834 – was Henri Arceneaux's history of Beau Rivage. Back in 1756, he wrote, Henri's father, Joseph was granted forty acres on the Atchafalaya River by Louis Billouart, the governor of New France. Joseph deeded the land to Henri in 1833, and by the middle of the next year, the house was under construction. Since he was a wealthy cotton merchant, Henri and Caroline spared no expense to make their home the most magnificent in the area. Before construction began, the couple had traveled by steamboat up the Mississippi, studying the gorgeous mansions along the river and bringing ideas back to their architect.

Henri's men built a dock, and before long there was a steady stream of boats arriving at what was now called Beau Rivage, offloading construction materials at first, and furniture from Europe, New York and New Orleans once the house was completed.

He detailed the months of construction, the celebration when it was finished, and the first of many lavish parties in the third-floor ballroom. When they tired of the serenity of Beau Rivage, Henri, Caroline and a couple of servants would board a steamboat at their dock and sail to Morgan City. There they would take one of the opulent riverboats down to New Orleans for a week of partying and dining with friends.

When she came to the entry for 1853, Callie learned whose marker she'd seen in the cemetery. On July 17, a girl was born in an upstairs bedroom that would be hers for as long as she lived. *We call her Maria,* Henri wrote, saying she was the most wonderful thing that had ever happened in his entire life.

Although Callie didn't know it, Maria's bedroom was the one where Mark had unsuccessfully tried to corner Anne-Marie.

As she skimmed the entries, there was no mistaking how much Henri and Caroline idolized their daughter. They were older – he was fifty-seven and she fifty when Maria was born – and Callie wondered if they had tried to have children earlier. She flipped pages to find the entries for Maria's death, since she had never known what happened.

Beginning in late 1862, Henri recorded one skirmish and battle after another as Union troops marched into south Louisiana. By the summer of 1863, things were going badly in St. Landry Parish. The Northern soldiers pillaged Opelousas and raided homes along the Atchafalaya River. Henri was determined that his would survive. He had the first-floor windows boarded up and the furnishings were moved into as few rooms as possible. He offered food, provisions and money to guerrillas who were roaming the countryside and fighting as mercenaries for the Confederacy. He housed a dozen of them on the third floor of Beau Rivage, and they managed to keep a couple of Yankee raiding parties away from the house.

Callie got goosebumps thinking how difficult this must have been for Henri, Caroline and Maria. He was defending his house and property, and perhaps their very lives. The tale was as exciting as a novel, and she was absorbed in this firsthand account of how people managed during the Civil War. There was one incident after another until she turned the page and came to July 17, 1863.

This was the date on the grave marker – Maria's tenth birthday. She took a breath and began to read, hoping to discover what had happened.

The Yankees landed at our dock around eight yesterday morning, Henri wrote on July 18th. The guards upstairs fired shots, but several soldiers made it to the front porch. Two of my defenders threw open the door and prepared to fire, but they were dead before they could raise their pistols. For the first time since the war began, two Yankees were inside my house, and they shot another of my guerrilla fighters dead on the stairway. More of my men were on the third floor, but I yelled for them to hold their fire. I hoped to get the Yankees off my property as expeditiously as possible.

Caroline and I were on the first floor and I shouted for Maria to stay in her bedroom. I raised my hands, and their leader, a colonel, requested food and water for his men. Caroline went into the kitchen and ordered the servants to set a table on the veranda. She would feed them lunch and hope they would go away.

"You have a beautiful home," the colonel said affably. "May I have a look around upstairs?"

I knew what he was doing. He was sizing up my house as a barracks for his men. He was going to count bedrooms. This had happened to other landowners along the river. The thought sickened me, but I had no choice. I told him my daughter was playing in her room and he promised not to bother her. Two of them tramped up my stairs and I could hear muffled voices as they invaded our privacy.

While they were upstairs, my servants removed the bodies of the downed guerrillas and washed down the floors. They put the bodies in a cart to be buried in the woods once the soldiers were gone. It was a tragedy to have men die in our beautiful home, but I thanked God my family had been spared – at least for now.

The men came back to the first floor, and at that moment I saw that Maria hadn't been upstairs after all. She'd been hiding in the music room. Apparently unable to contain her curiosity, she stepped into the hall and stared in shock at the soldiers dressed in blue who stood there.

She was in no immediate danger, but I was distraught that my beautiful daughter had to see the house occupied by Yankees. "Run!" I shouted to her. Why I did that, I will never understand, nor will I ever forgive myself. That single word will haunt me for the rest of my life. Maria obeyed. She sped out the door and ran across the lawn toward the river just as eight Yankees were walking from the dock up to the house. Two of them attempted to stop her. Maybe they were being playful, but maybe they weren't. They said something and I saw a look of terror on her face. I was too far away to hear and two stunned to react, damn my soul. The two soldiers and I stood on my porch and watched.

Maria tried to avoid them, but one reached out and grabbed her dress. I could see her sleeve rip as she tried to dodge him. He laughed and began to chase her. She must have been frightened out of her wits.

To his credit, the leader of that despicable pack – the colonel who stood beside me – shouted for his men to leave her alone, but it was too late. Terrified, she ran faster and faster as the soldier chased after her, laughing, apparently trying to give her a good scare.

"Stop! Stop!" I yelled, but she was overwhelmed with fear. She turned to see how close behind her the soldier was, and she lost her footing. I saw her tumble headfirst into the river.

Dear God! Dear God, my daughter was in the river!

The soldiers, Caroline and I rushed to the bank, but we couldn't see her. Their boat was moored there; maybe she had gotten trapped between it and the dock. Maybe she was trying to find a hiding place. I screamed and screamed for her to come out, that everything would be all right. The colonel ordered his men to find her and they fanned out along the shoreline.

In a few minutes I heard an awful, horrible, gut-wrenching shout that I shall never forget.

"I found her! Here she is!"

Forever etched into my memory is the image of that Union soldier in his blue uniform who carried in his arms the lifeless body of my wonderful child – my Maria – who was ten years old today. He handed her to me, and I held my child in her water-soaked blue party dress while tears streamed down my face.

The squad of soldiers went back to the house ahead of me. Caroline put her arm around me, sobbing and patting our baby on the forehead as we walked. The colonel expressed his condolences. He said he and his men needed food, but they would leave immediately after they ate. His compassion surprised me, although I said nothing. His men had killed my little girl.

I carried Maria into the music room. Heedless of her wet clothing, I laid her on the sofa and her mother straightened her dress and her hair. She looked as if she were sleeping, Caroline said as we held each other and cried.

I could hear the damned soldiers talking on the porch as if nothing had happened. I walked into the kitchen and saw a look of shock on the cook's face. Across the room, one of the soldiers had cut himself a big slice of Maria's birthday cake that Cook had prepared that morning. As he stuffed a piece into his mouth, something inside of me snapped.

Since the war began, I have taken to carrying a derringer pistol in my pocket. I can still see my hand bringing that gun out and aiming it. I shot that Yankee in the back of his head and his blood splattered all over my darling child's cake. Cook screamed. Caroline ran into the kitchen and so did the colonel.

I knew my life was over. I regretted that poor Caroline would suffer because of what I did. Not only had she lost her only child today, she was going to lose her husband too, for they would surely kill me now. They would likely burn the house too. I had done a horrible thing – not to the soldier, but to my wife.

To my amazement, the Yankee leader assessed the situation and walked out on the porch, where his men were milling about, waiting for orders. Then we heard nothing more from them. Caroline and I went to the window and saw the Yankees down at the dock boarding their boat. Five minutes later they were gone.

Callie put the book aside. Her stomach was churning as she thought of what torment Henri and Caroline had endured on that horrific day. She quickly thumbed through another page or two and stopped at an entry several days after Maria's tragic death. Reading it, she understood at last why there was a casket hidden in the wall.

CHAPTER TWENTY-NINE

August 13, 1863. I have tried to console Caroline, but there are no words that can mend a mother's broken heart. Day after day, she sits on the second-floor veranda, looking at the river. At first I was afraid the Yankees would see her, but although some boats have come by, no one stops at Beau Rivage. Perhaps the colonel declared our house under his protection after the tragedy his men caused. I have no idea, but nothing matters now except the depths to which my grieving wife has sunk.

I had the men clear a spot in the woods and ring it with a fence. Today I explained to Caroline that it would be a resting place for Maria, and for her and me someday in the future – a family burial plot on the grounds of this house she and I love so much.

Despite the difficulties in travel that the War has caused, two of my servants went into Baton Rouge with a letter of instruction and money for the undertaker. They returned with a casket. Caroline fluffed the pillow just so, and I gently put Maria inside. Caroline and I kissed our daughter and we closed and locked the lid. She will be at rest now.

From the next entries, Callie learned that one of Henri's servants engraved a headstone for Maria. Henri placed it in the spot he'd chosen for the family cemetery, but Caroline refused to let the child be interred. Her grief was so intense that she couldn't bear the thought of Maria being in the cold, dark earth. The casket sat in the music room for nearly a month. At last Henri gave in. Rather than create even more stress for his wife, he wouldn't bury the child. Instead, Maria would stay in the house forever.

As was the custom in many antebellum homes, Henri's architect had cleverly inserted hidden spaces here and there. Some were whimsical, like the staircase that ran up two stories inside the wall from the music room to the ballroom. It was simply a way for a person to disappear from one room and suddenly appear in another. Others were functional – they were secret places where valuable items – or people – could be hidden.

Henri and Caroline had chosen one of these spaces as their child's resting place. On August 29, 1863, a little over a month after Maria died, she was laid to rest literally within the walls of Beau Rivage. One hundred and fifty-five years later, Mark and Callie had found her.

Captivated by this true story, she read on. After the tragic event with Maria, the property had apparently been designated as off-limits by the Northern forces, because no Yankee ever set foot on the property again. Despite that, Henri described ever-increasing difficulties the War caused them. Before 1861, his had been a prosperous plantation with expansive cotton fields and a dozen men and women to help with the work. By 1864, many of them had left Beau Rivage because there was nothing for them to do and no money to pay them with. As Henri's spirits declined, so did his health. He wrote that he was rheumy – a word Callie had to look up – and had a persistent cough.

By December the journal entries were in Caroline's flowing handwriting. Things were getting very bad for the Arceneaux family. They had to ration food because the Union blockades had cut off supplies. In a demonstration of loyalty at the beginning of the war, Henri had converted all their liquid assets to Confederate currency. In early 1865, he took several thousand dollars to a bank in Opelousas and asked to exchange it for silver. His banker took Henri aside and brought the plantation owner up to speed.

"Confederate currency's no good anymore. Merchants only take silver, gold or greenbacks nowadays."

It annoyed Henri that greenbacks – the currency of the North – the United States – was good in Louisiana but Confederate money wasn't. What was the world coming to?

CALLIE: THE BAYOU HAUNTINGS

I cried when he came home and told me we were penniless, Caroline wrote. They had the land and the house, but they couldn't live on those things. Henri put all his currency in a strongbox and hid it in a secret place, but Caroline called him foolish. Her words were bitter. *You can't even buy a loaf of bread with all the Confederate money we have,* she said, but her husband stubbornly refused to allow talk that the South might lose the war.

Within a month, Henri could ignore things no longer. He heard that Yankee soldiers were forcing landowners to leave and then burning their houses, and he implemented a desperate plan he hoped would save their beloved Beau Rivage. He deeded the plantation to his brother, John, a physician in Philadelphia whose allegiance to the Union had caused a bitter separation between the siblings. Henri made sure the Yankee colonel who had kept the troops away knew that his house was now owned by a Union sympathizer.

It must have worked, Callie thought, since the house had been neither ransacked nor razed.

Caroline penned bitter words about the Union victory in May 1865. The humiliating defeat was more than her ailing husband could take, and he died three months later from what was probably tuberculosis, given the description of his symptoms.

When Henri died, their one remaining servant carved two headstones – one for Henri and one for her – and placed them in the family plot. Maria's stone would stand between theirs – a marker without a grave.

She buried her beloved husband and wrote a letter to his brother, John, asking that Beau Rivage be transferred back to her. That didn't happen. Caroline's angry words recounted how John's wife, Leonore Arceneaux – a full-fledged damned Yankee from Pennsylvania – arrived two months later with a toddler in tow and demanded that Caroline leave the house – *her* house – that now belonged to Leonore.

Callie was surprised that Mamère had never told her this story. Maybe it was too difficult for her – the betrayal of one brother by another, probably brought on by their choices

213

of sides in the Civil War. One important thing Callie appreciated was that Leonore had continued the journal. She took over the entries beginning in February 1866, the month of her arrival.

Her husband, John, never set foot on the property, preferring to live in the comfort and safety of Philadelphia instead of the South during the period of difficult reconstruction. Little innuendos here and there led Callie to decide that Leonore and John might have had marital problems. She flipped through months and years and learned that John ultimately deeded the house to Leonore, who neither returned to Philadelphia nor divorced her husband. John died in 1875.

Callie had wondered how Henri's wife had ended up in the family cemetery. The house belonged to her sister-in-law by now, but Leonore explained things by saying that when Caroline died in Opelousas in 1877, Leonore allowed the body to be buried in the family plot next to the tombstone of the child.

Since she had made entries herself, Leonore had obviously read the journal. She therefore knew Henri had interred his daughter's body inside a wall, but apparently she never found the hiding place.

CHAPTER THIRTY

Callie was working upstairs when she heard a car's engine and saw Uncle Willard arrive at the back entrance. She met him on the veranda.

"What do you want?"

"Calisto, I'm afraid I have some bad news for you and your friend. May I come in?"

More bad news? Was this about the restraining order? Surely not; they'd won the first round of that battle.

She turned and walked inside. He followed her and asked, "Where would you like me to sit?"

"Nowhere. Mark's not here. We can talk right here. That way when we're finished, you're closer to the door."

"Now, honey, you seem to be bitter, but all this stuff is just business. You never had a head for that kind of thing, but it was nothin' personal, as I'm sure you would realize if you'd quit acting so angry. What I have to say is going to take a few minutes. May we sit in the music room?"

"No, we can't. Start talking or get the hell out of my house."

"Once again it falls to me to be the bearer of bad news. You never had a head for business –"

"Knock it off, Uncle Willard! I'm sick of your attitude and your pretense. I beat you fair and square at the courthouse. Get to the point. Say what you have to say and leave."

"Have it your way," he shot back. "You took a book to the Darlington Gallery in New Orleans and its owner paid you ninety thousand dollars. He sent it off to England to have the experts look at it and he got a call yesterday with the results."

"How do you know that?"

"When you have connections, you learn a lot of things other people don't. Mr. Darlington is understandably upset – he paid you ninety thousand dollars on a contingency basis and now he's learned the book is a forgery. It's not even that old; someone made it look that way. He's quite angry; he feels as though he's been swindled – do you know what I mean? I tried to assure him you didn't do anything on purpose ..."

She was getting goosebumps. This wasn't right. "How are you involved in this?"

"The man needed a lawyer in St. Landry Parish to help him get his money back from a lady who lives in that same parish. He called me."

"You can't take that case. You have a conflict of interest because I'm your niece. Does Mr. Darlington know that?"

"There isn't going to be a case, darlin'. The man's clearly been wronged and you must make it right. She can't afford to let this sordid issue go to court. There could be criminal implications here," he said in the condescending voice that was making her angrier by the minute. "He's talkin' fraud and you have no choice but to pay back his money immediately."

She was seething with rage. Somehow, in some way, Willard had orchestrated this. She was certain the book was authentic. Mr. Darlington himself had been so convinced that he'd fronted her a lot of money. He wouldn't have done that if there was the slightest possibility something wasn't right. Darlington Gallery was a legitimate operation that had been in New Orleans for years. She was certain this wasn't about him – this was about Uncle Willard.

He pulled papers from his pocket. "This is a demand letter. He wants his money back by the day after tomorrow."

She looked at him in shock for a moment, and then said resignedly, "What do you want? You know where the money went. Fifty thousand plus of it went to you, to pay off Mark's note. We're using the rest; I don't know how much is in the bank right now ..."

216

"Around forty thousand, give or take," he answered smugly.

I suppose a bank director could find out things like that, she thought.

"Obviously I can't pay him back in three days. I need more time. I want to let another expert look at the book. What if Mr. Darlington's lying?"

Willard shook his head. "Maybe you're not understanding things. It doesn't matter if the book's real or not. He can demand his money back any time he wants. The book will be returned once you've paid him. Then you can do whatever you want with it."

"I asked you once, and I'm asking you again. What do you want from me?"

Willard smiled broadly. It was the same smile, Callie thought, that looked down on drivers from fifty billboards along Interstate 49.

"How am I goin' to get you out of this mess you've created for yourself, is that what you're askin'? Well, I have thought of a way I could help out. I don't usually get involved in messy situations like this, but since we're family, I'll make an exception. I'll pay the man his ninety thousand dollars. You can keep the forty grand that's in the bank right now, so you'll go back to Virginia a rich woman indeed compared to how penniless you were when you got here. All in all, it'll have been a very profitable few weeks down here in the bayou."

"And what do you get?" she asked, knowing the answer but wanting the despicable rat to say it.

"Everything. You're going to transfer over the land, the house and everything that's in it."

He walked into the hall and said, "Call my office. You'll need a notary when you sign the deed. I happen to have one on staff."

I'm sure you do. She watched him walk toward the door and glance toward the parlor.

"Hello there, young lady," he said. "Now who would you be?"

There was a pause, and then he said, "Don't say much, do you? Well, don't get too comfortable playing in this house. I'm afraid these people won't be here much longer."

The door slammed and Anne-Marie walked out of the parlor.

"I don't like him," the girl said. "He's going to hurt you."

"I think that's becoming crystal clear," Callie answered, seeing her hopes and dreams fading away.

Mark came back soon thereafter and she explained what had happened. "What am I going to do?" she asked. "He won't stop until he gets what he wants. He never wanted me to pay him the money in the first place. He's hell-bent on getting this property. I thought I'd beaten him, but now he's on a mission to take me down."

"What about the book? You think it's authentic, don't you?"

She replied angrily, "What the hell do I know about old books? I thought it was real because that guy Darlington jumped all over it. He couldn't wait to send it off to London to the experts. But none of that matters now. Uncle Willard's wrong – I do know something about business. I read the contract I signed. There's a paragraph that says he can demand his money back. I asked him about it. He assured me that we'd never be dealing with that issue, and not to worry about it one bit. It was standard language, he said."

Mark thought for a moment. "It probably is. It's not unreasonable from his standpoint; it protects him if someone tries to pull a scam on him. Regardless, we're in a jam because of the short time frame. We're back to square one – needing to raise fifty thousand dollars virtually overnight to get us out of this."

"I appreciate your saying this is your problem too," she said, squeezing his hand. "But it's not us that's in a jam – it's *me*. I've been a failure all my life. My father was never there, my mother could barely keep things together, and I'm sure she thanked the Lord the day I left for college. Two years later she was dead and I had nothing, not even a parent to talk to. I graduated and went to work for a two-bit newspaper, where I still work seven years later – although by now I've been fired, I'm sure. I live in a slum and I simply exist. Every day for me is just like yesterday and tomorrow. Nothing changes.

"When Uncle Willard told me I was going to inherit something from Mamère Juliet, I felt a tiny bit of hope for the first time in years. I hadn't kept in touch with her like I should have because she would have offered me money, and I didn't want her spending what she had on a failure like me. But I was hopeful she'd done something nice for me, something that would jump-start my life again. At first it made me angry she left me this old albatross. But the more I thought about it, and the more you were around, I realized that I needed to view this as the positive thing it could be, not something negative like everything else has been."

He put his arm around her and drew her close. "I know it's hard," he whispered, "and there has to be a way out of this."

"But there's not. I have no time and I've got to take the one single option I have. He wins, I lose. Simple as that. And he's right. I'll go back to Petersburg with more money than I ever had at one time in my entire life. Forty-something thousand dollars. Wow. Bet I can live on that for what – maybe a year? How pathetic."

She began to lose it and she put her head on his shoulder. She looked up when she felt his arm jerk away. Anne-Marie had disappeared when Mark came home, but now she was standing in the doorway. She walked across the room and stood by Callie.

"Get out of here!" Mark shouted.

With all that talking I was doing, I completely forgot about her.

"Let her stay. I may not be seeing much of her anymore."

"I don't like him," the child said, her face showing no emotion. "I can help you."

"Right, kid," Mark snorted. "Got a bunch of money stashed away over there in your daddy's mansion?"

"That was uncalled for," Callie said, extricating herself from his embrace. She pulled her hand from his and moved away.

"I'm not sure about you, Mark. I want you to leave Anne-Marie alone from now on because I don't like it when you treat her that way. Like I was about everything else, I was optimistic about you when I first hit town, but our relationship – or whatever you want to call it – never even began. I've made up my mind. I'm going to walk away in true Callie Pilantro style. I'm going to give up and give in, like I've done before. Uncle Willard can have the damned house and I'll go back to what I deserve. Start loading up your tools. I'll go see him tomorrow afternoon and sign the deed."

He tried to take her in his arms, but she pulled away.

"No, Mark. It's over. It never started, but it's over. Even if I wanted to, I can't let anything happen now. It's too late."

Clearly irritated, he said he'd be back in the morning to get his things. He huffed out and drove away.

Anne-Marie smiled, took Callie's hand for the first time ever, and led her down the hallway into the library. She took her to the bookshelf just to the left of the fireplace and said, "Press that button."

There was an indentation in the side of the bookcase that was so much a part of the decor, Callie would never have noticed it even if she'd looked closely.

"What is it?" she asked, knowing what the girl's response would be.

Anne-Marie smiled and hummed, and Callie pressed the button.

CHAPTER THIRTY-ONE

The shelf swiveled out noiselessly, revealing a small room behind it that was about six feet by twenty and ran behind several of the bookshelves. Inside there was a wooden table and a chair. On the table sat an oil lamp and a small metal box secured with a padlock.

The original lumber that Henri's contractor had used to build the house formed three of the rough, unfinished walls of this chamber. The fourth wall was the brick side of the library's fireplace. There wasn't much light, so she went back, got her flashlight, smiled at Anne-Marie and returned to the secret room.

At the far end of the narrow space where it abutted the fireplace, there was a stairway leading down to a very small door. She went down its narrow steps, her shoulders grazing the walls on either side.

This was made for small people, she thought. *Someone Mark's size would never fit in here.*

She expected to put some effort into opening the door, but to her surprise it yielded immediately, opening smoothly and silently. She stepped out and realized why she hadn't noticed the door from the outside. She was standing behind the thick hedges that ran along this side of the house, and the door was nestled up to the base of the fireplace at its junction with the house's wall. It was well-concealed and completely hidden in the hedgerow.

She stepped through the bushes and into the yard. Anne-Marie was there, watching silently. Callie wondered how she'd gotten out here, but she knew it was useless to ask.

"I think I just discovered how you come and go so easily. How long have you known the secret room was there?"

She smiled but said nothing.

"Thank you for showing it to me," Callie said. "What do I do next?"

"Just open the box, silly."

Callie went back into the little room, seeing what a simple, easy way it was to get into the house once you knew how. She thought Anne-Marie might have followed her, but the child wasn't there. It didn't surprise her – nothing about Anne-Marie did anymore.

She lifted the strongbox – for that was what it really was. Since it was made of metal, she'd expected it to be heavy, and it was. The padlock was very old and opened with a key. She looked around the room but didn't see one.

She stepped out into the library, intending to rummage through Mark's tools for a hammer and screwdriver, when her eyes fell on the old journal that she'd left on an end table.

The key's in there! I saw an envelope with a key in the back of the book!

She rushed back into the room and sat on the wooden chair she assumed had belonged to Henri. Had it been hidden here since the Civil War? Did Mamère Juliet know about this room? Did Leonore? She was convinced Anne-Marie used this room to come and go undetected, but she also might be the first Arceneaux to see it since the Civil War.

Giddy with anticipation, she put the key in the padlock and turned it. It took some effort, but in a moment the shackle snapped open. She carefully removed the lock and put it aside.

She raised the lid. The box was filled to the brim. She removed several pieces of yellowed paper from the top – documents of some sort – and she sifted her fingers down through the contents to see if there was anything different on the bottom. Suddenly she felt a tingle and looked around.

Anne-Marie was standing in the far corner at the top of the narrow stairwell. She was frowning. "He's going to hurt you."

"Hey, Callie," she heard a voice from the library. "I need to talk to you for a minute. I've got an idea."

She turned around just as Mark stuck his head through the narrow passage into the room. She quickly closed the strongbox as he stepped inside.

"What the hell is this place?" he said.

Anne-Marie was gone, and she wanted to disappear herself. She didn't want to share this discovery with him. Anne-Marie had brought her to this special place and it was Callie's secret, at least until she signed the paperwork at Uncle Willard's office tomorrow.

He looked around the room, taking it in. "This is incredible! The house reveals another secret! Tell me that box is full of gold and everything's going to be fine!"

She wasn't amused. "Why did you come back?"

"Have you opened the box? What's in it?"

She ushered him out of the room and into the library. "What are you doing here?" she asked again.

"I remembered something you told me earlier and wondered if you'd forgotten it with everything going on. You took those ten books to New Orleans, but you brought them back. The only one you left was the paperback that was supposed to be worth a fortune. Mr. Darlington offered you fifty thousand dollars for the ten books that you'd left with him earlier, remember?"

She nodded, seeing now where this was going. "The other six books I showed him were probably worth thirty more."

"Right. I know you don't want to part with anything you don't have to, but the books may be the easiest way to get some money fast. There's no authenticating this time – the man already offered you thirty thousand for ten books. Take a lot more to him. Take twenty or thirty – they'll barely be missed with the thousands of books in here. Give him ninety thousand dollars' worth, get your Poe book back, and everything will be fine between you and him. And between you and Willard, for that matter. He won't have anything to hold over you any more."

All that made sense. Selling a few dozen books wouldn't be a big deal if it would solve her problems. Maybe she was being too hard on Mark; he was still trying to help her find a solution. The optimism in his voice made her feel determined to work things out. It did no good to wallow in pity. She'd fight Uncle Willard for as long as she could.

"There's the ladder," she said, deciding that she was going to let him help. "Climb up there and pick the ones you think we could get the most for. I hate to sell the best ones ..."

"I wouldn't worry about that." He laughed. "They're all valuable, at least all the ones I've seen so far." He glanced at the end table where the family journal was. "What's that?"

"I found it earlier," she said, not wanting to get into all this now. "It's kind of a diary. I read parts of it. It's like a family history and I think I'll learn a lot from it."

"What does it say about Leonore?" he asked.

That was odd. Why did he want to know about her?

So she could find out what he was after, she lied. "I only read a few pages, all about the Civil War. I didn't see anything about Leonore. Why do you ask?"

"No reason. I was just looking at her picture up there on the wall and I wondered if there was any information about her." He pulled the ladder across the room and climbed up to the top shelves.

"You never told me what's in that box in the hidden room," he called down to her as he pulled out books.

"It's a secret. Maybe I'll tell you later." That was a stupid response, she told herself, but it would hold him off long enough for her to decide if she really would show him what she'd found. She wanted to trust him – God knew she needed someone to trust – and most of the time she did. But more and more, especially when he was unkind to Anne-Marie, she got this feeling that he wasn't what he appeared to be.

I have twenty-four hours left in this house unless Mark's miracle comes true. I don't need to start getting close to him anyway unless –

– unless everything works out with me and Beau Rivage. If that happens, maybe I'll think about Mark Streater. If it doesn't, I'll never see him again anyway.

Mark selected twenty books, sixteen of which were the ones she had already toted down to New Orleans and back. Now they talked logistics. Mr. Darlington had made her an offer on the sixteen books, but now he was demanding his ninety thousand dollars back on the paperback. They had limited options – they could find another dealer or two, but they were on a very short time frame and couldn't afford to waste a minute. Mark could go instead of Callie. That might help, Mark offered, since Mr. Darlington believed Callie had defrauded him. Then again, Callie could take her chances and go there herself.

Knowing something he didn't – the contents of the strongbox – Callie agreed with Mark's suggestion that he be the one to go to New Orleans. While he was away, she'd make a trip of her own. If the things in the box were worth something, then maybe – just maybe – she had another way to raise money quickly.

He took the twenty books and went home for the night. He planned to be on the road at daybreak, arrive at the gallery when it opened at nine, and return by mid-afternoon, hopefully with good news. When he got back, Callie would still have twenty-four hours to meet Willard's deadline for paying the money.

Alone at last, she took the strongbox into the parlor. She took out the documents that were on top, closed the lid and secured it with the padlock. She put the box behind one of the heavy curtains and took the papers into the kitchen to read.

She opened a beer, put a pizza in the oven and sat down.

She separated the papers into two stacks. One was a legal-sized formal document that had the words "Warranty Deed" and "Copy" at the top. She gave it a quick once-over;

it appeared to be a handwritten copy of the deed Henri had sent to his brother, John, when he transferred ownership. She set it aside for now.

She examined the other papers – a three-page letter in the same handwriting she'd seen in the journal. Henri Arceneaux had written it on August 1, 1865. She stopped, pulled up the photo of Henri's gravestone on her phone, and read his date of death – August 4, just three days after this letter was written.

She couldn't imagine the pain he must have been suffering, both physically – as disease was consuming his body – and mentally, as his beloved South had lost the war three months earlier. He explained that he had made a fortune in the years before the War. Like other plantation owners, he and Caroline were wealthy beyond their wildest dreams.

Callie knew that he had unsuccessfully tried to get his money converted to silver earlier that year, and she couldn't fathom the heartache this once-proud man felt now that he was bankrupt. His letter went on – the strongbox, he said, contained his entire life savings – more than forty thousand now-worthless Confederate dollars.

Henri talked about his decision to transfer the property to his brother, John, whom he detested because he'd abandoned his Southern roots and supported the Union. But John was his only chance to keep the house in the family, and Henri stated that he had willingly and voluntarily transferred his beloved plantation to his brother and sister-in-law in Philadelphia.

The letter was filled with such tragedy that it brought tears to Callie's eyes. These were her ancestors – her *people* – and she was learning so much in such a short time. It made for amazing reading even as it tore at her heartstrings.

She looked at the deed. Its date was January 5, 1865.

I, Henri Arceneaux, and Caroline Chapman Arceneaux, my wife, do hereby deed and convey the house known as Beau Rivage and forty acres of riverfront land, including all of the personal effects herein, to my brother John Samuel Arceneaux and his wife Leonore Streater

Arceneaux. Next there was a legal description of the land and a brief list of the furnishings, tools and equipment that were part of the transfer.

At the bottom were two signatures – one in a shaky hand that once had been bold and strong, and the other in a precise, feminine script. Henri and Caroline no longer owned the home they built and loved.

She ate her pizza and drank another beer. She was exhausted, completely overwhelmed by both her own precarious situation and that of her ancestor Henri. Like him, would she have to deed away this wonderful property because she didn't have the money to pay for it?

Callie went to bed and fell into a light slumber. Sometime after midnight she sat bolt upright in bed, her eyes open wide. It had finally come to her – now she knew exactly what was going on all around her. How could she have missed it earlier?

She fumbled for her phone and made a call, but it went to voicemail.

She got up, put on her clothes, and stuffed a few of the Confederate bills from the strongbox into an envelope. She grabbed two bottles of water and a toiletry kit, locked up the house, and soon she was driving along Interstate 10. Even with heavy truck traffic, she was in New Orleans before four a.m. She found a well-lit church parking lot, reclined her seat and slept in the car until daybreak.

She had a strange dream, one in which she told Anne-Marie that she was going to move Maria's casket. It can't stay in the house any longer, she had said. It's not normal to have dead people in your house.

Anne-Marie had smiled and replied that Maria liked being where she was very much. She loves this house, Anne-Marie had said.

The dream woke her, although she didn't remember much about it. She stretched and tried to find a better position in the cramped space. She also had a thought that she should move Maria's casket. Then she had a better one. *I'll leave her there for now. Maybe she likes being in this house, snug and safe inside its walls.*

CHAPTER THIRTY-TWO

Callie slept fitfully until daybreak, twisting and turning into one uncomfortable position after another. She gave up just before seven. She found a Starbucks, took her toothbrush and paste to the restroom and did the best she could to make herself look halfway human. She splashed water on her face and hair, pulled it back in a ponytail, and decided that was all she could do.

She ordered a latte and a muffin, and the caffeine gave her the wakeup jolt she required. She drove into the French Quarter, parked the Pontiac and walked to the Darlington Gallery. A sign in the window said it opened at nine. She had an hour to kill before she would see Mark. She found a sidewalk café down the street with a view of the gallery and ordered a chicory coffee.

Right at nine she paid her bill and walked to a spot across the street from the gallery. Five minutes later a lady she recognized from her earlier visit unlocked the door, flipped the sign from "Closed" to "Open," and went inside. She waited twenty more minutes, but Mark didn't show up. He'd promised to be at the gallery when it opened. Where was he?

There was only one way to find out. She went into the gallery and the lady gave her a warm smile. That was encouraging – Callie figured if Mr. Darlington himself had been here, the reception would have been much colder.

"I remember you," the lady said. "You had that exciting Poe book! What brings you back to town?"

"Actually, I was going to meet my friend Mark here."

"I remember your friend. I was the one that went to the bank and got the cashier's check to swap with him that afternoon when he drove down. Are you all planning a little getaway in New Orleans today?"

"No. Actually Mark has an appointment with Mr. Darlington."

"Oh dear," the lady exclaimed. "Let me check the schedule." She flipped through some papers on the counter, retrieved a calendar full of handwritten entries, and said, "Well, I'm not sure what the mix-up is, but I'm afraid your friend's appointment isn't on the books for today, and it really couldn't have happened. Mr. Darlington's out of the state, you see. He took a few days off and went to Atlanta to visit some friends."

"But what about the issue with the Poe book? I'm so sorry about all that ..."

The lady looked puzzled. "Your book? I'm not sure I understand. Mr. Darlington was really excited about it, as I think he told you. He sent it off to the British Museum, as he promised. Since it's so valuable, I tracked it yesterday. It's going to be delivered tomorrow morning."

"The authentication people haven't seen the book yet?"

"Not yet, but I assure you they'll be as amazed as Mr. Darlington was. It's not every day people get to hold a prize like that in their hands!"

"But what about Mr. Darlington's demand that I pay him back the money?"

Now the lady looked really confused. "Are you feeling well, dear? I think you must be mixed up. Mr. Darlington hasn't been here for several days. I haven't spoken with him since he left, and I can assure you that the last thing he wants is for you to give the money back. He's more exhilarated than I've seen him in years!"

Callie fumbled with an apology and said that she must have completely misunderstood. As she left the store, the lady wondered if that nice girl was taking medication that had addled her mind.

Confused and angry, Callie wanted nothing more than to simply go back to Beau Rivage, where she felt safe. But she had one more stop to make. She spent an hour at another shop in the French Quarter and then her business was finished.

As she drove home, a million thoughts swirled through her head. She had intended to confront Mark about what she'd learned yesterday – the thing that woke her in the middle of the night – but instead she'd discovered that not only had Uncle Willard lied to her, but so had Mark.

She felt more alone than at any time since she'd come to Louisiana. There was no one she could trust, and only she could decide what she should do next.

Callie sat on the couch in the library for two hours trying to understand. Both of them had lied, so were he and Uncle Willard working together? If so, why? What was worth all this trouble just to get an old mansion and forty acres? She needed more information, but there was no one left to confide in.

Around four she heard Mark's Jeep pull up, and she walked out on the back porch as he took out the box of books.

"Hi," he said.

"What did Mr. Darlington say?"

"Let's go inside and talk. I need to put this down and get a beer. I've been on the road for six hours and I'm exhausted."

"I can only imagine. Was the traffic bad?"

"Yeah, and there was a wreck in Metairie that held me up. I still made it by nine, thanks to my leaving half an hour earlier than I planned."

He asked if she wanted a beer too, but she said no. In a moment, he joined her in the library.

"So tell me the news. Is he willing to buy the other books? Are my problems over?" She almost choked on the words, knowing he was going to lie and wishing everything could be different.

"I'm sorry, Callie. What I have to tell you is going to hurt, and I'm sorry. Mr. Darlington's furious about the book. I explained that there was no way you could have known it wasn't authentic. You relied on his expert opinion and he was the one who offered the money. But he doesn't see it that way. He said he hired Willard because he wants nothing more to do with you. You can deal with his attorney, and once you pay back the money, he'll call it even. If you don't pay him, he says he's going to have you arrested."

Callie brushed away a tear and let Mark take her hand. She had to play this out to the end.

"So I guess the people at the British Museum knew immediately that it was a fake. They couldn't have had it very long – it's only been a few days since we left it with Mr. Darlington."

"He said the expert called him within an hour after he got it. He didn't give me the details, but he said once the book comes back, he'll give you the paperwork that explains their findings."

"What about the other books you took to show him? I guess he wasn't interested in those either."

"That's putting it mildly, I'm afraid. He almost threw me out of his shop. He used the old 'fool me once' line."

"And did you see other dealers?"

"Yes, two more. Neither of them would offer anything up front. Both were willing to take them on consignment and give you sixty percent whenever they sell. But we don't have time for that, unfortunately. I really struck out today and I feel awful about it."

She looked him in the eyes, dropped his hand and said, "Is there anything else you want to tell me?"

Her words surprised him and there was a tiny alarm bell somewhere in his mind. Something wasn't right with her.

"I think that's about it. What did you do today?"

"I drove to New Orleans, Mark. I went to Darlington Gallery to find you."

"You did what? Why did you do that? You didn't trust me, did you?" His words were fierce and harsh, but also anxious. She knew he must be scrambling to create a story.

She laughed. "Trust you? Yes, when I drove to New Orleans I trusted you. I wanted to talk to you about something else entirely – something I discovered yesterday."

He answered quickly. "Then I guess you know that Mr. Darlington and I changed our appointment. I should have told you and saved you a trip, but I had no idea you'd go yourself. He offered to meet me halfway so I wouldn't have to drive so far. We met south of Baton Rouge."

"What about that six-hour drive and the wreck in Metairie? Why did you tell me that? You weren't in Metairie at all."

"I, uh, I was trying to make you feel sorry for me, I guess. It's been a hard day for me too. I wanted to come through for you. You didn't go into the gallery, did you? That wouldn't have been a good idea since he's so angry."

She ignored his question. "Where were you today, Mark? The truth. Where were you all day? Mr. Darlington didn't meet with you. He's been in Atlanta for days, according to the lady at the shop."

"Okay. Here's the truth. I didn't think this plan would work. I didn't think the books would bring nearly what we'd talked about ..."

"You chose to screw me over by not even taking them to New Orleans. You were going to let me think you did, but since I'm running out of time, there wouldn't be anything I could do to save Beau Rivage. What's going on, Mark? What's your involvement in all this? Are you and Uncle Willard conspiring against me?"

"I don't know what you're talking about."

"I trusted you. I thought you were on my side and we were working together. But this morning in New Orleans, everything I believed about you vanished before my eyes. I'm sure you know all about the Poe book. There's no demand letter – no angry Mr. Darlington who wants his money back – and the book hasn't even gotten to London yet, so nobody has begun to authenticate it. Everything you and your partner Uncle Willard told me is a lie."

"Callie, I didn't know any of that! Please believe me. Now that we know he's lying, we can stop him. I'll help you. We can do this together."

She let him ramble, hearing his words pour out like water from a garden hose. He clutched at every straw, used every angle he could think of, and even told her how much he cared for her. When he paused, she walked out of the room to get a beer. When she came back, Anne-Marie was standing in the hall. Mark couldn't see her, but she gave Callie a smile. Callie smiled back; she had known that the girl would be here for her.

Callie took a seat across the room from him. "I told you that I went to New Orleans to talk to you about something I found out yesterday. Do you want to know what it was?"

"Yes," he answered, thankful for any break in this perilous conversation.

"Before the end of the Civil War, my ancestor Henri deeded the house to his brother, John, who lived in Philadelphia. Do you remember that?"

"Sure."

"John died, and his wife, Leonore, inherited the house. Leonore was my grandmother's grandmother. Do you remember that?"

"Yes, of course," he answered, looking at her quizzically.

"Who was Leonore, Mark?"

"What? What do you mean, who was she?"

"Remember the box in the secret room? There was a copy of the deed inside – the deed where Henri transferred Beau Rivage to his brother, John, and his wife, Leonore Streater Arceneaux. Her maiden name was Streater, just like your last name is. Who was she, Mark?"

He hung his head. "What do you think you're doing?"

"Answer me! For once, tell me the truth."

He jerked his head up and glared at her with fire in his eyes. "She was my great-aunt. There, now you know. Are you satisfied?"

"Hardly," Callie replied evenly. "I want to know everything. Start from the day I first saw you and tell me exactly what you're doing. Oh, and don't forget Uncle Willard. I'll guarantee you he's in your story too."

CHAPTER THIRTY-THREE

"All of this is rightfully mine."

Callie paused, waiting for more, but he sat back and crossed his arms defiantly. His face was set and determined, and any trace of the friendly, try-to-be-helpful man she'd known was gone now.

"That's it? Everything that's happening is because you think I screwed you out of your inheritance?"

"Damn right. If it hadn't been for Leonore Streater, your family would have lost Beau Rivage. The Yankees would have burned it to the ground, like they torched so many others. Henri deeded this albatross to his brother – whom he hated, by the way – because he wanted to save his precious house. John couldn't have cared less about the place, but Leonore dumped him and moved down here. She invested her own sweat and a lot of cash to keep it up. *She* was the one who saved your ancestral home, and she should have left it to her brother Paul, my great-grandfather. Instead, she willed it to her son, so it ended back up with the Arceneaux clan instead of the Streaters.

"Just like my great-aunt did years ago, another Streater watched over this place after your grandmother Juliet died. That would be me. I came out here three times a week and scared off the vandals. I ran boatloads of beer-drinking teenagers off the property. Even when it started deteriorating, I was prepared to come in and save it, but I had to wait until the will was read because I didn't know who it was going to belong to. It was going to be one of you, that was for sure. Keep it in the family, that's what old Juliet did. Just like my great-aunt should have, damn her hide.

"Willard knew I was watching the place. After the will was read, he told me that the new owner was you – a grandniece from up north somewhere who hadn't set foot in

St. Landry Parish for years. It was a lucky break that I knew you and you called me for help. I thought at first you wouldn't give a rat's ass about this place. You were dead broke, and by your own admission you hadn't even come back to see your grandmother when she was alive. But now this place that rightfully should have been mine was yours. And then, amazingly, you decided to try to make something out of it."

Callie mulled over what he was saying. "You gave me a place to stay, you helped me out financially, and you came out here and worked beside me to fix the place up. It was your idea that we borrow the money for improvements. You intended even then to take it away from me, didn't you? Is that where Uncle Willard came in? Did you get him to help you steal the plantation from me?"

He laughed mirthlessly. "Steal the plantation? How can you steal what's rightfully yours? I didn't have to take it away from you, Callie. You didn't have twenty dollars to your name. I'd inadvertently put the perfect plan in place when I suggested I borrow money and you mortgage the property. We used my bank – which also happened to be Willard's bank. He told the directors you couldn't pay it back and he did what a good bank director should do when a family member has a problem. He assumed the bank's risk by buying my note and your mortgage. When he explained that's what he was going to do, I thought it was foolproof.

"I never suspected there was anything valuable in the house. Once I learned about the books, Willard and I had to figure out another plan, because if you started selling them, it was going to screw up everything. You homed in on the Poe book that was going to be your salvation, but Willard didn't intend to let you win. He refused to take your money. If that damned Judge Freed hadn't decided to be a do-gooder for the first time in his career, there wouldn't have been a restraining order, and Willard would have owned the house. I was supposed to get half for everything I'd done and to compensate me for the fact that I should have inherited it in the first place."

"And you believed him, after seeing what he did to his own grandniece?"

"I still believe him. He's done nothing to hurt me."

"I guess that's true," she admitted. "But you've let him tear me to shreds. How can a person act so caring and be so evil? I thought at first there might be something between us, and even after I saw how you treated Anne-Marie, I hoped things might work out. Boy, how could I have been so wrong!"

"Anne-Marie's a creepy trespasser who brings nothing but trouble with her. If I see her again, I'll make sure she doesn't come back here."

Callie recoiled and shouted, "What exactly does that mean? What kind of monster are you?"

"Just keep her out of my sight. That's what it means. I'm no monster, but she knows how to push my buttons and I'm not standing for it anymore."

She stared at him blankly. How could she have been so stupid? How could she have missed so much?

"Open the bookcase," he commanded. "I want to see what's in that metal box."

"Open it yourself."

"You know I don't know how. Listen to me! You're going to do what I say or else –"

A quiet voice behind him said, "Leave her alone."

He whirled and saw Anne-Marie standing in the hallway. He broke out into a wide grin. "Well, well, look who's here. I've been hoping you'd show up." He walked toward her, but she went down the hall into the music room. He ran after her as Callie bounded behind, screaming for him to stop. They burst into the room just as the door to the hidden stairway closed.

Mark ran to the master staircase and bounded up two at a time. Callie opened the door where Anne-Marie had gone and whispered, "Come back down here, Anne-Marie! He's going upstairs." The girl popped back into the music room, took Callie's hand and led her to the library. She pushed the button, and when the case swung out, they ducked inside and closed it behind them.

They rushed down the stairs and went through the door into the side yard. Holding each other's hands, they began to run toward the woods. Just as they ducked into the trees, they heard a yell from the porch. He'd seen them!

"Hurry," Anne-Marie said. They ran along the narrow path until they emerged on the far side of the woods. As they rushed towards the shack, the girl let go of Callie's hand and ran inside. Spike tried desperately to break his chain as Callie ran past and stopped at the doorway. She yelled, "Hello? Is anyone home? Help me, please!"

Anne-Marie's father emerged, wearing the same stained, torn clothes as the last time she was here.

"What do you want?"

"A man who was at my house – he's chasing us. Please let me come inside!"

"Who all's he chasin'?"

"Anne-Marie and me."

"I don't know what the hell you're talkin' about, lady. Ain't nobody standin' here but you."

"She was with me. She ran into your house just before I yelled. Can we please go inside? I'll explain everything."

He turned and she darted into the meager living room and closed the door.

"I'm sorry to bother you, but the man – his name is Mark Streater – I think he was going to hurt Anne-Marie and me. We ran over here."

"Why'd you do that?"

She paused a moment. She was here because Anne-Marie led her here. "Because this is where she lives."

The man's eyes bored a hole through hers. "Listen to me clear. I don't know if you're crazy or what, but nobody by that name lives here. I don't know what you're talkin' about. You can stay here for a minute, but then you have to get out."

Callie rushed through the house to the child's room. "Ask her," she yelled. "She'll tell you." She threw open the door where the same blond-haired girl sat in a chair and gazed out the window. The man came in behind her and grabbed Callie's arm roughly.

"Anne-Marie! Tell your father what happened!"

The girl turned slowly, smiled at Callie and began humming.

"I'm about to call the sheriff. There ain't no Anne-Marie in this house. My daughter ain't left the house in years. She ain't right. I told you that before. She's been sittin' there all day long just like yesterday and the day before and last week. I think you're havin' a spell or somethin'."

"What's her name?"

"Maria. Her name's Maria, if it's any of your business. Now get out. If you got man problems, they ain't our problems. Don't never come back here."

There was no sign of Mark outside the shack. Callie walked through the woods, wondering what this revelation meant. The autistic child's name was Maria, the same as Henri Arceneaux's daughter who drowned in 1863. But so what? It was a coincidence, right? What else could it be?

When she got back to Beau Rivage, Mark's Jeep was gone. So was the box of books she thought he'd taken to New Orleans.

CHAPTER THIRTY-FOUR

For the second night in a row, Callie slept in her car. She was terrified to stay at Beau Rivage after the confrontation with Mark. As much as she'd wanted to believe he was on her side, she now saw what he really was. She was afraid not just for herself but for Anne-Marie too, but the girl seemed to know how to stay out of sight when she needed to.

She rolled down the car window when she saw Lanny coming down the sidewalk on his way to work. She explained that they had to talk. They went to Starbucks and over a glorious latte that revived her in minutes, she explained what had happened yesterday.

Lanny took notes as she recounted his ranting tirade and the revelation that he and Willard were in cahoots to steal the plantation. She told him how terrified she had been when he screamed at her and the little girl – whom she described as a neighbor child who was visiting – causing them to flee for their lives.

"Do you believe he wanted to hurt you or the child?"

"At that moment, I believe he would have. He snapped – do you know what I mean? He got madder and more red-faced as he told me what he and Willard were involved in. But do I think he's really like that? I hope not, but Mark Streater's certainly not the man I thought he was. He's full of anger and he really might have hurt us."

"Have you been to the police? Do you want a restraining order? With what you've told me, you deserve one, but a judge would bring in Mark for his side of the story before you'd get it. Frankly, a restraining order packs no punch except for the fear angle. If he's worried that he'll be arrested for coming around, he might stay away. But sometimes people who are that angry simply ignore the order. Sometimes they do really bad things to other people ... and themselves."

She answered that she hadn't contacted the police because it would simply be his word against hers. No one else had seen it except Anne-Marie, and Callie couldn't count on her to say anything at all. And no, she didn't want a restraining order. She agreed with Lanny that it would probably be a waste of time.

Then he asked if she owned a gun.

"No," she replied. "I've never had a gun in my life. Do you think I need one?"

"You can't defend yourself if you don't have a weapon."

"Come on, Lanny. I'm not going to shoot anybody. I'm sorry, but that's just not me. I'm not that worried about him. He lost it completely but maybe he'll be sorry eventually for what he's done. If that happens, he'll come back to make it right."

He warned her not to be naïve. And that morning before she went to Beau Rivage, she bought a gun.

Four days later she met with Lanny again. She was staying at the house, she was armed with a .45 pistol and she hadn't seen Mark. The next day after he chased her through the woods, he had cleaned out the joint bank account, stealing over fifty thousand dollars that was rightfully hers. She was okay financially. All it had taken was a call to Mr. Darlington, who gave her another advance. This time she had gone to the authorities and there was a warrant for Mark's arrest on charges of larceny and fraud.

She told Lanny that every time she came to Opelousas, she made a point to drive by Mark's office. It was always shut down tight, regardless of the time of day. She went by his house too, but likewise it was closed up and his Jeep was gone. As much as she hoped for retribution, every day that passed made it seem less likely.

"I'm certain now that he's mentally deranged," she admitted. "I hope I never see him again."

They talked about her uncle Willard. He had called, asking her to come in and talk things over, but she refused, telling him to talk to her attorney from now on if he wanted anything from her. He feigned confusion, asking what on earth could be wrong with her, and with the satisfied click of a button, she had hung up on him.

Lanny said, "I'm doing research on disbarment proceedings. We have your uncle dead to rights. He lied to you when he said Darlington Gallery was his client, he lied about the book being worthless, and he attempted to coerce you. You know now that Mr. Darlington hadn't talked to him at all. Willard must be worried about the ramifications of what he did, even though I doubt he thinks you would try to take down your uncle. You're certain you want me to keep working on this – right? He could retaliate and you know how vindictive he is."

"Damn right. I say let him fire his best shot. I hope you aren't worried that helping me is going to affect your future. It could get nasty."

"I'm in. I have nothing to lose, and if I can prevail against a legend like Willard Arceneaux, I'll be somewhat of a legend myself. Hopefully that'll help land me a job with a good firm. It won't be down here in Cajun country, where memories are long, but in New Orleans or Shreveport – maybe even Baton Rouge or Monroe – I'm certain I can begin a career with a reputable firm who appreciates that I've stood up for the law and the rights of little people against bullies."

She picked up groceries, and as she drove back to Beau Rivage, her phone rang. It was Mr. Darlington, the dealer from New Orleans, who said he had good news for her. But first, he added, he wanted to apologize for the apparent mix-up that led her to believe there was a problem.

There was no mix-up, she thought bitterly. *That was the collusive effort of Mark Streater and my uncle to force me out.*

Darlington told her that her book *Tamerlane and Other Poems* had been positively authenticated as the thirteenth known copy from Poe's original printing in 1827.

243

The last one to sell, he reminded her, was in poorer condition than her copy, and Christie's auctioned it in 2009 for over six hundred and fifty thousand dollars. He asked for her permission to leave the volume in England for safekeeping. It would stay in the vault of one of the major auction houses until it could be auctioned.

She agreed and thanked him for his help. Based on the authentication, Darlington offered her another hundred-thousand-dollar advance. She thanked him and said she was good for now, but if the auction was delayed, maybe she would accept his offer later.

At last everything seems to be going in the right direction, she thought to herself as she walked around the house, checking on the workmen who were giving Beau Rivage a fresh coat of white paint. She told the crew chief how quickly the house was becoming a showplace again.

She watched as a black BMW came up the road from Point Charmaine and through her gate. She stood in the yard until it stopped and two men in suits and ties got out.

"Miss Pilantro?" one asked.

"I'm Calisto Pilantro. Who are you?"

He handed her a business card. "I'm Marvin White and this is Thomas Baines. I'm with Interstate Southern Acquisition Corporation in Shreveport. Mr. Baines and I have recently become aware of a critical issue that involves both our company and you. May we talk to you for a moment?"

She led them into the library and offered coffee or water, which they declined. She saw from his card that Marvin White was the executive vice president of Interstate Southern, a company she'd never heard of. She sat in a chair across from them and waited to find out what brought some corporate bigwigs from Shreveport down here to St. Landry Parish.

"With your permission, I'd like to give you a little background about why we're here," he began. "When Juliet Arceneaux passed away late last year, we were contacted by an attorney in Opelousas with a business proposition."

She smiled. "I'm going to take a wild guess and say that was Willard Arceneaux."

"It was indeed. Mr. Arceneaux advised us that he was the executor of his sister's will and, by virtue of that fact, he controlled the future of this plantation. Based on certain assurances we received from Mr. Arceneaux in writing as part of a binding agreement, our company paid him a retainer to act as our attorney in the transaction he was offering. You might think it was an odd combination – hiring an attorney to represent our company who's also acting as the executor for this property, but our in-house counsel approved it after receiving certain assurances from Mr. Arceneaux. At that point, we entered into a contract and paid him more money – a one-million-dollar deposit against future monies we would owe Juliet Arceneaux's estate once the transaction closed."

"I'm not following you. What was the transaction that you were working on?"

He looked at the other man and frowned. "I'm sorry. Mr. Arceneaux told me that you were aware of our involvement, but like other things he said, that was obviously incorrect. Interstate Southern is one of the largest owners of gaming properties in the southern United States. Mr. Arceneaux promised to deliver this property to our company so we could build a casino right down there in the front yard on the Atchafalaya River."

At that point, the man turned to his associate and asked him to explain the rest. Mr. Baines handed her a card that identified himself as a partner in the law firm of Baines and Crabtree in Chicago.

"Until ten days ago," he began, "Mr. Arceneaux claimed that the will was missing and that the property would remain in his hands as executor until it turned up. He showed us the deed filed in the parish courthouse that showed Juliet Arceneaux had owned the property since 1949, and she inherited it from her mother, Anne. What Mr. Arceneaux failed to tell us was that you were the present owner of the property, thanks to a deed filed by your grandmother shortly before her death last year.

"This matter has progressed slowly for some time while Mr. Arceneaux advised us he was researching the law in order to effect a transfer from his sister's estate. Once we learned you were the true owner – strictly because we did a routine search of the records, I might add – Mr. Arceneaux's new story was that he was in negotiations with you to reach an agreement under which we would purchase the property. He referred to you as his niece. Was that an accurate statement?"

"Probably one of the few you got from him," Callie replied with a smile. She could see the lawyer no longer believed anything Uncle Willard had said. "I'm his grandniece, but all this is news to me."

"Unfortunately, we can see that now. Once Mr. White learned that Mr. Arceneaux had – shall we say – been less than honest about the ownership situation, he employed our law firm to look into all aspects of Interstate Southern's contract. And that's what brings us here today. As late as yesterday morning, your uncle assured my client that you had agreed to sell, and he was merely wrapping up the terms to present to us."

He paused for a moment and then said, "I have no idea what your relationship with your uncle is, Miss Pilantro, but I'd like to know if the statement Mr. Arceneaux told us yesterday about you is accurate."

Callie shook her head. "As I said, I never heard any of this before. As to how my uncle and I get along, he's been making moves against me in hopes I'd lose this place. He bought the mortgage from the bank I borrowed money from to begin restoring the house. I tried to pay him with a cashier's check, then in cash, and he refused to take payment. Every judge in this parish is in his pocket, but thank God I found one who had the guts to do the right thing and issue a restraining order. He's pulled some other despicable things in cahoots with a man who was supposed to be my friend, but you didn't come here to talk about me. What can I do for you – short of selling you the plantation, of course?"

The casino executive said, "That would be the ideal situation for us, and we're prepared to make you a generous offer for the forty acres. The house would remain the showpiece of the property. We'd build a riverboat casino where the dock is today, and we'd spend whatever it takes to restore Beau Rivage to its former grandeur. It's easy to see that you love this place," he added. "I saw it once before, just after your grandmother died, when Willard gave me a brief tour."

She was shocked at his plans for the plantation, but she kept her thoughts to herself. "I was worried about the house when I first got it," she confessed. "I didn't have the one thing this place needed lots of – money. I scraped by, no thanks to my uncle, and I discovered there were a few things in the house that could be sold off to raise what I needed to finish. That's where I am today, and I must admit that until you showed up, I never seriously thought about letting it go. I still don't think I would, but I guess it never hurts to listen. So that's what you wanted from me?"

The lawyer answered this time. "Not entirely. We'd like you to join us in a lawsuit my firm is preparing to file against your uncle. To be perfectly honest, I believe his actions demonstrate criminal intent, and given what you've told us today, this may be a matter for the district attorney. In my opinion, he's defrauded both Interstate Southern and you."

She said she wanted to talk to her own lawyer and, presuming he agreed, she'd be happy to do anything she could to help them fight her uncle. Baines promised to email her a proposal she could share with Lanny Weinstein.

Marvin White said he would send her his company's business plan and their formal proposal to develop a casino at Beau Rivage. He also asked her to carefully consider a purchase offer he would include.

When she received the Chicago lawyer's letter and an agreement she needed to sign, she went over everything with Lanny. He told her she should go for it, and she eagerly joined the battle. Still bitter over his deception, she was happy to help bring her shady uncle to justice. *Maybe he'll even get some time in the slammer*, she fantasized, even though she knew she'd likely never see that day.

CHAPTER THIRTY-FIVE

Regional media and some of the national news networks ran special reports announcing that Willard Arceneaux, the Cajun Crusher, had been arrested at his home in Opelousas at five a.m. He was booked into the county jail and ignominiously thrust into a cell to await a court appearance later that morning.

The newscasters didn't point it out, but the smiles of satisfaction from the local officers who carried out the predawn raid couldn't be missed on the TV broadcasts. They could have picked him up mid-morning and taken him directly from his house to the courtroom, but there were many people in law enforcement who'd waited their entire careers to see the arrogant, overbearing lawyer get what was coming to him. Rousing him from bed by banging on his door and ensuring cameras were rolling when he was taken out in handcuffs – his hair tousled and messy and his face unshaven – the cops did everything possible to make Willard's trip to the jail something he and the public would remember.

Lanny woke Callie with the news. He told her Willard was charged with bribery of a public official, embezzlement, and mail and wire fraud. Most of the charges arose from his past associations with judges, high-ranking police officials and even a couple of state legislators. The injustices against Callie were addressed too, resulting in additional charges of attempted extortion and criminal conversion of property.

As he indicated he might, Thomas Baines had taken Interstate Southern's grievances to the district attorney, and Callie had met with him too. Two weeks had passed without a word, but suddenly things were happening. The first prop had been jerked from the supports that until today had kept Willard Arceneaux on top of the world.

Interstate Southern's Chicago lawyer knocked out two more props before the day was over. On behalf of Callie, he filed a civil suit accusing Willard of the same crimes – fraud and the like – but also alleging breach of fiduciary duty as executor of Juliet's estate. To make matters worse for Willard, Interstate Southern Acquisition Corporation filed a twenty-million-dollar lawsuit against him.

By the time the six o'clock news aired, the journalistic feeding frenzy had completely consumed Willard Arceneaux. Released on a million dollars bail and no longer in possession of a passport, Willard sneaked off to Houston, seeking anonymity but finding instead that his smiling face on those billboards was also familiar to Texans. He couldn't find peace anywhere on land, so he chartered a yacht out of Galveston and stayed below deck for several days, emerging only to eat, drink and gaze at the calm waters that he wished represented his future.

On the fifth morning, he came on deck bright and cheerful for the first time. He asked the captain to take him back to land. He disembarked, settled his tab for the boat rental and drove back to Louisiana. The captain would later tell the police he seemed like a man who had found the answer he'd been looking for. He had changed literally overnight from a pitiful, despondent creature to a man on a mission.

CHAPTER THIRTY-SIX

What a great day this has been, Callie thought as she relaxed on the porch with her usual glass of wine. She looked down toward the Atchafalaya and tried to picture a low-slung riverboat out there, with patrons walking along a path winding across the yard to the casino, their cars parked in a concrete lot to the back of the house. She'd sat out here a couple of other times since those men had visited her. Sometimes the scene seemed reasonable, but other times she reminded herself her ancestors – including her grandmother – would have been horrified at the idea.

Until the men came, she hadn't seriously considered selling the place, because she never thought anyone would pay anything for a two-hundred-year-old house that constantly needed upkeep. Now all that had changed, and she had to weigh the pros and cons. Did she want to stay in St. Landry Parish forever, or would she be content to go back to another life? Once the house was ready for visitors, would she be happy running a bed-and-breakfast or a tourist attraction? Would it be satisfying, and could she make any money at it? These were the things on Callie Pilantro's mind.

One incredibly positive thing she had learned was that for the first time in her life, money was no longer a constant worry. Her ancestor Henri had left that strongbox filled with his entire fortune – forty thousand dollars in Confederate currency – and he had died a pauper because the money was worthless.

A hundred and fifty years had passed, and Confederate States of America currency had become highly prized by collectors. She had visited a New Orleans coin and stamp dealer the day she went down to find Mark, and she learned that most of the bills in the strongbox were valuable.

The denominations ranged from fifty cents to five hundred dollars, and some of the ones issued early in the War – 1861 or 1862 – were extremely rare and in almost perfect condition. She had sold eleven bills to the New Orleans currency dealer for thirty thousand dollars that day, and there were stacks and stacks left in the strongbox.

After dinner, she went to the parlor, pulled the drapes and prepared for bed. She'd already cleaned the bedrooms upstairs, and she could move anytime she wished, but she'd become fond of this room that had been her safe place since she first came to Beau Rivage. She fell instantly into a deep, dreamless sleep.

———

He had sat in the woods for hours. He had watched her rocking to and fro on the porch, enjoying a glass of wine, as she had done on so many other evenings at Beau Rivage. He knew how much she loved that view of the river.

He looked through the kitchen window and watched her making dinner. She sat at the table and ate, and he pictured the happy thoughts of the future that must be in her mind. Her fortunes had turned the moment she realized that Beau Rivage was worth a fortune – if she was willing to part with it. She would do that, he believed, because she had no ties to this parish or this land. She didn't care about family or history or what was fair. She would sell the property and be gone as quickly as she had arrived.

He was surprised to see that she wasn't concerned about keeping the drapes closed. She wasn't afraid anymore, although now was when she should be afraid. He watched her undress and leave the room. He knew she was heading to the bathroom to wash up before bed, and in a moment she was back, standing at the window, unaware that his eyes were upon her. She reached for the cord and drew the curtains. And then she was gone.

As he had done the other nights, he settled in to watch and wait.

———

Run, Callie! Run!

Her eyes snapped open. Dazed, she tried to clear her mind. Had someone called her? Was she dreaming?

Run! Run now!

Anne-Marie stood in the hallway, pointing to the back door.

Callie reached for her shoes, but Anne-Marie ran to her side and grabbed her hand. They raced down the hall toward the library and the safety of the secret room, but suddenly Callie heard a sound. She turned and watched the doorknob move – someone was trying to get inside. A dark shadow moved across the glass pane next to the door, and then there was another sound. He was pushing against it, trying to force it open!

Anne-Marie pulled her into the music room and opened the door to the secret staircase. They crept inside and started up, but Callie whispered, "I need my phone! We have to call for help!"

"I'll get it," the girl said. "Go upstairs and wait for me."

"You can't go back in there! He may already be inside!"

Anne-Marie darted through the doorway and closed it before Callie could stop her. Terrified that the child had put herself in danger, she climbed the stairs and waited at the top. In seconds she heard footsteps coming up the stairs, and she breathed a sigh of relief as Anne-Marie turned the corner and handed her the phone.

Callie dialed 911 and a dispatcher promised to send help right away.

"Did you see anyone?" she asked Anne-Marie.

"He's not in the house, but I know it's him. I told you he was going to hurt you."

"How can you be sure if you didn't see him? It's Mark, isn't it?"

Why did it take me so long to realize what Mark really was? And why didn't I grab the gun when we ran?

The child put a finger to her lips and pointed down the stairway. From somewhere below they could hear noises.

At first there were footsteps, then the sound of something heavy being moved around.

He's in the house!

She held her breath, hoping and praying that the door at the bottom of the stairs didn't open. The hidden stairway would be one of the first places Mark would look.

There were muffled sounds – voices, perhaps – and a heavy thud. Then she heard two distinct popping noises.

For a second she felt relieved that the deputies were here, but then she realized they couldn't have come this quickly. Maybe the sounds weren't gunshots ... but she knew deep inside that they were, and she was in a perilous situation.

"He's going to hurt you."

She held Anne-Marie's hand and waited for several long moments. The house was silent. At last she decided to see what had happened. She went downstairs and opened the door quietly. In the half-light, she made out something lying in the hallway. She listened carefully, but the only sound was the ticking of the grandfather clock.

She crept across the music room. As she stepped into the hallway, an enormous blast of light from the chandeliers momentarily blinded her. Mark stood by the open back door, his hand on the light switch. Next to him on the floor was a person dressed in black. The figure wasn't moving.

She recognized her uncle, pushed past Mark and dropped to her knees. "Uncle Willard! Uncle Willard!" She shook him, but he didn't move.

"My God!" she screamed, jumping up and backing away. "Did you kill him?"

Mark answered quietly. "He came here to kill *you,* Callie. Now he won't be able to hurt you anymore."

"How do you know that? Why are you here?" She had to keep him talking until help arrived.

His eyes looked distant and his voice was a monotone. "I'm protecting you. Thanks to me, you're safe now." She saw the pistol in his hand as he slowly walked toward her. She knew she was next. She backed away again, slowing moving toward the library.

"Where have you been?" she asked, hoping to distract him until she could get to the bookcase. "You weren't in town. I haven't seen you anywhere."

He smiled, but his eyes were cold. "Were you looking for me? That's nice to know. I was here all the time. I've been watching you."

This was a different person than the Mark she had known. His words made her tingle as if something evil and nasty was crawling on her skin. He took another step toward her and she turned and ran.

He was right behind her. "I'm glad you came in here. Open the bookcase." His voice sounded mechanical, like the words were being replayed from a low-quality recording.

That was exactly what she had hoped to do. She might have escaped, but now he was too close.

"Why do you think Uncle Willard was going to kill me?"

"Because he wants all this for himself. He wants everything, don't you know that?"

"But his career was ruined. He was probably going to jail."

Mark laughed. "Not anymore."

Just then Anne-Marie appeared in the doorway behind him. Callie looked at her in shock and shook her head. "Run away!" she shouted.

Mark turned and raised the gun.

With Mark a few steps behind her, Anne-Marie darted down the hall. Before Callie could stop him, he raised the gun and fired. Anne-Marie was just three feet away from him, and Callie watched in horror as the bullet went through the back of her blue dress and into her body.

Callie screamed and hit his arm with such intensity that he dropped the gun. "You're next," he said, hitting her savagely in the jaw with his fist. As she fell to the floor, he stooped to retrieve the gun.

"Hold it right there! Don't make a move for that weapon! Hands in the air!"

Dazed, Callie looked behind Mark and saw two deputies in the open doorway. One held a shotgun and the other a pistol, both trained on Mark. He raised his hands above his head and they took his pistol and restrained him.

Callie had never experienced such pain. Her jaw throbbed, but she managed to pull herself up. She had to see about Anne-Marie. She got to her feet unsteadily and looked down the hall. She wasn't there – she must have made it into the parlor. Even as she hoped that was true, Callie knew in her heart it couldn't have happened. Callie had seen Mark shoot her in the back point-blank.

But there was no body. No blood. There was a broken pane by the door where Mark's bullet had passed through, but Anne-Marie wasn't there. Sobbing uncontrollably, Callie called her name over and over until one of the officers put his arm around her and carefully led her to her couch. Through her pain and her tears, she tried to explain that there were two dead people in the house, not one, and the deputy sat with her and patted her hand. The other officer handcuffed Mark and took him to the squad car, and then he joined his partner to wait for backup.

Callie asked if she could see her uncle again and the deputies suggested that wasn't a good idea. It was a crime scene, they explained, and they had to be careful not to disturb the evidence. She nodded and dabbed at her eyes.

Thirty minutes later an ambulance arrived to take Callie to the hospital for an examination. When it was finished, a doctor gave her the news that she'd be very uncomfortable for a while, but fortunately there was no fracture. As soon as he left her, a detective and a sergeant from the state police stepped inside. She explained everything that had transpired, and the detective asked if she could name the victim.

"One is my uncle Willard Arceneaux," she answered. "The other one – the child – is named Anne-Marie. Her last name's Dupre, I think. I can tell you where she lives."

The men glanced at each other for a second, and the detective began to question her about Mark. She told them everything that had happened from the time she arrived in Opelousas a month ago.

CALLIE: THE BAYOU HAUNTINGS

"How did Mr. Streater happen to be in your house at 2:20 in the morning?"

She said that Anne-Marie – the dead child – had awakened her. They heard noises and saw the knob turning, and they hid in the staircase. She heard two shots and thought it was the sheriff. She came out, found her uncle's body and saw Mark holding a gun. He was acting very strangely and he said he'd been watching her to keep her safe.

"Was this girl Anne-Marie living with you? Is that why she was able to wake you in the night?"

"Not exactly. She comes and goes," Callie answered. From his facial expression, she could see the detective wasn't accepting her story, but there was no logical way to explain Anne-Marie. She told them the girl lived nearby and had found a secret entrance, which she had recently shown to Callie.

She was glad when they finally went back to asking about Mark. She told them how he'd confessed that he should have inherited the house. He had a dark side that he kept secret, she explained, adding that she and the child had once run for their lives through the woods to escape him.

They asked exactly what happened when she found Mark standing by Willard's body. She described how she felt and how terrified she had been that he would kill her too.

"What's going to happen to him?" she asked. "He said he killed my uncle because he was protecting me. Do you believe him?"

"What do you believe?"

"I don't know what to think. I can't believe Uncle Willard would have hurt me. He tried to cheat me and steal my property, and he lied so many times, but I don't think he was the kind of man to do harm to his own grandniece."

"What about Mark Streater? You said he has a dark side. Do you believe he could have hurt you?"

That was the question she'd been asking herself since she found him standing in the hallway.

"I hardly know him, to be honest. We were friends in high school, but that was years ago. I reconnected with him when I got to Opelousas because I didn't have anyone else to turn to. It sounds foolish now, but I took him at face value. Could he have hurt me? I would have said no until recently. Tonight – if the deputies hadn't come in time – I'm certain he would have killed me." The minute she blurted out those words, she was surprised she'd confessed them, but they were true. In those frenzied moments, she had seen at last what he really was.

When they wrapped up, the detective said she wouldn't be allowed back into the house until the crime scene investigators were finished. There would be a lot of activity out there for several more hours, he explained.

She was afraid to ask, but she had to know one more thing. Anne-Marie's body was in the house somewhere. Even if she'd managed to crawl away, she couldn't have gotten far.

"Is she dead?"

"Who, ma'am?"

"Anne-Marie. The child in the blue dress. Did he kill her too?"

"There's only one victim, Miss Pilantro."

"But I saw him shoot her in the back. The bullet went on and broke the glass next to the door. I saw it!"

He patted her hand. "I'll let the investigators know. If there's another victim, they'll find her."

The detective went to the ER nurses' station and informed them that Callie needed to stay put for a few hours. She had no place else to go, she was on pain medication and she was delusional. He left his number; he'd come back to take her home once she was cleared to leave.

CHAPTER THIRTY-SEVEN

Callie brought a basket of groceries to the counter at the Krotz Springs store. As the proprietor checked her out, he said, "As I recall, you're the girl who inherited Beau Rivage. There's a letter for you at the post office."

He said it had an insufficient address and was technically undeliverable, but it was still there. He'd been waiting until the next time she came in.

"Everybody knows everything in a little town, I guess." She laughed, wondering how he knew there was a letter for her.

"That's a fact, but actually I'm the postmaster. The Krotz Springs post office is right over there." He pointed to the rear of the store where there was a USPS sign hanging over a window. He handed over her change, walked to the back and brought her the letter.

This is the first time anyone's written me a letter since I came here, she mused, looking at the envelope. It was from the Louisiana State Museum in New Orleans and it was addressed to "Owner, Beau Rivage Plantation, Krotz Springs, Louisiana."

Two weeks later Callie sat at a long wooden table stacked so high with files, books and papers that she could hardly see the twentysomething female sitting across from her.

She introduced herself as Margot and apologized for the mess. "I'm on a project right now involving some of the old plantations along the Mississippi River. I'm trying to separate fact from legend, and it's turned out to be no small undertaking." She explained that many stories were handed down through generations of family members and – like most legends – there were embellishments and exaggerations along the way that made the tales more interesting. She was working on her PhD in history at Loyola University, and she'd gotten a summer job with the Louisiana Historical Association doing what had turned out to be a fascinating project.

It sounded interesting, and Callie asked if she'd debunked anything exciting that people had claimed was true. Margot laughed and said in fact she had, but she was under a strict confidentiality agreement about what she'd learned. The genteel Cajun families of southern Louisiana were fiercely proud of their heritage and they didn't need anybody telling them that Grandpa, known for years as a fine, upstanding citizen of this parish or that, was really a cheating card sharp who dallied with his neighbors' wives now and then when their husbands were out of town.

Callie laughed. She was enjoying the company of a female her own age – something she hadn't found since she'd come to Louisiana – and she was excited as Margot revealed why she'd written a letter asking the owner of Beau Rivage to come to the museum.

"There are literally millions of items here that go all the way back to the 1700s," she explained. "The Civil War archives are chock full of things like land transfers, military commendations and letters from soldiers sent to wives back home. There are medals, weapons, canteens – everything you can imagine, some of which are on display next door in the public areas of the museum.

"As I said, my concentration is on antebellum mansions along the Mississippi, so I skipped over tons of things that were off the subject. Anything about New Orleans itself, or the northern part of the state, or even the parishes over where Beau Rivage is, weren't germane to my project and got shuffled to one side. If I had taken time to look at those too, I'd have been here for years. You can't believe how much stuff there is."

She reached to one side of the desk, picked up a stack of old documents that were bound together with a string, and set it in front of Callie. "Most of what I came across was one-off – and what I mean by that is that there would be a letter about a soldier in Alexandria mixed in with a bunch of stuff I needed about Oak Alley Plantation. I'd put the letter aside and keep the Oak Alley things. But one day I came across a box that was sent down here in 1887 from Opelousas to be stored with the historical archives. I wasn't aware of any mansions in St. Landry Parish that fit my project, so I should have put it aside, but for some reason I opened it instead. When I did, I found this thick bundle of papers with Beau Rivage's name on the top of it."

Margot added that she had taken a brief look without untying the string, and she saw some legal documents that might be historically important to someone. Deciding that it wouldn't take more than a few minutes and a forty-nine-cent stamp, she'd let the owner of Beau Rivage know there was something he or she needed to see.

Callie was pleased to get the stack, regardless of what it contained. These days she was trying to locate items from the plantation's history that would make interesting additions to the house tour and displays she was planning. She offered to buy Margot's lunch as a token of her gratitude and to get to know her better, but the girl declined. There would be time for casual lunches once she was back in school; right now, she couldn't afford the time away from her project. Callie thanked her and they agreed to keep in touch.

Back at Beau Rivage, Callie unwrapped the voluminous stack and took it from the top. She gave each document a quick look and put it in one of two piles – things to look at soon, and things that could wait until later. Margot had been right – there were lots of family records showing births, deaths, marriages and confirmations. She smiled when she came across a party invitation. Henri and Caroline had been cordially invited to another plantation along the river for a dinner and dance. The date was October 1862. The Civil War was under way, but these folks were apparently in their Scarlett O'Hara, devil-may-care mentalities. There might be an uncomfortable situation somewhere, but out here on the river, things were just dandy.

It only took an hour to finish, and she had a small stack of things to go through, and a pile that could wait. She got a yellow pad and began to record names, dates and types of documents, one by one. There were many names she hadn't heard before – shirt-tail kinfolk, as people in the South called them. Cousins, nieces and nephews, great-aunts and uncles, relatives who had died in infancy or as children – the Arceneaux clan had carefully kept its family records. Callie was thrilled to see the hoard and was already thinking how to display some of the documents.

She saw a birth certificate and was about to write it down on her pad, but suddenly she looked more closely and recoiled in shock.

Anne-Marie Arceneaux. Born at Beau Rivage Plantation, St. Landry Parish, Louisiana. July 17, 1853. Parents: Henri Arceneaux, age 57, and Caroline Chapman Arceneaux, age 50.

At last she put things together. Even after learning that the child's death certificate listed her name as Anne-Marie, she was puzzled. She thought there were twins at first, but now she recalled Henri's journal. When their daughter was born, Henri didn't record her given name. He said, "We call her Maria." It was a nickname. Here was the birth certificate. The circle was complete.

The child in the casket was Anne-Marie Arceneaux, the same child who had protected her from Mark Streater.

Callie's mind spun with crazy thoughts. According to the police, there was only one victim at Beau Rivage that night – her uncle Willard. Callie's insistence that a child had been shot too was chalked up to her confusion and stress. But why had Callie not seen her since?

Many times, Callie had wondered who Anne-Marie was referring to when she said, "I don't like him. He's going to hurt you." She'd thought at first she was referring to Uncle Willard, but was it really Mark? His evil intentions had ultimately been revealed. But what about her uncle, who had tried time and again to steal the property from her? No one could explain why Uncle Willard had been at Beau Rivage in the middle of the night. Was he the one trying to open the door, and had Mark already been inside? No one knew for sure, and Mark wasn't talking.

Anne-Marie was there to protect me, Callie thought, remembering how the child had helped her hide on that awful night. *Now Mark's in jail and he can't hurt me anymore. Neither can Uncle Willard, so maybe Anne-Marie thinks she isn't needed here any longer.* The thought made her sad; she felt a closeness to the odd girl – like she was family.

From a common-sense standpoint, Callie knew why Anne-Marie hadn't come back. She was dead. She absolutely had to be. Mark had shot her squarely in the back. Body or no body, it was a fact. Callie had seen it with her own eyes. So why did Callie keep expecting to see her standing in the hallway? She was gone. Forever. Wasn't she?

She wasn't gone forever, and Mark couldn't have killed her. She died on July 17, 1863 She's been dead the entire time I've been here.

After seeing the girl's birth certificate, Callie addressed the enigma scientifically. She filled pages in a notebook with things she knew about the girl, and more pages with things she had observed but didn't understand. Then she listed crazy, out-of-the-box ideas that might explain what was going on. She didn't allow herself to be constrained by sensibility or rational thinking. She put down stuff she'd never believed in and knew nothing about – astral projection, ESP, mind control, out-of-body experience and the like. Nothing was off-limits.

After a couple of days mulling things over, she thought she knew everything. In a twenty-first-century world it was as far-fetched as they come, but thinking logically about Anne-Marie didn't work. There was nothing logical about her.

Callie wanted to know the truth. To find it, she had to visit the girl who lived on the other side of the woods. She might get nowhere, but she had to go if she was ever to know if her theory was correct. As she approached the house, Spike barked his head off and tugged at the chain until it seemed he'd choke himself. The woman stepped out to see what all the commotion was.

"He ain't here," she said to Callie.

"That's good. I'm here to talk to you. Did you hear about the murder at Beau Rivage?"

The woman looked at her through blank eyes and didn't say anything.

"Your daughter was there. She protected me and saved my life. You must tell me about her. Please help me. I need to understand what this is all about."

"He don't want me to talk to you."

"But he's not here. I promise I won't tell him we spoke. Please help me."

The woman turned and walked into the house. Unsure if she was supposed to follow, Callie followed her to the girl's room and went inside. There was the child, staring out the window as always. She was wearing a frilly blue dress – *that* blue dress. Callie looked for a bullet hole in the back, but she it knew it wouldn't be there.

"She ain't right. My husband told you that. She ain't talked to anyone but herself in a long time. She just sits there. Sometimes she hums or smiles, and once in a while I've heard her talk to herself. Carryin' on a conversation with nobody, know what I mean? But ever' time I walk in, she stops."

"Her name is Maria. That's what your husband told me."

The woman said nothing.

"Her birthday's July 17th, isn't it?"

The woman turned, her face ashen. "How'd you know that? What's this all about? My husband ain't gonna like this ..."

"Please don't be afraid. I want to explain something. This is going to sound crazy, but I think your daughter is somehow able to project herself and become someone else. I don't know how, but I'm convinced she is Anne-Marie Arceneaux, the child of the people who built Beau Rivage in 1835. They never called their daughter by her real name.

They nicknamed her Maria. She was born on July 17th. Do you see the connections here?"

The woman was obviously having difficulty processing all this, and Callie understood why. This was heady stuff that would be hard for anyone to grasp, especially this poor soul.

"None of that means nothin'," she said after a pause. "You're just makin' up a bunch of bull. She sits here all day long. She ain't nobody else but her. That's crazy talk. There's somethin' else, ain't there? What are you really after?"

"I want to talk to Maria for a couple of minutes. That's all."

"She don't talk. I told you that."

"Please, may I have a moment alone with her?"

The woman shrugged her shoulders and rolled her eyes. She walked out of the room and Callie knelt at the window beside the child.

"Thank you for helping me. You saved my life and I can never thank you enough."

Nothing.

"Anne-Marie, I don't know exactly how you do what you do, but you heard what I told your mother. There was no twin, was there? Anne-Marie and Maria are the same person – and somehow you project that child today. Am I understanding, or am I totally wrong about everything?"

The girl whispered something to herself.

"What? I'm sorry, but I didn't hear you."

She turned and smiled at Callie. Then she spoke in that now-familiar voice. "I said she's not my mother."

Callie took her hand and squeezed it. "It's you! I knew it was you and I've missed you. I've gotten used to you showing up at the oddest times and helping me figure things out. Will you please come back and see me?"

Maria turned back to the window and began to hum softly. Callie let her hand go and said, "Thank you for everything you did for me. I want to tell you something I've decided to do. I'm going to bury your casket in the woods.

You can be at peace there, resting between your real mother and father."

She turned her head slightly, smiled and whispered, "I would like that."

CHAPTER THIRTY-EIGHT

If he hadn't had all those problems recently, Willard Arceneaux's funeral would have been more grandiose and far better attended. The pews of St. Andrews Catholic Church would have been packed with people who were in his debt for one reason or another. Since his ignominious fall from prominence, there were maybe a hundred people who chose to come pay their respects. Callie debated whether to go; no one would have wished for a relative like Willard, but in the end, she decided to do it for herself. He was gone – out of her life – and it was a celebration for her.

She waited until the last minute, walking down the aisle and standing at the end of the pew on the second row where her cousins Madeline and Carmine were seated. They refused to acknowledge her presence and didn't move a muscle, forcing her to push roughly past their knees to take a seat. She left plenty of room between them – today there would be no hugs, no conversation and no shared tears.

The priest went through his ritual, one Callie hadn't seen since her mother's funeral years ago. Church wasn't a part of her life anymore, and she'd bought a pantsuit just to have something to wear today. When Carmine went to the podium to read a scripture verse, Callie thought how shallow her words seemed. Madeline was next and she gave a tearful eulogy that was almost nauseating in its effusive praise for her beloved father. What a wonderful, giving, saintly man he had been, she blubbered, and Callie wondered how many others besides herself knew that it was all an act. Willard had never been close to anyone – not his deceased wife, his girls or anyone else in the family. As far as she knew, he had had no real friends. Willard Arceneaux's life could be summed up in one sentence – it's all about me.

After what felt like hours, it was over and the three of them were led up the aisle by an usher. The girls stayed in the vestibule to greet the sparse crowd of mourners, but Callie walked straight out. She'd done her familial duty and she damned sure wasn't going to the cemetery to endure more of this fake sniveling from Carmine and Madeline.

For the past few days, the news reports had been all about Mark Streater. He'd been charged with involuntary manslaughter in the death of her uncle. The DA decided against going for murder, since Mark's claim all along was that he was protecting Callie, even though he was a trespasser in her house himself, and she had considered him a threat.

Mark had been released on a half-million-dollar bail. He'd paid the bail bondsman's fee by giving him a second mortgage on his fixer-upper houses, and within twenty-four hours he was gone. His disappearance led to speculation that he was mentally unstable, that he had murdered the famous lawyer in cold blood and was carrying out some secret vendetta against Callie.

Callie would worry about him for a while, but when reports surfaced that he'd been seen in Cabo, or Guadalajara, or Puerto Vallarta, she decided life was too short to look over her shoulder all the time. He was gone for good, she told herself.

When it came to burying Anne-Marie's casket, she debated whether to call the funeral director in town and have a proper burial, but she decided against it. Revealing that there was a body in the house would only lead to questions. Maybe there'd be an investigation and a lot of red tape Callie didn't need. She knew who was in the casket and all she wanted was to give the child the final resting place she'd been denied for over a hundred and fifty years.

She went into town and hired four men who were milling around outside a 7-Eleven waiting for day jobs. She set them to work digging a grave and she paid them a hundred dollars each to keep their mouths shut about the coffin they hauled from the house and buried. It was all on the up and up, she promised, explaining that she'd found it in a secret wall and wanted a proper burial for her ancestor.

That evening she walked to the family plot and put flowers on her grave. She said a prayer and told Anne-Marie she loved her.

A rustle of wind in the trees sounded for the world like a voice that was echoing the words back to her. *I love you.*

Since Henri's Confederate currency held no memories, it was something she could easily part with. She kept a dozen bills to display inside the no-longer secret room, and she consigned the rest to the dealer. After a well-attended auction, she received a check for nearly two million dollars, which allowed her to finish the house project and have plenty left over.

When she turned down his offer, Marvin White, the executive from the casino company, told her she was passing up a once-in-a-lifetime opportunity. "The casino will be built somewhere on the Atchafalaya," he promised, "and if you don't reap the benefit, then one of your neighbors will." She thanked him for his interest and let him walk away. Six months from now Beau Rivage would be the newest tourist destination in Cajun country – a beautifully renovated antebellum mansion with original furnishings and ghostly stories of bodies hidden in the wall and secret rooms and stairways. The five second-floor bedrooms would be rented to overnight guests; Callie would live in the ballroom and serve as host and B&B cook for people who came to experience life on the river.

The civil lawsuit she filed against her uncle hadn't gone away when he died; it merely became a matter for his estate instead. Willard's attorney advised Madeline and Carmine that they should let sleeping dogs lie. Surely they didn't want a trial, where a jury would hear sordid details about their father's business dealings. Although he might not have cheated anyone, the lawyer said, the other side was going to make it sound like Willard Arceneaux was the devil incarnate.

BILL THOMPSON

Lanny Weinstein called Callie one afternoon and advised the estate was willing to settle all disputes between her and her uncle. They were offering a million dollars and she took Lanny's advice to counter for three. She ended up with a check for two and a half million and a terse letter from her cousins informing her they never wanted to see her again.

When she read it, Callie's face broke out in a grin. That suited her just fine.

MAY WE OFFER YOU A FREE BOOK?

Bill Thompson's award-winning first novel, *The Bethlehem Scroll*, can be yours free. Just go to
billthompsonbooks.com
and click
"Subscribe."

Once you're on the list, you'll receive advance notice of future book releases and other great offers.

Thank you!

Thanks for reading *Callie*. I hope you enjoyed it and **I'd really appreciate a review on Amazon, Goodreads or both.**
Even a line or two makes a tremendous difference so thanks in advance for your help!
Please join me on:
Facebook
http://on.fb.me/187NRRP
Twitter
@BThompsonBooks

Made in the USA
Las Vegas, NV
24 March 2024

87650255R00154